THE TENDER KISS . . .

Yves was not the man who could offer her the happy-ever-after future she deserved. But maybe if he postponed his return to London a few days he could give her that gift of seeing herself through his eyes—the gift of knowing that she was a beautiful, desirable woman. An overpowering feeling of tenderness welled within him, and gripping her slender shoulders with both hands, he drew her to him.

Rachel had not expected such a move on Yves's part, but she went willingly into his arms. She was not sure what had prompted his sudden show of affection; she would not ask. She would simply snatch this one wondrous moment of inexplicable joy from the endless tedium of her life and savor it again and again in the long, dull years ahead.

Yves lowered his head and his mouth touched hers with melting gentleness. Then amazingly his arms tightened about her, and groaning deep in his throat, he raked his tongue across her lips until they opened to his sensuous exploration. Instantly she was awash with the same dark, bewildering longings his first kiss had evoked. . . .

The Yorkshire Lady

Nadine Miller

A SIGNET BOOK

SIGNET
Published by New American Library, a division of
Penguin Putnam Inc., 375 Hudson Street,
New York, New York 10014, U.S.A.
Penguin Books Ltd, 27 Wrights Lane,
London W8 5TZ, England
Penguin Books Australia Ltd,
Ringwood, Victoria, Australia
Penguin Books Canada Ltd, 10 Alcorn Avenue,
Toronto, Ontario, Canada M4V 3B2
Penguin Books (N.Z.) Ltd, 182–190 Wairau Road,
Auckland 10, New Zealand

Penguin Books Ltd, Registered Offices:
Harmondsworth, Middlesex, England

First published by Signet, an imprint of New American Library,
a division of Penguin Putnam Inc.

First Printing, January 2001
10 9 8 7 6 5 4 3 2 1

PUBLISHER'S NOTE
This is a work of fiction. Names, characters, places, and incidents either are the
product of the author's imagination or are used fictitiously, and any resemblance to
actual persons, living or dead, business establishments, events, or locales is entirely
coincidental.

To Pat and Peter O'Toole
Treasured friends whose steadfast
affection is one of the great
blessings of my life.

and

In memory of Bob Longfellow
Whose gentle spirit lives on in the hearts
of all of us who knew him.

Prologue

London, England, August 1816

"**H**owever much the traitor may deserve it, a public trial of a peer of the realm charged with treason is unthinkable. Furthermore, I must ask that you cease your persistent questioning of public officials."

Yves St. Armand recognized the finality of Lord Castlereagh, Marquess of Londonderry's statement, but he chose to ignore it. *"Mon Dieu, pourquoi?"* he demanded, so enraged he unconsciously lapsed into his native tongue.

"Because, sir, your questions could spawn dangerous rumors in the wrong places."

Yves had known something was in the wind when he'd received an invitation to visit White's Club in St. James as the guest of one of the most powerful men in England. Now he knew what that "something" was. It was all he could do to resist telling the British Foreign Secretary his ultimatum fell on deaf ears.

With the war finally over, he had come to London to seek out, and bring to justice, the English nobleman who had betrayed him and another French Royalist who had acted as General Wellesley's agents at Napoleon's court. He had no intention of leaving until he had accomplished his mission.

Castlereagh hailed a waiter and ordered two glasses of the excellent brandy for which White's was justifiably famous. "England is a powder keg waiting to explode," he explained once the waiter had departed. "The same miserable conditions exist today in such places as The Rookeries and Seven Dials as those that ignited Paris in '79."

Yves refrained from comment, though he found it difficult to imagine Madame Guillotine holding sway in Hyde Park—or condemned British aristocrats dragged through the streets of London in tumbrels.

"The problem is exacerbated by countless numbers of discharged soldiers desperately searching for a scrap of bread to fill their empty bellies," the Foreign Secretary continued. "The few voices raised in their behalf in Parliament are drowned out by louder voices of greed and self-interest. Nor does it help that our Regent lives like an India nabob. Hatred of the aristocracy mounts by the day, and rightly so."

"Are you saying that you honestly believe the public disclosure of an English nobleman who sold military secrets to Bonaparte could kindle a spark that would set London aflame?"

"It is possible." Lord Castlereagh's solemn expression lent added meaning to his words. "If what I have been told of your past history is true, you of all men should understand why we dare not let such a trial become a tool in the hands of rabble-rousers."

Yves shuddered at this reminder of the blood-crazy mob that had been driven to murder his parents and grandparents by just such rabble-rousers. He had been but six years old at the time, but the horror of that night during the Reign of Terror would remain with him forever. Still he had to ask. "Then for the sake of peace, Whitehall—and you—are willing to let the traitor go unpunished?"

Castlereagh's vivid blue eyes flashed with anger. "On the contrary, we will leave no stone unturned until the necessary proof is found to convict the traitor."

"You have a suspect?" Yves interjected, his heart racing at the thought of getting his hands on the unscrupulous devil.

"As a matter of fact, we have four men under investigation at the moment."

"Their names, *s'il vous plait,*" Yves said, his voice hoarse with emotion.

"Not so fast. First, I want your word you will treat such information with the utmost discretion—and that should you be the one to find proof that one of them is indeed guilty, you will immediately turn it over to me."

Yves frowned. "To what purpose?"

"I will personally see that the traitor is quietly dispatched to the prison colony in Van Dieman's Land to spend the rest of his life at hard labor. I think you will agree even hanging would be preferable to such a fate."

Yves hesitated, but only for a moment. "Very well, you have my word. I am, as you say, the last man on earth who would willingly risk unleashing the rabid dogs of revolution."

Castlereagh glanced around to make certain no one was within earshot. "Other than myself, only four noblemen, highly placed in Whitehall during the war, were privy to the information that was passed to the French in the spring of 1812. We feel fairly certain one of them is the traitor. But that could be a false assumption, which is why we must have absolute proof before we take action."

Yves clasped his glass of brandy with taut fingers. "Do *you* doubt that one of the four is the man we seek?"

Castlereagh shook his head. "No, I do not, but my judgment could be clouded by my eagerness to see the villain get his just desserts. My favorite cousin was a major in the company of Light Dragoons that was ambushed at Salamanca, thanks to information the traitor supplied Bonaparte. He, and all the brave men who served with him, died in the crossfire of French bullets."

"Then tell me the four names and I swear I will not rest until I find the proof you need to send the guilty bastard to Van Diemen's Land—or to hell."

Castlereagh cleared his throat. "None of the men in question have personal ties to France. Ergo, it would seem logical that the motivation for the heinous act was the money Bonaparte was willing to pay for such information. One of them—the Marquess of Haversham—has been a close friend of mine since we were boys together in Ireland. I know him to be both an honorable man and one with great personal wealth. I cannot imagine he would betray his country for money."

"And the others?"

"Oddly enough, all three sought government positions because their finances were at low tide—and all three came into mysterious windfalls during the summer of 1812. To date, neither my people nor Bow Street have come up with an explanation for this amazing coincidence."

Yves's fingers beat an impatient tattoo on the table. "Their names, my lord?"

"The first is Viscount Blevins, a quiet, studious sort of fellow who is more at home in the halls of Oxford than the ballrooms of London. But he is a possibility, since he is known to be an avid collector of ancient manuscripts and being addicted to the pastime myself, I can attest to the exorbitant cost of such treasures.

"The second is Baron Thornton, a true pink of the *ton* and my first choice as a suspect until I went out of my way to become better acquainted with him. Now I seriously doubt the fool has the imagination or daring to be a spy . . . unless, of course, his excessive prettiness is merely an act to cover his true identity."

"Which it well could be," Yves said, remembering his own portrayal of a dim-witted, fashionable fop during his years at the Emperor's court. He studied the Foreign Secretary's haggard face. "And who, pray tell, is the final suspect?"

"Edgar Hanley, the Earl of Fairborne," Castlereagh said in a voice devoid of all expression. "A handsome, good-natured man, liked by everyone in the *ton*—and a particular favorite of the Regent. My colleagues all consider him the least likely suspect of the trio—a feeling I shared until just recently."

"What made you change your mind?"

"He is ordinarily in residence at his townhouse in Grosvenor Square and very much a part of the London scene. But according to the Bow Street runner monitoring him, he is currently visiting an elderly aunt in Yorkshire and courting a wealthy cit named Rachel Barton. This strikes me as an odd thing for one of Prinny's crowd to be doing at the height of the Season. Nor would I expect such a dashing fellow to make a woman the runner described as a 'complete dowd' his countess."

Yves frowned. "Unless he is desperate to find another source of income now that the war is over and Napoleon safely on St. Helena."

"My thinking exactly, which makes him my prime suspect at the moment. For how better to recoup one's fortune than to marry a simple countrywoman who has inherited one of the most profitable woolen mills in Yorkshire? Under English law, everything she owns will belong to him the instant the marriage lines are signed." Castlereagh frowned. "I pity the poor innocent. Fairborne is said to be quite the charmer where the ladies are concerned."

Yves shrugged. The fate of the dowdy heiress was no concern of his. He stared out the window at a lamplighter making his rounds as the city of London prepared to greet another night. "I can only investigate the suspects one at a time," he said thoughtfully. "Like you, I find the Earl of Fairborne's recent conduct extremely suspect, so I believe I shall concentrate my efforts on him at the moment and leave the others to Bow Street. If he is presently in Yorkshire, this might be the ideal time to search his townhouse."

Castlereagh nodded. "It might indeed. Unfortunately, such a search would have to be done illegally since none of the four is officially under suspicion. Ergo, Whitehall cannot condone it; nor can Bow Street."

Yves shrugged. "Luckily, I am not burdened by such compunctions."

"Still, what you suggest is inherently risky." The Foreign Secretary studied Yves with grave eyes. "I hope you realize how risky, my friend. The fact that you are the Comte de Rochemont, and a citizen of France, will not save you from imprisonment, or worse, if you are caught in the act of housebreaking. Nor could I lift a finger to help you. In truth, I doubt even your mentor, the Duke of Wellington, would dare speak for you under such circumstances."

"I am no stranger to risk," Yves said softly, "and I learned long ago to never count on anyone but myself. I am well aware that the traitor, whoever he may be, has to know the part I played in the war against Bonaparte. Nevertheless, I came to London, planning to be very much in evidence, so as to draw him out."

"You play a dangerous game, my friend."

Yves smiled. "But one to which I am accustomed."

"So be it then. If you are determined on this course, I will put you up for honorary membership in White's. Fairborne has been a member here for many years."

"*Merci,* my lord. An excellent idea. The quickest way to drive a rodent out into the open is to crowd him in his nest."

"It is the least I can do. Were it not for men like you, the Corsican might have one day dwelt in Carlton House."

Yves rose from his chair, embarrassed by Lord Castlereagh's fulsome praise. "Thank you, my lord. But now if you will excuse me, I have been invited to dine at the home of my friend, the Earl of Stratham—after which, I believe I shall enjoy a late night stroll to Grosvenor Square."

Lord Castlereagh stood up as well. "One moment, if you

please. I have divulged my personal reason for wishing the traitor apprehended. I would know yours as well. I sense there is more to it than his betraying your identity to Bonaparte."

Yves blinked, surprised by the Foreign Secretary's keen perception. "Amalie de Maret, the woman I loved, learned of the Englishman's betrayal before I did," he said, taking a white-knuckled grip on the back of his chair. "She was shot by one of Fouchet's minions while trying to warn me. I swore on her grave I would never rest until I had avenged her death. The Frenchman who pulled the trigger has long since met his Maker, but the English traitor still walks free."

Chapter One

Rachel Barton had been in London a total of twelve hours, and already she regretted letting herself be talked into becoming a houseguest of the Earl of Fairborne. She had visited the great, sprawling city twice before and decided it was not at all to her liking. But the earl had been so insistent she had found it impossible to say no to his invitation.

In truth, she felt honored that a charming fellow like Lord Fairborne had sought her out as a friend. She was well aware that many people found her extraordinary height and razor sharp mind a trifle offputting. Her own father had declared she need never worry about being besieged by fortune hunters for no man would be so lost to reason he would leg-shackle himself to such an "odd duck."

She wished her cantankerous parent had lived long enough to know that at the ripe old age of four-and-twenty she had received an offer—and from a wealthy nobleman with no need of her money. For miraculously, the earl had asked the local vicar to introduce him to her, and after knowing her but three weeks had asked for her hand in marriage. She sighed. In such a romantic way too. He had raised her fingers to his lips and declared, "In you I have found a woman who can be my soul mate as well as my helpmate."

She didn't doubt his sincerity; the earl was the most honorable of men. But she had to wonder how he had come to that amazing conclusion. She couldn't remember their ever having discussed anything more serious than the cut of his new coat or the bloodlines of his pair of Cleveland Bays. On the few occasions when she had attempted to discuss the subject closest to her heart—the reforms she was putting into effect at the mill, he had politely informed her that noblemen did not involve themselves with trade.

Still, it was her first offer, and likely to be her last. She would always feel deeply grateful to the man who had made it. For one rash moment, she had even been tempted to say yes—for he had kissed her and she had found the experience exceedingly pleasant. She suspected she would find other aspects of the husband and wife relationship equally enjoyable.

Her father's widowed cousin, Mrs. Verity Dalrymple, who served as her companion, had urged her to accept the earl. "Snap him up, my girl," she'd said with her usual embarrassing frankness. "The handsome fellow is everything any woman could want in a husband and what's more, he's tall enough to look you in the eye."

But in the end, despite Verity's urging and her own secret longing for a husband and children, she had allowed reason to prevail. For she was not just any woman. She was the owner of one of the largest mills in Yorkshire, as well as the flocks of sheep that supplied the wool for its looms. She had more than her own future to consider. She would have to know a man a good deal longer than three weeks to trust him with the welfare of the more than two hundred families who depended on her for their livelihood.

Reluctantly, she had informed her suitor that she would need time to consider his offer. After which, she could scarcely refuse his plea that she and Verity visit London so he could show her the many advantages of becoming his countess.

So, here she was lying wide awake, late at night, in the elegantly appointed bedchamber the earl had instructed his housekeeper to assign her. She had to laugh at the irony of it all. If he but knew it, there was nothing more apt to make her refuse his offer than the thought of spending the rest of her life sleeping in bedchambers such as this. The satin sheets, gold leaf wallpaper, and priceless antique furniture only served to remind her that a plain Yorkshire countrywoman posing as a countess would look very much like a mudhen pretending to be a peacock.

She missed her comfortable old house and her books and the quiet joy of working in her garden early on a summer morning. Most of all, she missed supervising her mill and sharing in the lives of the people who worked for her. They were her "family" and filled the empty spaces in her lonely heart. She sighed, wondering how long she must stay in the city before she could leave without hurting the earl's feelings.

The clock on the mantel struck midnight and Rachel gave up all hope of sleep. Remembering the impressive collection of books she'd seen in Fairborne's library on her tour of the house, she donned her comfortable flannel wrapper and slippers, and candle in hand stepped into the corridor. She tiptoed past the room where Verity slept, past the earl's suite, down a flight of stairs, and along a hall to the bookroom.

"So far, so good," she congratulated herself as she approached the door she sought. But the instant she cracked it open, a draft of air extinguished her candle.

"Damn and blast," she grumbled, echoing her father's favorite epithet. Someone had apparently left a window open and now she was stranded. For there was no way on earth she could find her way back to her bedchamber in the dark.

Then she saw it—a faint glow seeping through the crack between the door and the jamb. She pushed the door open and to her surprise, saw the shadowy figure of a man bent over the bookroom desk, apparently searching through the contents of one of the drawers.

The light she had glimpsed came from a candle which was shielded from the draft by a screen composed of three large books standing on end in the middle of the desk. She smiled to herself. Only a man would have thought of such a solution to the problem. A woman would simply have closed the window.

But how humiliating to appear before the earl in the dead of night clad in nothing but her night rail and wrapper. What would he think of her? She wished she could magically disappear and save them both embarrassment. But all she could do was make the best of a bad situation.

"Do not let me disturb you, my lord. I just came for a book because I couldn't sleep," she said briskly, and saw his head jerk up like a rabbit caught in a hunter's sights.

"But I shall need to light my candle off yours . . ." She gasped. Even in the dim light of the single candle, she could see he was not the fair-haired, brown-eyed earl. Though he was tall like Fairborne, this man's unfashionably long hair was black as a raven's wing and his strange silver eyes searched for her in the shadows like a hawk staking out its prey. He was, in fact, so darkly beautiful he reminded her of one of Satan's fallen angels in a painting she'd once seen in a Benedictine abbey near York.

"Who . . . who are you? What are you doing in the earl's

bookroom?" she stammered and immediately regretted her questions. For his coldly calculating gaze swept over her as if she were a troublesome insect he was considering swatting out of his way. She bit back the urge to scream, belatedly realizing she had happened upon a thief in the process of robbing the earl. She'd had no previous experience with thieves; they were unheard of in her Yorkshire village. But it stood to reason any man embarking on such a career would be both desperate and dangerous.

As if to prove her judgment of his species correct, this particular thief proceeded to pick up the candle, skirt the desk, and advance toward her in a most menacing way. "Stay away from me," she commanded, hoping desperately he was not a defiler of women as well as a thatchgallows.

She backed toward the door, willing to brave the dark hall rather than be caught in the pool of light created by the burglar's candle. The very thought of the violence to which he might be driven by the sight of a woman in her present state of dishabille made her blood run cold. Words like "ravish" and "violate" raced through her fevered mind.

"One step farther, sir, and I swear I will scream loud enough to wake everyone in this house and every other house in Grosvenor Square," she declared in her best no-nonsense tone of voice.

"I would not advise it, madam. I have no wish to harm you but, as you can see, we are in a delicate situation here."

Rachel's mouth fell open. The mysterious fellow spoke perfect English with a refined, upper class accent. Almost too perfect. He scarcely sounded British. Still, she took comfort in the fact that he had the bearing of a gentleman.

Furthermore, now that she thought about it, if it was burglary he had in mind, he must be very new at his trade. Only a rank beginner would search for money and jewels in a desk drawer. He must have recently fallen on hard times and been forced into a life of crime to survive.

"Your threats do not frighten me, sir," she declared, hoping desperately the tremor in her voice was not as noticeable to him as it was to her.

The devil they didn't! Yves could almost smell the woman's fear. He felt sickened by the realization he had sunk so low as to terrorize helpless women to obtain the evidence he sought. One more crime he could lay at the traitor's feet.

He raised his candle to take a closer look at this servant of the earl's who had stumbled upon him at the most inopportune time. For servant she must be. No woman above the rank of housekeeper would consider owning, much less wearing, such a hideous wrapper.

Yet, oddly enough, the garment suited this female. She was a head taller than the average woman and pencil-slim. Her face, while not actually homely, was plain as an English pudding and her light brown hair was skinned back into a thick plait that would have better suited a novice in a convent than a woman of mature years. In truth, except for her remarkable height and a pair of expressive gold-flecked brown eyes, she was one of the most forgettable women he had ever encountered.

"I demand to know what you are planning to do with me," she demanded in a no-nonsense voice that sounded more like that of a schoolmistress than a common servant.

"For one thing, madam, I will surely throttle you unless you keep your voice down," he threatened, reaching past her to push the door shut. She jumped back, banged her head on the wall, and screamed. As he'd feared, he soon heard footsteps in the hall outside the bookroom.

Quickly snuffing the candle, he shoved the annoying housekeeper into a recessed area between two stacks of bookshelves and clamped his hand over her mouth. She wriggled like a worm on a hook and unfortunately, there was a great deal of her to wriggle.

With one hand still clasping the candleholder, the other covering her mouth, he had no hope of controlling her unless he used his body to wedge her into the narrow recess. A mistake. She evidently mistook control for ravishment, because she began thrashing about in earnest and making frantic squealing sounds deep in her throat.

"You leave me no choice, madam," he murmured and silenced her squeals by covering her mouth with his. He felt her stiffen, felt her fists pound against his chest and her lips compress against her teeth. The poor woman obviously thought she was being attacked by the worst kind of fiend, and there was nothing he could do to alleviate her fears. For at that very moment, the door burst open and two men entered the bookroom. Unless he instantly subdued the Amazon housekeeper, he would be in serious trouble.

He took the only course left to him—the one course that had never failed him in his dealings with women. He gave himself over to kissing her with all the sensuous expertise of a lusty Frenchman who had spent his youth in the arms of some of the most accomplished courtesans in Paris and Vienna. As if by magic, the Amazon's lips softened beneath his and the tension in her body relaxed.

Behind him a voice said, "I thought I heard a woman scream."

Another, thick with Celtic brogue replied, "As did I, milord. But 'tis plain 'twas only the wind howling like a banshee through this open window."

"Devil take it, I'm certain I closed the blasted thing before I went up to bed," the first voice replied. "Ah well, no harm done."

One of the men closed the window Yves had purposely left open to allow for a quick exit if necessary. Moments later the door clicked shut, the voices died away, and the footsteps receded down the hall.

Yves lifted his head and breathed a sigh of relief—and heard an echoing sigh deep in the throat of the woman whose body was crushed against his. Shock rippled through him as he realized the ungainly housekeeper had literally melted in his arms when he'd kissed her. From her passionate, but clumsy, response, it was all too obvious she was a complete innocent—a revelation that only added to his sense of guilt.

Gently, he began to extricate himself from the embrace. But her arms wound around his neck and her lips moved tentatively against his as if inviting him to once again deepen the kiss. Unexpectedly, desire shot through him, hardening his body and firing his hot, Gallic blood.

Mon Dieu, what was he thinking of? This tall, gauche beanpole was not the kind of woman to stir his senses. His taste ran to diminutive sophisticates with dark hair and sweetly curvaceous bodies—women who, in one way or another, reminded him of Amalie.

He stepped back and put her firmly from him. "I must light the candle," he whispered and winced at her plaintive whimper. He had always felt contempt for men of his class who forced their attentions on helpless female servants. Yet he had defiled this innocent woman as surely as if he had seduced her.

The thought haunted him while he groped his way to the fireplace and lighted his candle with a glowing ember. It haunted him even more when he glimpsed the look of shock in the house-keeper's eyes. He drew her out of the alcove and with a hand firmly beneath her elbow, led her to one of the armchairs facing the fireplace.

"I must leave now," he said.

She nodded.

"Will you be all right?"

She shook her head. "I doubt I shall ever be 'all right' again, but please do leave. You are in grave danger. Surely you are aware that many magistrates in England consider theft a hang-ing offense."

Her candor stunned him; her concern for his safety shamed him. There was more to this ungainly woman than met the eye. He was painfully aware he should beg her forgiveness for tak-ing advantage of her innocence. Instead, he simply said, "I shall keep your warning in mind in the future, dear lady," and exe-cuted the same courtly bow he had once accorded the Empress Josephine. Then, without further ado, he opened the window and slipped out into the shadowy garden.

As he walked through the darkened streets toward his hotel, he viewed the events of the previous hour with mixed emotions. On the one hand he had been interrupted before he could find the evidence for which he searched. On the other, he had proved the Bow Street runner's information outdated. The Irishman in the bookroom had addressed his companion as "milord." Evidently the earl had returned to London sooner than expected, which meant Yves would have to alter his plans accordingly.

Strange as it might seem, he did not consider the earl's house-keeper a menace to those plans. True, she could alert the earl that a "burglar" had broken into his bookroom. But he doubted burglary was all that uncommon in postwar London. All in all, the night's work was not an entire fiasco.

He was less than a block from the Pulteney Hotel, where he was stopping while in London, when he remembered he had left the three books standing on end in the middle of the earl's desk. He cursed softly. When had he grown so careless? A slip like that could have cost him his head at the emperor's court.

He refused to admit that a gangly, flat-chested British house-keeper could have thrown him so off-balance he would make such a crucial mistake. Still, remembering his unexpected stab of desire when he'd kissed her, and the wounded look in her fine dark eyes when he'd bid her farewell, he was grateful she was a member of the servant class and someone he would never have occasion to meet socially.

He wished he could find a way to apologize for his shabby treatment of her. But how could he when he didn't even know her name?

Rachel noticed the three books shortly after the black-haired burglar disappeared into the night. Once she was certain her legs would support her, she returned the large, leather-bound volumes to the bottom shelf of the bookcase from whence they'd come and tidied the desk to make certain there was no evidence of the stranger's having rifled it.

If anyone had prophesied but a few hours earlier that a law-abiding citizen like herself would go to such lengths to protect a common thief, she would have judged them mad. But she could not bear the thought of the handsome Frenchman ending his life on a gallows. For because of him she had experienced what she could only term an epiphany. She had entered the bookroom a callow spinster; she would leave it a woman awakened to her own profoundly sensual nature. But how cruel a joke! What could the Creator have been thinking to endow a plain-as-dirt countrywoman with longings she could never hope to satisfy?

Still, she owed the black-haired stranger a debt of gratitude. Never mind that he had only kissed her to keep her quiet. He had given her a glimpse of the wildly wonderful passion a woman could experience with such a wicked rogue—and she felt strangely liberated. Now that she possessed such worldly knowledge, she was in a much better position to make an intelligent decision about the Earl of Fairborne's offer.

She wished she could tell the stranger she was glad he had opened her eyes to such knowledge. He had looked so guilty and unhappy when he bade her good-bye. But how could she when she didn't even know his name?

Chapter Two

The Earl of Fairborne was a conscientious host. Too conscientious to Rachel's way of thinking. He apparently felt dutybound to entertain her every waking minute of every day. It was the last thing she wanted; she'd even gone so far as to beg him to spend an occasional evening at his club during the fortnight she'd been his houseguest. In truth, she sorely missed her privacy and found the endless round of sightseeing, theater parties, and carriage rides in Hyde Park unbelievably exhausting.

But even as she made a halfhearted attempt to dress for yet another evening of entertainment, the voice of her conscience whispered that she might feel a good deal less exhausted if she could sleep through one entire night without dreaming of the daring, black-haired burglar she'd caught in the act of robbing the earl's townhouse.

For dream of him she did every time she laid her head on her pillow. With shocking realism she relived the moments when his lean, hard body had pressed hers into the narrow alcove and his warm lips had sent shivers of awareness racing through her.

The chaste kisses Lord Fairborne gave her each night at her chamber door only added to her feelings of guilt about her erotic fantasies. There was no doubt about it; she was a wicked, depraved woman—not worthy of polishing the boots of the fine, upstanding man who had offered her his heart and his name.

"Have you naught but this plain, brown frock to wear to Vauxhall Gardens this night, mistress?" Mary Tucker, the abigail provided her by the earl's housekeeper, interrupted Rachel's self-chastisement with her usual complaint about her new mistress's meager wardrobe. "'Tis a shame to cover your pretty silk underclothes with the drab thing," she added as a parting shot.

"In case it has escaped your notice, Mary," Rachel said

patiently, while I may enjoy the feel of silk against my skin, I am still a plain, brown kind of woman on the outside."

"Such talk is pure gammon, miss, if you don't mind me saying so. Any woman can turn a man's head with the proper gown and hair style."

Rachel couldn't help but note that while Mary tended to be a bit pale and mopish, she was still an exceptionally attractive young woman. Her eyes were large and very blue, her hair a mass of golden curls, and her curvaceous body looked ready to burst the seams of her modest uniform in the most intriguing places.

"An interesting philosophy," Rachel said with a smile. "But I fear even Michelangelo had to start with a superior piece of marble to create one of his masterpieces."

Mary scowled. "Well now, I don't know what this Michael what's-his-name has to do with anything, miss, but I do know you've as fine a pair of eyes as ever I've seen and nice, thick hair what just wants proper dressing, for all it's a mousy sort of color."

Verity Dalrymple looked up from her embroidery. "The girl is right, you know, and if you're thinking that dowdy frock will make you look shorter, it won't. So, you might as well wear something colorful with a neckline that shows a bit of bosom—especially when you're escorted by a man as well turned out as the earl. I'm surprised the dear fellow hasn't suggested you visit a good mantua maker while you're in London."

As a matter of fact he had, but Rachel was not about to admit *that* to her two critics. "I shall consider it," she said crossly. "In the meantime, I'll wear my second best brown chintz. It will do for strolling about a public garden."

If the truth be known, she'd stopped thinking about her appearance on her fourteenth birthday, when her father had enrolled her in Miss Frogmire's Academy for Young Ladies. Such thoughts were much too painful. It had been bad enough that she'd been plain of face and a head taller than any other girl. To compound her problems, her speech had been peppered with the thees and thous common to Yorkshire farmers and mill workers. As a result, she'd been subjected to the cruelest kind of ridicule.

She'd determined then and there that the best course of action for a social misfit like herself was to become as inconspicuous as possible. From that day forward, she had worked diligently to improve her speech and made certain the gowns she wore were plain, serviceable, and not apt to draw attention.

Verity scowled at her over the rim of her spectacles. "When my dear Wilfred and I resided in London, we frequently visited Vauxhall. It is much more than a public garden, and everyone who goes there dresses to the nines. If you must wear that drab gown, you should at least brighten it up with one of my pretty embroidered collars. Furthermore, you should demand that lazy abigail of yours dress your hair more fashionably. It is high time the girl did something to earn the generous salary the earl pays her."

Not for the first time, Rachel found herself sorry she had insisted Verity consider herself family instead of just a hired companion. The woman had taken that as an invitation to speak her mind freely, and she had a knack for always saying the very thing one did not want to hear.

Too tired to argue, Rachel agreed to wear the proffered collar and even agreed to let Mary clip and curl a tendril of hair at either side of her face. "There now, that's ever so much better," the young maid said when she had finished her barbering.

Rachel stared into the cheval glass and found herself amazed at how much softer her features appeared with the minor change in her hair style—how much brighter her eyes looked because of the colorful collar.

Her spirits rose even higher when the earl, or Edgar as he insisted she call him, complimented her on her changed appearance—though she did feel he went a bit too far when he called her a "goddess of beauty who graces the night with her radiance." Still, it was her first real compliment, and now she had another reason to be grateful to this kindest of men.

Darkness had fallen by the time she and Edgar reached Vauxhall Gardens. "We are in luck," he said, gazing at the starstudded heavens. "It is one of those rare summer nights in London when a breeze has carried the smoke of the city upriver."

"The stars look close enough to pluck them out of the sky," Rachel agreed, her pulse quickening in anticipation of the evening ahead. She was an avid gardener and while a public garden in London was a poor substitute for her own precious flowers and shrubs, it would be a welcome change from cobblestone streets.

She soon discovered, however, that Vauxhall was nothing like any other garden she had ever seen. Oh there were neatly tended flower beds here and there and a great many ancient trees. But unlike the trees on her property in Yorkshire, these were hung with hundreds of small gas lanterns that rivaled the twinkling lights of the firmament. In truth, the park was a fairyland of marble statues and temples, man-made caves and grottos, and cascading waterfalls designed to stir the imaginations and titillate the senses of the hundreds of pleasure seekers escaping the heat and congestion of the city.

For a change, Verity had not accompanied them. "Run along, you two lovebirds," she'd said with a broad wink for the earl."I want to remember Vauxhall as I saw it on the arm of my darling Wilfred, and it is not as if a lady mill owner needs to guard her reputation like a nobleman's daughter."

Rachel had cringed at this less-than-subtle attempt to throw her into the poor man's arms. But now she was glad her companion had chosen to stay at home. It was clear Edgar had planned the evening very carefully, and Verity would have ruined it with her vulgar chatter.

To begin with, they had crossed to the south bank of the Thames by scull. "Less convenient than the iron bridge, but infinitely more romantic," Edgar had explained, with such a tender smile, Rachel had felt her eyes pool with sentimental tears.

Then it turned out he had reserved a private supper box in the colonnade bordering the dance floor so they could watch the couples waltzing beneath the stars. Rachel wished with all her heart she could join them, but she had never learned to dance. Her father had considered such lessons for a girl her size a waste of good money. A pity, she thought, for she'd not tower over Edgar if she danced with him. Nor would she tower over a certain tall black-haired burglar if she waltzed in his arms.

Good heavens! From where did that shocking thought come? A decent, law-abiding woman was not supposed to daydream about a common thief—particularly when she was being wined and dined by a fine gentleman like the earl. Deeply ashamed, she thrust aside all thought of silver eyes and warm, sensuous lips, and firmly resolved to devote the rest of the evening to being a perfect companion for her gracious host.

The task was not a difficult one, for with every passing minute, his meticulous planning for the outing became more evident. No sooner had they seated themselves than a waiter appeared out of nowhere with a tray on which reposed two glasses of what the earl assured her was the finest sherry available. It was Rachel's first taste of the golden wine and she found it rather disappointing. She decided she might be more impressed with the "fine, nutty flavor" if the stuff didn't smell so much like the vat of sheep dip in which she deloused her flock of prize Wensleydales each spring.

The elegant supper of cold chicken, thinly shaved ham, and plump strawberries was more to her taste, but she scarcely had time to eat it with so many of Edgar's friends stopping by their table to say hello. It was plain to see Edgar was a popular member of London society. Once again Rachel found herself wondering why a man who could have his pick of the most beautiful women of his own social class should want her for his countess. But want her he obviously did. The dear man held her hand while they listened to the music of Handel and watched the tightrope artists and jugglers and daring equestrians.

He held it even tighter when the spectacular fireworks display began. Another first. She had always wondered what it would be like to entwine her fingers with those of a man. Now she knew. It made her feel delightfully feminine and—there was no other word for it—cherished.

Wrapped in the quiet joy of the moment, she told herself this pleasant kind of companionship between a man and woman had to be what true contentment was all about. The fiery, heart-stopping emotion she'd experienced when the black-haired stranger kissed her had been nothing more than a reflection of that wanton part of her own nature that was best kept buried deep inside her.

"Shall we take a stroll through the gardens before we leave, my dear?" Edgar asked when the fireworks ended.

Rachel smiled at her gentle suitor. "I should like that above all, my lord . . . Edgar." She sensed he had arranged their lovely evening with a purpose in mind. Once again he was about to ask her to marry him, and this time she was tempted to give him the answer he desired.

Arm in arm, they strolled the softly lighted Lovers' Walk together with the other couples of a like mind. Rachel listened to the happy murmur of voices, the music of laughter echoing through the trees, and for the first time she felt a part of the life around her—not just a lonely outsider watching from a distance.

It was enough; it was, in fact, the miracle she had never

expected to happen. She told herself how lucky she was, how grateful she should be that such a kind, generous-hearted man wanted to give her the home and children for which she had always yearned. What did it matter that she and Edgar appeared to have little in common? Surely two decent, well-meaning people could find a similarity of spirit—no matter how diverse their individual goals might be. She would simply explain to him that managing her mill was very important to her. Surely he would understand, even if he had no interest in such things.

She glanced up as they approached another couple strolling toward them. They had passed any number of such couples, but somehow these two people caught her eye. Perhaps because they were so remarkably beautiful and so perfectly suited to each other they drew admiring attention from everyone around them—perhaps because they were as different from her and Edgar as midnight was from morning.

The woman was a small, raven-haired beauty with huge dark eyes and a surprisingly voluptuous figure for one so slender. Her daringly décolleté gown of some diaphanous blue material shimmered in the lantern light as she walked, and she clung to the arm of a tall man whose hair was as jet black as her own.

Rachel blinked. There was something shockingly familiar about the beautiful woman's escort—something about the way he moved, the way he tilted his head when he listened to her.

She blinked again and felt her breath catch in her throat, her heart skip a beat. But not until his bold gaze raked her from head to toe as they passed on the narrow path, was she absolutely certain he was the wicked rogue who had haunted her dreams for the past fortnight.

It took her a moment longer to realize that he and the earl had exchanged curt nods. "Are you acquainted with that man?" she asked in as normal a voice as she could manage.

"He's a French aristocrat—the Comte de Rochemont, or some such title."

"A c-count?" Rachel stammered. "The man is a French count? Whatever makes you think that?"

"I don't think it; I know it." Fairborne ground his teeth. "I was introduced to him at my club a few nights ago. He had just been made an honorary member—something I find rather appalling. One does not expect a foreigner, especially a Frenchman, to become a member of one's club. But apparently he is well to grass, unlike most of his kind, who are hard put to find two coins to rub together. Rumor has it his grandfather managed to hide the bulk of the family fortune before the revolutionaries could get their hands on it."

Rachel stared at the earl with mouth agape. Something did not ring true here. Why would a wealthy French aristocrat resort to burglary? She shivered as the disquieting thought crossed her mind that it might have been something other than money and jewels he was searching for in the earl's desk.

She'd heard it said the French were a wily lot and not to be trusted to honor the peace. Could the devious fellow have been looking for important papers concerning Edgar's work at Whitehall?

She wasn't certain exactly what it was Edgar had done during the war. He was such a modest fellow, he never bragged about his accomplishments. But from the little he'd divulged, she'd gathered he had played a major part in planning the defeat of Napoleon Bonaparte and had been the one to convince Lord Castlereagh that St. Helena was the logical place for the Corsican monster's final exile.

Rachel's heart thudded painfully and her thoughts spun as wildly as one of the crude wooden tops her mill hands whittled for their children. Could Bonaparte be planning another escape? Could the papers in some way aid that escape if they fell into the wrong hands? Dear God, had she inadvertently been a traitor to her country because a handsome Frenchman had hypnotized her with a kiss?

A glance at the earl's face told her the unexpected appearance of the Comte de Rochemont had upset him every bit as much as it had her. "I take it you do not like this French count," she ventured tentatively.

"I am an Englishman, with an Englishman's distrust of the French."

Rachel choked on the massive lump of guilt that had lodged in her throat. "Are you saying you think he may be in London on some dangerous political mission?"

Fairborne stopped in his tracks. "What the devil makes you ask that?"

"N-nothing in particular," Rachel stammered, startled by the unusual harshness in his voice, the odd look in his eyes. "It is just that one hears so many conflicting reports about the Gallic nature."

"And with good reason. I hate to say it, my dear, but the truth is the only good Frenchman is a dead Frenchman."

Rachel stared at him, aghast. "Surely you cannot mean that!"

"Indeed I do, and I am not the only Englishman to think so." The earl massaged his right temple, evidently to ease a burgeoning headache, as they resumed walking along the shadowy path. "But thank God for small blessings. For a moment there, I feared the pawky fellow might expect me to stop and exchange the usual amenities with him—which would, of course, have been disastrous."

"How so?"

"It would have necessitated the two of us introducing our companions as well. Luckily he recognized you for what you are and went on his way without causing any undue embarrassment."

Rachel stiffened. "What am I, my lord—that this French count immediately recognized?"

"Why, a lady, of course, which is more than can be said for that flamboyant creature hanging on his arm." A scowl black as a thundercloud crossed the earl's handsome face. "Jacqueline Esquaré is one of the most notorious women in London."

"Notorious? In what way?"

Fairborne's scowl grew even darker. "At the risk of offending your innocent ears, she is a courtesan. Or, to put it in plain English—a high-priced French whore, whose demands for expensive baubles would bankrupt all but the wealthiest of noblemen."

"Oh!" Rachel felt numb with shock. They walked on, but her euphoric mood was gone—irrevocably shattered by the appearance of the mysterious Frenchman and the beautiful courtesan.

Edgar seemed every bit as upset as she was by the unexpected encounter. She hazarded a peek at his stern profile and the rigid set of his shoulders and decided it would be prudent to wait until the following morning to confess she'd neglected to mention she'd caught the Comte de Rochemont rifling his desk a full fortnight earlier.

She sighed, certain of one thing only. She would not be faced with making a decision about an offer of marriage from her noble suitor this night.

*   *   *

"You are acquainted with the Earl of Fairborne, *cheri*? I did not know this." Like a slashing blade, the sharp edge of Jacqueline Esquaré's voice penetrated the fog engulfing Yves.

He managed a terse, "I was introduced to him Thursday last."

"Then why so grim a face? Edgar Hanley is much too charming a fellow to have offended you at first meeting." She studied Yves with eyes nearly as black as her gleaming tresses. "Surely it is not that brown stick of a woman on his arm who makes you tremble with rage."

Yves quickly collected his scattered wits. "I am not trembling with rage," he said coldly. He was, in fact, reeling from shock. One glimpse of the tall woman at Fairborne's side and he'd instantly realized his mistake in labeling her the earl's housekeeper. She had to be the Yorkshire heiress the Bow Street runner had termed "a complete dowd." She certainly fit the description; the nondescript gown she wore at the moment was every bit as unattractive as the wrapper she'd had on the first time he'd seen her.

But what was she doing residing at Fairborne's London townhouse? Had the blackguard already seduced her? If so, she had learned little from the experience. He would wager everything he owned that the woman he had kissed had been a complete innocent—albeit a passionate one. Not that he cared one way or the other; the morals of a dowdy English spinster were not his concern.

"It *is* the woman. I see it now." Mockery sharpened Jacqueline's melodic voice. "*Mais pourquoi?* Of what interest to you is the brown stick heiress from Yorkshire? You do not share Fairborne's pressing need for money."

"I have no interest in a tall, gawky Englishwoman," Yves declared. "How could I?" He favored Jacqueline with a seductive smile and dutifully mouthed the words she expected to hear. "My taste runs to delicate, black-haired Frenchwomen like you— women whose eyes are dark pools of desire in which a man can drown and die happily."

It was not precisely a lie. While he felt nothing but disgust for Jacqueline's coldly avaricious nature, he couldn't help but be attracted to a woman who bore such a strong physical resemblance to his beloved Amalie.

He paused a long moment. "But it strikes me you are surprisingly well versed in the earl's affairs. Should I be jealous?"

Jacqueline gave a noncommittal shrug of her slender shoulders. "The Earl of Fairborne has been madly in love with me since the first moment he saw me," she stated with her usual lack of modesty. "But it is over between us."

Yves managed a look of surprise, though, in truth, it was her involvement with the earl that had prompted him to make overtures to her in the first place. He had been waiting for just such an opportunity to quiz her about her former patron.

"The man must be a fool to give a woman like you her congé," he said tongue in cheek.

Sparks flashed in Jacqueline's dark eyes. "He did not give me up; I gave him up when he failed to pay my landlord and my modiste. What else could I do? It was obvious he did not have the funds to support a woman with my needs."

"And when was that?"

"My rent was due on the first day of June. Would you believe it, I had to pay it myself—and my modiste as well, or the selfish pig would not have completed my gown for the annual cyprian's ball." She sighed. "It was most sad; I liked Edgar very much and I agreed to consider taking him back once he recouped his fortune by marrying the heiress."

Yves scowled at the beautiful woman clinging so possessively to his arm. "That seems a rather shabby way to treat the heiress."

Throaty laughter spilled from Jacqueline's rosebud lips. "Since when has the Comte de Rochemont become such a sensitive fellow?" She raised a delicate eyebrow. "For what other reason would any man take a woman like her to wife?"

"None I can think of, now that you mention it," Yves said quickly. Jacqueline Esquaré was a breathtakingly beautiful woman; she was also a jealous little cat who had spent a lifetime perfecting the wiles that made her one of the most sought-after cyprians in London.

It would never do to admit that kissing a plain woman like Rachel Barton had made his pulse race like that of a green lad with his first woman. The "cat" had a deep-seated prejudice against plain women. He knew for a fact it galled her that at the ripe old age of nine-and-twenty her plain-faced rival, Harriette Wilson, enjoyed the patronage of such men as the Dukes of Wellington and Argyll.

He suspected it disturbed her even more that, thanks to the generosity of one of her powerful patrons, Harriette commanded her own box at Drury Lane, from which she regularly held court in plain view of all of fashionable London. Yves was not averse to leasing a like box for Jacqueline if it fit in with his plans to goad the Earl of Fairborne into acting recklessly.

Jacqueline lowered her incredible black lashes. "I may not take him back after all if you beg me not to, *cheri*."

Yves laughed. "Providing I do not run out of money."

"*Exactement.*" Jacqueline gave an indignant sniff. "I was not born into a fortune, as you were. I cannot afford to be sentimental when I must keep up present appearances and save for my old age as well. I doubt any of the noblemen who clamor for my favors now will offer to take care of me once time has robbed me of my beauty."

There was no disputing the logic of her reasoning. Yves halted their progress along the shadowy path long enough to raise her slender fingers to his lips. "I salute your Gallic practicality, Jacqueline," he murmured. But even as he did so, he had to wonder if Lord Castlereagh's suspicions about Fairborne were justified. Was this man who callously planned to strip Rachel Barton of her fortune to support his lust for a beautiful trollop the same one who had caused Amalie's death?

A chilling thought crossed his mind. If they were one and the same and if Castlereagh was right about English law, Fairborne would have little use for the dowdy heiress once the marriage lines were signed. In which case, the naive countrywoman from Yorkshire might very well lose more than her fortune before all was said and done.

Chapter Three

Rachel rose from her bed after a restless, wakeful night, determined to confess all to the earl. But how much easier it would be to do so if only she could think of a plausible reason for waiting so long to tell him she had surprised the Comte de Rochemont in the act of rifling his desk.

Over and over she rehearsed how she would go about the humiliating task. "By the way, my lord, I believe I may have forgotten to mention that . . ." or "There is something I have been meaning to tell . . ." But each new approach she came up with sounded more lame than the last.

Finally she decided there was nothing for it but to get on with the sorry business. But how ironic! After waiting a lifetime for an offer, she had risked alienating the kindest and most honorable of suitors simply because a handsome stranger had kissed her and addled her wits. Not that she intended to mention that in her confession.

Grim, but determined, she entered the breakfast room, only to have the footman on duty hand her a note from the earl, stating he had business in the city, but would return home in time to join her for dinner. He added that his town coach was at her disposal and he hoped she would have a pleasant day.

"Damn and blast," she muttered as she poured herself a cup of tea to calm her frayed nerves. Now she would have to stew in her own misery another ten or twelve hours before she could unburden herself. She was not accustomed to wrestling with a guilty conscience and she found the experience most unpleasant.

"So, what shall we do to entertain ourselves until the earl returns?" Verity asked when Rachel showed her the note.

Rachel thought for a moment. "I believe I shall visit Hatchard's Bookstore. I have a list of books I should like to take back to

Yorkshire. Then, if I have time, I'll take in Ackerman's Art Library or possibly make a tour of Westminster Abbey."

"Good heavens, how dull!" Verity shuddered. "In that case, I believe I must beg off my duties as your companion and take to my bed. I feel a headache coming on."

"A wise decision," Rachel agreed, more grateful than she cared to admit for a day to herself. Without further ado, she ordered the carriage and hurried to her bedchamber to gather her bonnet and gloves before Verity could change her mind.

"Take me to Hatchard's Bookstore please," she directed the young coachman.

He stared down at her, a blank look on his round, freckled face. "Have ye any thought where that might be, mistress?"

"I was told it is on Piccadilly Street."

"Well then that solves me problem. For I knows Piccadilly well enough. I've driven the earl there often." He scratched his head. "But I'm certain 'twas never to a bookstore."

How odd, Rachel thought. When she'd mentioned her desire to visit Hatchard's to Edgar, he had claimed it was one of his favorite haunts. But remembering his extensive library of leather-bound books, she could see his noble taste was limited to the classics, most of which she already owned.

Knowing the dear man as she did, she suspected he had been loath to point out that only someone who found Fanny Burney every bit as enjoyable as Plato would need to patronize the eclectic bookstore. Once again she had to wonder what in heaven's name a wealthy, sophisticated nobleman like the Earl of Fairborne had found to admire in a plain Yorkshire countrywoman.

Her first glimpse of Hatchard's convinced her it was all she had heard and more. Entranced by the sight of shelf upon shelf of every kind of book imaginable, she stood just inside the entrance and breathed in the wondrous scents of leather and paper and printers' ink until she realized she was attracting the attention of the other customers.

Quickly claiming a small-wheeled cart a passing clerk parked nearby, she wandered through the stacks, gathering the books on her list and a dozen more that would keep her entertained through the long Yorkshire winter.

What seemed only minutes later, she glanced at the small, gold chatelaine watch pinned to the shoulder of her gown and blinked in disbelief. She had spent more than two hours at the pleasant occupation—while the poor coachman and pair of spirited horses waited outside on the hot, dusty street.

Guilt-stricken, she hurriedly wheeled her precious collection toward the front of the store just in time to hear a familiar rich, male voice ask the counter clerk, "Have you by any chance located the book I ordered Tuesday last?"

Rachel brought the top-heavy cart to a grinding halt, spilling four of the books onto the floor.

"We have indeed, sir," the clerk replied, "and here it is—*The Legend of the Chevalier de Bayard* by Christian Trenholm."

"*Mais oui, Le Chevalier sans peur et sans reproche.* It will be interesting to see how an Englishman views one of France's greatest heroes. And how much do I owe you?"

Rachel didn't hear the clerk's answer. Abandoning the cart, she slipped back out of sight and held her breath until she heard the door close behind the Frenchman. Then, heart pounding, she crept back to the cart, picked up the scattered books, and once again headed for the counter.

The clerk glanced up as she approached. "Good heavens, madam, let me take care of that for you," he shrieked at the top of his voice. Rushing forward, he wrested the cart from her hands. "I assure you, Hatchard's does not expect its lady customers to do manual labor. We are pleased to supply floor clerks and stock boys to carry out such tasks."

Rachel's cheeks flamed as a furtive glance about her confirmed that every eye in the store was on her. She was so accustomed to doing for herself, it hadn't occurred to her that London ladies would never think of wheeling heavily laden carts through the aisles of bookstores.

To add to her humiliation, the clerk who had rushed to her assistance was a diminutive fellow. The top of his head barely reached her shoulder and he looked no bigger around than a willow twig. In truth, she felt like an elephant trailing a mouse as she followed him to the counter.

She could hear the rustle of voices behind her—and here and there a ripple of laughter. Words like "Amazon" and "country bumpkin" scalded her ears and heated her cheeks. She had long ago learned to ignore the stares and comments her unusual height occasioned. But this was different; it was difficult to ignore the fact that she had amused a crowd of jaded Londoners with her provincial Yorkshire ways. She had obviously made a monstrous social blunder by London standards, but there was nothing for it but to grit her teeth and wait while the clerk slowly and meticulously tallied up her numerous purchases.

At long last the sale was recorded, the money paid, and two stock boys conscripted to carry the books to the carriage. "Hatchard's thanks you sincerely for your patronage, madam," the clerk said, never cracking a smile. But his moustache twitched suspiciously and more than ever, he looked like a bright-eyed little mouse.

Rachel swept the cheeky fellow with a look that brought an instant flush to his sallow cheeks, and head high she marched from the store with what little dignity she had left. "Put the packages on the seat facing the rear," she directed the floor clerks and waited beside the carriage while they did so.

"Will that be all, madam?" one of the clerks asked.

"Yes, thank you," she replied and wondered why the two still stared at her expectantly.

"I believe this is what they are waiting for." The Frenchman she had thought she'd avoided detached himself from the lamppost on which he'd been leaning and tossed each of the clerks a coin. "For services rendered," he said, smiling into Rachel's eyes. "'Tis an old established custom in both London and Paris. I doubt the poor devils could keep body and soul together without it."

Doffing his high-crowned beaver, he made Rachel the same courtly bow as when he'd taken his leave of her in the earl's bookroom. "Good morning, Miss Barton. How nice to see you again."

"G-good morning," she stammered, her heart thumping wildly in her breast.

"What a happy coincidence that we should both be visiting Hatchard's at the same time," he remarked. But a devilish glint in his strange silver eyes made her wonder just how much a part chance had played in their meeting. The thought that this mysterious French count might be monitoring her comings and goings sent chills down her spine.

"Allow me," he insisted when she made to enter the carriage. Placing a hand beneath her elbow, he handed her up as easily as if she weighed but a feather, then stepped back onto the curb.

"Thank you," she murmured, wondering how he could have learned her name—until it occurred to her that spies were probably good at that sort of thing.

"Where can I take ye now, mistress?" the patient coachman asked, peering down at her through the trap.

She was tempted to say "Back to Grosvenor Square." But that would never do. Whatever trepidation she might have concerning the Frenchman, she was not about to let him frighten her into hiding behind the walls of the earl's townhouse.

"Do you know where Ackerman's Art Library is?" she asked.

"No, mistress, can't say as I do."

"Then what about Westminster Abbey?"

The coachman grinned. "Aye, that I know, as does every other man who calls himself a Londoner. The abbey it is then. I'll have ye there in no time."

Rachel waited until he had closed the trap and set the coach in motion before she cast a furtive glance out the window. The Count de Rochemont still stood on the curb, a thoughtful frown on his face as he stared at the departing coach.

She shivered. What was there about this mysterious Frenchman that affected her so strangely? Why did his slightest touch elicit disturbing sensations she had never before experienced? Even now, suspecting what she did about him, she could feel heat pulsing where his long, elegant fingers had gripped her arm— feel her legs tremble just as they had that night in the bookroom.

Rachel had little knowledge of men. But Verity had warned her that London abounded with handsome, unscrupulous rakes who could charm any woman into abandoning her principles. She had to believe that one such man was a certain silver-eyed Frenchman. For there was no denying a few of her principles had gone a-begging as a result of the handsome rogue's kiss.

But all that was behind her. With one last glance at the Comte de Rochemont, she consigned him to perdition. Then settling back against the comfortable squabs of the earl's carriage, she vowed to enjoy every minute of the rest of her precious day. Considering what she must confess to Edgar when next she saw him, she suspected the evening ahead would be anything but pleasant.

Yves watched the Earl of Fairborne's dark green town coach pull away from the curb, leaving a street urchin in Hatchard's employ to remove the pile of steaming horse droppings left by the pair of grays.

"Enjoy your luxurious transportation while you can, mademoiselle," he murmured as the coach melded into the stream of traffic on the busy street. Just that morning he had learned that though the earl had been in possession of the expensive carriage slightly more a year, he had never paid a single farthing to the carriage maker.

Unless a miracle happened, Browne and Forbes, Ltd., would soon move to repossess, and once that happened, all of his other creditors would converge on him like wolves on a wounded sheep. Yves intended to make certain the dowdy Yorkshire heiress did not provide that miracle by letting Fairborne get his hands on her fortune.

He had dealt with men of the earl's ilk time and again at the emperor's court. The more desperate their finances became, the more apt they were to grow careless—and careless men invariably made mistakes.

When Fairborne tipped his hand, Yves would be ready for him. Then if it turned out he was indeed the traitor who had caused Amalie's death, Yves vowed to see him quietly dispatched to Van Dieman's Land. If, on the other hand, the earl proved to be merely a fool with a weakness for gambling hells and French trollops, that would be another matter entirely.

But first things first. Yves was all too aware he needed Rachel Barton's cooperation to complete his investigation of Fairborne, and to that end he needed to have a serious talk with her. He was sorely tempted to follow her to Westminster Abbey, but he decided against it. From the look on her face just now, she was already leery of him, and it would never do to give her the impression he was stalking her.

He shrugged. Another "coincidental" meeting should not be too difficult to arrange if the naive provincial persisted in wandering about London without her elderly companion or her maid, as any well-bred lady would do. He had only to continue greasing the palm of the earl's underpaid butler to keep advised of the lady's plans.

But what argument could he put forth to convince a plain-faced commoner she should not jump at the chance to marry a handsome, charming nobleman? Remembering her surprising compassion when she thought him a common thief, he suspected she was much too trusting and good-hearted to comprehend the evil that lurked in the hearts of scoundrels like Fairborne.

Then he remembered something else about Rachel Barton. She had responded to his kiss with the innocent passion of a woman yet to be awakened to her own deeply sensuous nature—an awakening the earl was apparently not providing. If the butler was to be believed, Fairborne was playing the part of the perfect gentleman in his courtship of the heiress.

Such a woman would be highly susceptible to the seductive charms of an experienced rake—and few men could boast the erotic expertise Yves had gained at the emperor's decadent court. If all else failed, he would simply have to seduce her.

It was not, he admitted, the most honorable of alternatives. Nor was it one he would normally employ. Introducing an innocent to the mysteries of the flesh had never appealed to him.

But desperate circumstances required desperate measures. He salved his conscience with the thought that the dowdy heiress would be better off losing her virtue to him than losing her fortune as well as her virtue, and possibly even her life to Fairborne, if the earl turned out to be the villain Yves suspected.

Rachel couldn't remember when she had been so frustrated. The earl had not returned to the townhouse for dinner, as promised. Nor had he returned by the time she and Verity retired—nor even at midnight when she'd laid down her book and extinguished her bedside candle. But he had to have come home sometime during the night because for the second morning in a row, she found a footman waiting with a note for her when she entered the breakfast room.

Edgar apologized for yet another day's absence from her side, but assured her he would conclude his urgent business in the city in time to escort her to the theater that evening.

"Whatever shall I do with myself until he returns?" Rachel murmured, passing the note to Verity.

"If you've the brains God gave a flea, you'll spend the time acquiring a decent wardrobe," Verity said, adjusting her lace cap more firmly on her iron gray curls. "If the earl went into raptures over a simple embroidered collar, you could have him eating out of your hand if you had a good mantua-maker stitch you up a few fashionable gowns."

"I have never had the slightest desire to have any man eating out of my hand," Rachel protested. "And my wardrobe is perfectly adequate for Yorkshire. The most I need is a new bonnet to wear to church and maybe a colorful shawl to compliment my best gray chintz."

Verity selected another muffin from her plate, broke it in half, and slathered it with butter and apricot jam. "Well you don't need my help to purchase such paltry items. Furthermore, my aching joints warn me it is going to rain, and my health is much too delicate to allow me to traipse from store to store in inclement weather."

Rachel could scarcely believe her luck. Another whole day to herself! She actually felt guilty about leaving Verity alone—so guilty she suggested her companion pay a visit to her spinster sister. "I am certain Miss Patience would be delighted to see you," she said. "I shall direct John Coachman to drop me off on Bond Street and pick me up three hours later. That will give him plenty of time to deliver you to Bloomsbury Square."

Miraculously, Verity's "delicate health" took an instant turn for the better at the thought of a comfortable coze with her favorite relative, leaving Rachel to enjoy her day of freedom without a single qualm.

Thus it was that two hours later she found herself alone on Bond Street, admiring the bonnets displayed in the window of the shop her abigail had recommended. Compared to most of the other shops on the street, it was a very modest establishment, but Mary had assured her that it was where all the most fashionable ladies of the *ton* currently purchased their bonnets.

A discreet sign reading BONNETS BY MADAME FRANCINE occupied one corner of the small window, reminding Rachel that the proprietor was a French emigrée from Paris—one of many, it would appear. According to Mary, every good chef in London was a Frenchman and every good bonnet or mantua-maker a Frenchwoman.

"But why should you care, mistress?" the young abigail had asked in all innocence. "It's not as if we was still at war with the Frogs."

Rachel had reason to question the truth of that last statement, but she had to admit the bonnets in Madame Francine's window were exquisite. One in particular appealed to her. A lustrous pale green straw, it boasted a flat crown trimmed with yellow silk roses and a narrow brim that was secured beneath the wearer's chin with a deep, green velvet ribbon. It was, she decided, just the thing to minimize her height, yet still be in the first stare of fashion. Without a moment's thought, she entered the tiny shop and asked to try it on.

Madame Francine was nothing like Rachel had pictured her. She was a tiny, gnomelike woman with a sadly twisted body, brown raisin eyes, and hair as black and glossy as a piece of polished ebony. Rachel's first thought was that she looked more like the evil sorceress in a children's folk tale than a famous bonnet-maker.

But as Rachel soon learned, appearances were deceiving. With amazing quickness, considering her infirmity, Madame divested Rachel of the umbrella that Verity had insisted she carry, seated her on a chair before the shop's only mirror, and retrieved the bonnet from the window. Then with the careful precision of an artist completing a masterpiece, she placed the green and yellow bonnet on Rachel's head and adjusted the ribbon beneath her chin.

Rachel held her breath as the bonnet-maker stepped back to view her handiwork. She had the distinct impression that if Madame did not like what she saw, she would simply refuse to make the sale—and for reasons she could not entirely explain, Rachel had her heart set on that particular bonnet.

"You have chosen well, mademoiselle," Madame declared at last in her heavily accented English, and Rachel felt an unaccountable thrill over her nod of approval.

But as if wanting to make certain of her judgment, the bonnet-maker moved about the tiny room with the aid of her cane, studied Rachel from all angles, and solemnly pronounced, "It is the perfect bonnet for a tall, willowy woman like yourself."

Willowy. What a lovely word. Rachel beamed from ear to ear. Heretofore, the most complimentary thing she had been called was a skinny bluestocking. She chose not to think of the other labels she'd heard applied to her over the years.

"I'll take it," she said, smiling at her reflection. There was no doubt about it—from the neck up she looked positively elegant.

"A wise decision, mademoiselle, and naturally you will want to wear it immediately." With a grimace that left no doubt about her opinion of Rachel's old bonnet, Madame Francine consigned the offending article to a hatbox, which she secured with a piece of string. "Now, if you will give me the name and address of the man to whom I should send my bill, we can conclude this most excellent sale."

Rachel raised an indignant eyebrow. "No man is responsible for my purchases. Like you, I am a woman of business and pay my own bills," she declared—then nearly fainted when Madame named her price.

She had been warned that London prices were atrocious, but it had never occurred to her that one small bonnet could cost more than the last three gowns her Yorkshire dressmaker had stitched for her. But it was too late. She had seen herself in the mirror and for once her feminine instincts won out over her practical mind. Grimly, she dug through her reticule and counted out the requisite pound notes.

Madame's dark eyes widened in surprise as her hand closed about the money. "It is not often my customers pay so promptly. Most of the ladies who buy my bonnets are the wives or mistresses of noblemen and the rule of thumb appears to be the loftier the title, the longer I must wait for my money."

"How fortunate for you then that I have not a drop of noble blood."

"More fortunate than you know. For this money you have paid me will go toward my quarterly rent on this mouse hole in which I create my masterpieces." With a satisfied smile she placed the pound notes in a tin box, which she locked with a key that hung from a chain around her neck.

"Now, mademoiselle, because you have been so honorable in your dealings with me, I shall reward you with a piece of good advice, free of charge."

"Advice? About what, madame?"

"I am gifted with what we who work in the fashion trade call 'the eye' and I cannot help but notice that this brown, high-necked gown you wear simply does not suit you. You are, as the saying goes, 'hiding your light' beneath the dreadful garment."

Rachel flushed. "I am a mill owner from Yorkshire, Madame Francine. The revealing fabrics and décolleté necklines that London ladies prefer would be sadly inappropriate for me. My dressmaker has one pattern that fits me and whenever I am in need of a new gown, she produces one in whatever color and fabric I request."

Madame shrugged. "Then request these gowns with the neckline brushing your ears be made in rich fabrics and beautiful colors. Surely even in the provinces one is allowed a bit of color."

That much Rachel could not deny. Nor did she think it appropriate to mention that considering her outlandish height, she was more comfortable wearing drab colors. Madame had, after all, supplied her with a charming sobriquet.

The little bonnet-maker obviously took her silence as an invitation to proceed with her "free advice." From a pile of swatches on a nearby table, she chose a square of sky blue velvet and held it beneath Rachel's chin. Next she held up a twilled silk the color of spring grass in a Yorkshire meadow.

"Just as I thought," she declared. "These are the colors you should be wearing—the colors with which nature would surround your counterpart, the willow, not the mud in which it is planted."

Rachel chuckled at the Frenchwoman's choice of words. But she had to admit the fanciful analogy drove the point home.

Madame cocked her head and studied Rachel with her shrewd dark eyes. "You will never be one of the porcelain beauties you *Anglais* prize so highly," she said gravely. "But with a little effort, you could be striking as only a woman of your magnificent height can be."

She sighed. "What I would not give to have been born with your long legs and straight back. But I can see that what I suggest is too much too soon for you. Very well, then begin by wearing a colorful silk shawl over your drab gowns until you feel more courageous."

Rachel frowned. She had never equated her desire to remain inconspicuous with cowardice. She had simply faced the truth of who and what she was and lived accordingly.

But that was no concern of Madame Francine's. Putting aside her disturbing thoughts, she smiled at the little Frenchwoman. "I thank you for your sage advice, and oddly enough, I had planned to buy both a bonnet and a shawl today."

"Then do so, mademoiselle, by all means. But be certain the shawl you purchase is as perfect for you as is the bonnet I created. There is a kind of magic in such perfection."

Rachel nodded. "I promise I will not settle for less," she said as she collected her hatbox and umbrella. Then bidding farewell to the odd little bonnet-maker, she stepped out onto Bond Street to enjoy an hour or two of window-shopping.

Unfortunately that was the only kind of shopping she could enjoy at the moment since she had but two farthings left in her reticule after the purchase of her pricey bonnet. Ah well, if she should see a shawl she favored, she could always return on the morrow to purchase it.

Meanwhile, she had nothing but time on her hands—an unexpected luxury she intended to enjoy to the fullest. And so she did—wandering from shop to shop, inspecting all the wondrous items displayed in the windows.

She glanced up from a particularly interesting display of fine crystal to find two fashionably dressed ladies on the opposite side of the street staring at her as if she were some sort of oddity. Now that she thought about it, she had received more than a passing glance from any number of people in the past few minutes. Two well-dressed gentlemen had even gone so far as to tip their hats and smile at her in a most friendly fashion.

What could have occasioned this sudden interest on the part of Londoners? On the whole, she had found them to be a rather hard-nosed, unfriendly lot. Surely something as simple as a new bonnet couldn't make that much difference. Unless, of course, it was one of Madame Francine's "perfect bonnets."

She chuckled to herself. If the proper bonnet could make this much difference, she wondered what might happen if by some chance she should find the perfect shawl as well. Would Madame Francine's promise of magic come true?

With an inexplicable feeling of expectation, she continued her walk down Bond Street, gazing into every window she came to. Then just when she had decided it was time to return to where she had arranged to meet John Coachman, she spied a shop, no larger than Madame Francine's, tucked in between two tall buildings.

The shop window was tiny; there was room to display only one item—a silk shawl so beautiful it literally took Rachel's breath away. A wonderful profusion of delicate yellow and white roses bloomed against a background of the same pale green as her bonnet and a wide fringe of darker green bordered the softly scalloped edge.

It was the "perfect shawl" Madame Francine had admonished her to seek out and as with the bonnet, she felt an overwhelming desire to own it. A strange thing indeed, since she had never before taken the slightest interest in such items of apparel.

But something about the silken shawl spoke to her spark of femininity—that intense hunger for beauty that dwelt deep inside her—as did the flowers in her Yorkshire garden and the paintings on her walls.

If she'd had the money at hand, she would have marched into

the shop and purchased it instantly, no matter the cost. There was nothing for it but to return to the townhouse and get the "emergency money" she'd hidden in the toe of one of her half boots. She dared not wait until tomorrow, lest her "perfect shawl" be gone.

She turned from the window, determined to hurry back to the arranged meeting spot just as three young men, walking arm-in-arm, approached her. From their intricately tied cravats, ridiculously high shirt points, and flamboyant waistcoats, she assumed they were what Edgar had termed "pinks of the *ton*" when he'd pointed out similarly attired young blades at Vauxhall.

"Well now, what do we have here?" asked one of them—a pimply faced fellow in a mulberry jacket with platter-sizes buttons and shoulders too wide to be those endowed by nature.

"Have your eyes gone bad on you, Percy? 'Tis an Amazon, by jove, and a cit as well from the looks of her." The tallest of the trio, who was still a head shorter than Rachel, doffed his high-crowned beaver and executed a sweeping bow. "Your servant, Madam Cit," he said with absurd gravity.

The one called Percy raised a quizzing glass to his eye. "Upon my word, I do believe you've the right of it, Clyde."

The third, and shortest, of the three clasped a hand to the puce corded waistcoat covering his narrow chest. "Zounds! I think I am in love." He hiccoughed loudly. "I have always lusted after tall women and you, madam, are the tallest female I have ever seen."

Rachel raised a haughty eyebrow. "And you, sir, are the most ill-mannered male I have ever encountered."

"She has you there, Reggie," the one called Percy declared, and all three roared with laughter.

Rachel instinctively covered her nose to escape the stale alcohol fumes that suddenly enveloped her. "You are foxed and it is but an hour past noon," she said coldly, backing as far away from the odiferous trio as the window at her back would allow.

"Au contraire." Reggie tugged a gold watch from his waistcoat pocket and held it up in front of his face. "By my reckoning it is still the shank of the evening and we've yet another party awaiting us at a friend's bachelor quarters in St. James Street. I insist you attend as my guest." He chuckled. "Or should I say my trophy."

"I most certainly will not, and I shall thank you to step aside so I may be on my way."

To Rachel's surprise, all three instantly moved closer, forming a tight ring around her.

Reggie's eyes narrowed to angry slits. "You dare to refuse my invitation? Perhaps you are not aware that I am a member of the nobility, Madam Cit?"

"As are we all," Clyde chimed in. "Has no one ever told you that you should show respect for your betters?"

"My betters?" Rachel willed herself to control her temper. The three young lordlings had apparently spent the night carousing and were drunk as wheelbarrows. She had seen her father in a like condition often enough to know that reasoning with drunks was an exercise in futility.

Still, she must somehow rid herself of the silly fribbles before they caused her any more embarrassment. She took a firmer grip on her umbrella, but she sincerely hoped she would not have to resort to violence. Not that it would bother her in the least to raise a lump or two on their noble heads, but passers-by were already casting curious glances her way.

"You are asking for trouble, young sirs," she said, deciding her best hope to settle the bumblebroth peacefully was to call the young troublemakers' bluff. "I am expecting a friend who should arrive any minute. He will not take it kindly if he thinks you are annoying me—and he is not the sort of man you would wish to anger."

Percy and Clyde clutched each other and moaned in mock terror and Reggie uttered a bark of laughter that told her he was no more impressed by her puny threat than were his two companions. In fact, he moved forward to where his nose was but an inch from her breast and the heat of his breath penetrated the thin fabric of her summer gown.

"I tremble with fear at the thought of this 'friend' of yours, Madam Cit," he said, leering up at her with bloodshot eyes.

Rachel's fingers curled around the handle of her umbrella but before she could raise it, a familiar black-clad figure bore down on the little group, lifted Reggie by the scruff of his neck, and deposited him some three feet away from her. The two other lordlings stumbled over each other's feet in their haste to join him.

"Are these children being troublesome, Miss Barton?" the

Comte de Rochemont asked in a quietly dangerous voice. "If so, I shall be happy to teach them a lesson or two concerning how to behave around a lady."

Rachel collected her scattered wits. "That will not be necessary, sir," she said, wishing she could somehow sink out of sight before the crowd of spectators gathering around them grew any larger.

The count transferred his gaze to the three hapless culprits. Pale as ghosts and with mouths agape, they stared at the tall, angry man who confronted them.

"W-we meant no harm, sir," Clyde stammered. "We were just having a little fun and as usual, Reggie went too far. He tends to get a bit mean when he tangles with John Barleycorn. But Clyde and I keep a tight rein on him. We'd not have let him do her any harm."

"Devil take it, it goes without saying if I'd known the cit had friends in high places . . ." Reggie pulled a handkerchief from his pocket and wiped his perspiring brow. "I mean, I'm not stupid. "

The count's scowl grew darker. "A paltry excuse to say the least. No gentleman would abuse any woman for any reason—certainly not for sport."

He turned back to Rachel. "What say you, Miss Barton, will apologies from these scapegraces suffice, or do you demand your 'pound of flesh.' "

Rachel swallowed hard. "Apologies will do,'" she said, and silently watched while, one by one, her tormenters bowed and mumbled incoherent apologies, then like three small, whipped dogs scurried out of sight.

The excitement over, the crowd quickly disbursed, leaving Rachel alone with her gallant rescuer. Outwardly, she maintained a calm facade, but a sinking feeling in the pit of her stomach warned her that the mysterious Frenchman presented a far greater danger to her peace of mind than did any torment inflicted by three foolish young lordlings.

Chapter Four

An uncomfortable silence descended once Yves and the heiress were left alone. She had not yet deigned to look at him, but stood straight as a ramrod, her chin tilted at a haughty angle more befitting a duchess than a commoner from Yorkshire.

Any other woman he knew would be in hysterics after the ordeal she'd been through. Miss Barton managed to appear calm, almost detached. He had to admire the woman's fortitude, if not her stupidity, in wandering about London without proper escort.

Still, he had to believe he had made headway toward his goal. Thanks to information relayed by Fairborne's butler, he had been in the right place at the right time. For how better to gain a woman's trust than to come to her rescue—especially a simple countrywoman trying to cope with the frightening complexities of life in London.

As if proving him correct, she turned her head and met his gaze. "Thank you for your intervention in an annoying situation," she said stiffly. "But I assure you, it was not necessary. I am quite capable of taking care of myself."

"Indeed!" This lukewarm response was not what he had expected for his efforts on her behalf. "And how, may I ask, had you planned to ward off the unwanted attentions of the three inebriated dandies?"

She held up her umbrella. "I was just about to add a lump or two to the head of the one called Reggie when you burst on the scene. The other two were timid rabbits who would have run for cover once they saw their comrade routed."

He couldn't fault her appraisal of the situation; he had judged it the same. But he found it a little disconcerting that a woman should think with such cool logic. He smiled. "Still, I cannot help but feel it was a good thing I arrived when I did."

"Another of your happy coincidences?" She studied him

through narrowed eyes. "Tell me, sir, which of the earl's servants have you bribed to keep you informed of my comings and goings? And why should you care what I do and where I go?"

Again she surprised him. He had not expected the dowdy heiress to be so clever—or so spirited. It was obvious he would have to watch his step with this "simple countrywoman."

"Your questions deserve an answer and I have every intention of giving you one," he said, with what he hoped was a convincingly sincere smile. "But first things first. Since our meetings so far have all been 'accidental' we have never been properly introduced. Allow me to—"

"I know who you are," she interjected, "and you obviously know who I am." She frowned. "But I would be interested in learning why the three young lordlings instantly recognized you and why they viewed you with such awe. Or was it fear?"

Yves frowned. "I am not unknown in London." As a matter of fact, since the Duke of Wellington had insisted he ride beside him in the victory parade two years earlier, he had been recognized much too often to his way of thinking. But, of course, Miss Barton had not been in London at that time.

Anger flared in the lady's expressive eyes. "An evasive answer if ever I heard one. Undoubtedly your explanation as to why you were in the earl's bookroom in the dead of night will be even more vague. I do not like mysteries and since you seem determined to remain one, I see no point in continuing this discussion. Good day, sir. The earl's coachman awaits me."

So saying, she turned on her heel and marched off down Bond Street with her long-legged stride—but not, Yves observed, before she cast a last, longing look at the colorful shawl in the shop window. It would appear the sharp-tongued heiress had a feminine side as well as a coldly logical one. He could see she had already acquired a fashionable new bonnet, and he suspected she would have purchased the shawl had she not been inhibited by his presence.

Filing that interesting bit of information away for future use, Yves hurried to catch up with her. "I shall escort you to your carriage, Miss Barton," he said when he drew abreast of her.

"That will not be necessary."

"On the contrary, a woman walking alone on the streets of London invites the kind of unwelcome attention you have just encountered. Since you appear to be without either companion or maid at present, I insist on seeing you safely to your destination."

Rachel stopped in her tracks and glanced around her. The Frenchman was right. Every woman on the street was either accompanied by another woman or had a uniformed maid trailing behind her.

Damn and blast! She had broken yet another of the rigid rules of etiquette observed by London ladies. Although, now that she thought about it, the rule was not limited to the capital. Even in the remote part of Yorkshire where she lived, the wives and daughters of noblemen and country squires were always accompanied by their maids when they shopped in the village.

She had simply ignored the custom and gone her own way. Now, at the advanced age of four-and-twenty, she was deemed a hopelessly eccentric spinster more suited to the world of commerce than to normal womanly pursuits. But how galling to be reminded of her social shortcomings by this contemptible foreigner.

"All things considered, I believe I am better off without your escort," she said, and casting a fulminating glance at the cheeky fellow, strode off again.

Startled by her vehemence, Yves could only stare after the prickly woman. Then gathering his wits, he nimbly dodged an aging dandy and two fashionably dressed matrons to again catch up with her. "I assume by 'all things' you are once again referring to the odd circumstances of our first meeting. If you will give me the chance, I can explain why I was in the Earl of Fairborne's bookroom a fortnight past—but not, if you please, during a foot race down Bond Street. What say you to sharing an ice at Gunters. We can talk there."

The heiress stopped again and drew herself up to her full height, which put her eyes on a level with his. "You must be mad! I'll have you know I am a loyal British citizen. Nothing could induce me to consort with the likes of you."

Yves stared at her in disbelief. "*Sacré bleu!* Are you inferring you think me an enemy of England? If so, why have you kept silent about finding me in such a compromising situation?"

"How do you know I have?"

"Because I have met the earl at his club any number of times since and it was obvious he was not aware of my 'secret.' "

Rachel lowered her eyes to avoid his piercing gaze. "I did not know until we met at Vauxhall that you were a Frenchman."

"Ah yes, I am French; ergo I have to be a minion of the devil. If so, your Duke of Wellington must answer to the name of Lucifer. For I acted as his agent at the emperor's court during the war—incognito and without compensation I might add—as did other French aristocrats who had reason to despise the murderous peasants with whom Bonaparte surrounded himself."

"*You* were an agent for the Duke of Wellington? A likely story! I may be a simple countrywoman, sir, but I did not come down in the last rain."

Yves struggled to control his rising temper. This sharp-tongued woman was beginning to get on his nerves. "It so happens His Grace is in London at the present time," he snapped. "I know that because I was his aide at the Congress of Vienna and we returned to London together. I shall be happy to introduce you to him so he can corroborate my 'story.' "

The Frenchman's offer took Rachel by surprise. She suspected he was weaving a tale out of whole cloth, certain a gullible countrywoman would accept his outlandish claim without question.

"Very well," she said, looking him straight in the eyes. "If the Duke of Wellington personally vouches for you, I will agree to listen to your explanation of your odd behavior."

"I will hold you to that, Miss Barton, and hope you have the good sense to remain silent about what you know until you have heard what I have to tell you."

The Frenchman studied her intently, a devilish look in his pale, worldly eyes. "But remember, while the duke can vouch for my sterling character, he cannot be held responsible for everything that occurred on that fateful evening."

"Such as?"

"The kiss we shared. I take full responsibility for that. Although, as I remember it, you appeared to enjoy the experience every bit as much as I did."

Rachel gasped. "How dare you, sir! You may be a French aristocrat, but you are no gentleman."

"But the very British Earl of Fairborne is a perfect gentleman, I suppose."

"He is indeed, and the kindest and most honorable of men as well."

Yves wondered how vigorously the heiress would defend her

noble suitor if she knew he was angling to marry her, and her fortune, so he could keep a certain French courtesan in the style she demanded—a courtesan he was at that very moment visiting.

"I will say this for you, Miss Barton," Yves said with wry humor, "you are either the most naive woman I have ever met—or the most foolish."

"Well, I never—"

"That, too, was obvious when I kissed you—and because you are such a 'babe in the woods' I shall strive to forgive your childish insinuations."

Moments later they arrived at the spot where John Coachman waited with the earl's carriage. With his usual graceful bow, the Comte de Rochemont took his leave of her, and Rachel doubted that anyone observing them would guess they had spent the last few minutes trading insults. The annoying fellow would probably have kissed her fingertips, had she not had her umbrella in one hand and the hatbox in the other.

"*Au revoir* for now, mademoiselle," he purred, like a great, black cat toying with a mouse. "But I look forward to seeing you at the theater this evening. I understand you and the earl will be the guests of Baron Thornton."

Rachel was still seething when she arrived back at the townhouse in time for afternoon tea. Luckily neither the earl nor Verity had returned, so she opted to have a quiet cup in the privacy of her bedchamber.

"You look tired, miss," Mary observed when she delivered the tea. "You should have a nice lie-down before time to dress for dinner."

Rachel nodded her agreement. "I think I shall. Shopping in London can be an exhausting experience." She glanced toward the bonnet that still held pride of place on her dressing table. "Albeit a rewarding one if one is lucky."

Still, nothing could induce her to return to Bond Street that afternoon—not even the knowledge that the shawl was just what she needed to impress Edgar tonight. Mary was right. She needed a long nap before she faced the arduous evening ahead, and if the shawl was gone tomorrow, she would take it as an omen that she was never meant to own it.

In truth, the thought of encountering the bewildering Frenchman again had so dampened her enthusiasm for her first taste of

London theater, she was tempted to plead a headache and beg off. If only they were not attending as guests of some fellow who had served with Edgar at Whitehall during the war.

She had just finished her tea, removed her half boots, and stretched out on the bed when she heard a tap at her door and Mary's voice. "'Tis I, Miss Barton. A package just arrived for you and I've brought it up."

"A package?" Rachel sat up and dangled her legs over the side of the bed. "Who in the world would be sending me a package?"

"The lad who delivered it said 'twas a delivery of a purchase you made in a Bond Street shop."

"But how can that be. I wore my bonnet, and I ordered no other." Rachel stared at the flat, brown package Mary carried. It was obviously not a bonnet.

"Shall I open it, miss?"

"Yes, please do. I cannot imagine what it could be."

Mary tore off the wrapping and laid the contents on the bed. "Oh, miss, 'tis the most beautiful thing I've ever seen."

Rachel stared with disbelieving eyes at the colorful swath of silk Mary had spread out on the coverlet. "My shawl!" she gasped. "My perfect shawl! But how could it . . . who could have?" But, of course, she knew instantly who had sent it. She had sensed the Frenchman's sharp perusal when she'd sneaked a last look at it.

But what had prompted him to do anything so outlandish? Surely a professed expert on propriety must know she could not accept such a gift from a stranger—particularly one she distrusted. He was taunting her, of course, and she would have to find a way to return it. But thanks to the cursed fellow and his bizarre sense of humor, the lovely shawl could never be hers.

She watched Mary circle one of the delicate rosebuds with her forefinger. "How could you forget you had purchased anything so lovely, miss? I never could."

"I guess I had a momentary lapse of memory." Rachel cleared her throat. "I recalled seeing it in the window and then . . ." She let her voice trail off before she had to tell an actual lie.

"You paid for it and left the package sitting on the counter. I've done the same thing meself, though not with anything as grand as this."

Mary lifted the shawl and draped it over the back of a chair.

"'Tis a blessing the shopkeeper was honest enough to send it round, for 'twill do wonders for that plain gray evening gown of yours. You'll put those fashionable ladies at the theater to shame, and that's a fact, miss."

The theater! Damn and blast. Rachel had forgotten all about that. Mary would naturally expect her to wear the shawl and she couldn't—not when she was certain to encounter that devilish Frenchman.

She would simply have to dismiss Mary as soon as she finished dressing for dinner and hope the little abigail remained in the servants' quarters for the rest of the night. It was not too impossible a hope. From the dark smudges beneath the girl's lovely blue eyes, Rachel had to assume she would be grateful for an early night.

Verity did not return from visiting her sister in time to partake of dinner—and luckily so. The usually pleasant meal was an unqualified disaster.

To begin with, the butler announced that the French chef had resigned without notice and he had been forced to hire a replacement, sight unseen. Rachel had to wonder if all aristocrats had so much trouble with their domestic help. She could recall at least six of the earl's servants who had quit or been sacked in the three weeks she had been in London.

The new chef was definitely not up to the standard of his predecessor if the overcooked filet of salmon and undercooked loin of pork were examples of his culinary skills. But strangely enough the earl, who was usually the first to complain if his food was not perfectly prepared and served, simply ignored the inedible fare spread out before him. Absentmindedly he raised his fork to his mouth and as absentmindedly chewed and swallowed.

But it was his unusual moodiness that puzzled Rachel the most. One minute he sat morose and silent, seemingly unaware of his surroundings; the next he threw himself into plying her with extravagant compliments as if his very life depended on charming her. The earl was definitely not himself and she could only assume his business in the city had not gone as he'd planned.

She did her best to remain calm and sympathetic, but with each passing minute the food congealing on her plate grew more unappealing and the earl's mood swings grew more erratic. Then just when she thought she could contain herself no longer, Fairborne ordered the hovering footman to remove the covers, signaling the miserable ordeal was over.

Rachel quickly excused herself to return to her bedchamber, where she tidied her hair and collected her plain, but serviceable shawl before descending the stairs to where the earl waited in the entryway. She had vowed to confess her shameful duplicity before this evening was over, but considering his present frame of mind . . .

With a sigh, she accepted the moody fellow's proffered arm and breathed a silent prayer that after such a bizarre beginning the balance of the evening would remain blessedly uneventful.

Silently, the butler handed the earl his gloves and high-crowned beaver. Silently, the footman opened the door. But before they could step out into the beautiful, moonlit night, Rachel heard the sound of hurried footsteps—caught a glimpse of vivid, silken color. Her heart sank like a pebble in a pond.

"Wait, mistress," her conscientious little abigail called. "I can scarce believe it, but you've gone and forgotten your lovely new shawl again."

Yves raised his opera glasses and surveyed the other private boxes in the Royal Theatre at Drury Lane with the satisfaction of a master showman who had set the stage for a particularly fascinating act of drama.

Every seat in the theater was taken—every box overflowing with the usual subscription holders and their guests. The combination of *Hamlet, Prince of Denmark* as the main production and the long-limbed Italian actress, Vestris, performing in the comedy had drawn every theater enthusiast in London. One of them was Baron Thornton, Fairborne's host for the evening, and another of the suspects Lord Castlereagh had mentioned.

His lordship had been correct in labeling the pretty fellow a "true pink of the *ton*." Not even in the jaded social life of Paris had Yves seen anyone comparable. He adjusted his glasses and took a closer look. Thornton's dark hair was tightly curled and glossy with oil, the points of his collar so tall he was in danger of losing an eye if he made a sudden turn of head, and his cravat an intricate work of art. His jacket of vivid blue satin sported padded shoulders and a sharply nipped-in waist; his pantaloons were a buttery yellow and his waistcoat a wondrous creation composed of large gold and silver checks. Between it and the chains, seals, and fobs decorating it, he outshone every jewel-bedecked dowager in the theater.

He was, in short, a trifle too much to be believed, and Yves had to wonder if the flamboyant fellow was really as shallow and frivolous as he appeared, or if a devious mind could be hiding behind the paint and powder. He made a mental note to investigate Baron Thornton with the same meticulous care as that he accorded the Earl of Fairborne.

Thornton's box was in the second tier to the left of the stage. In the box directly above him, London's most notorious cyprian, Harriette Wilson, held forth with her usual coterie of admirers. But the rigid set of her shoulders told Yves that La Wilson was sorely peeved about something—that something undoubtedly being Jacqueline Esquaré. For Jacqueline now occupied a first tier box to the right of the stage and had already gathered her own court of besotted noblemen.

Yves had no interest in the rivalry between the two barques of frailty. He had set Jacqueline up for one reason only—to goad the earl into making a desperate move.

A flash of color at the back of Baron Thornton's box signaled the arrival of his guests and Yves quickly trained his glasses on his unsuspecting prey. As usual the earl was a model of sartorial splendor in green and gold. But surprisingly he failed to put his female companion in the shade because Miss Barton's slender shoulders were draped in a silk shawl so elegant it immediately drew the envious attention of the two ladies in the adjacent box.

Yves shook his head. Would the woman never cease to astound him? He had purchased the shawl and sent it round to Grosvenor Square on a whim, never expecting the prickly female to wear it in public. In fact, he had halfway expected her to ferret out where he lived and return it to him forthwith.

Curious, he concentrated on her face. She looked unusually pale, and the moment she was seated, she made a furtive search of the theater. Yves nodded his head when her gaze lighted on him. To his amusement, she immediately dropped her opera glasses and slumped in her chair as if hoping to make herself invisible, despite her colorful shawl. The woman made no sense. Why, if she found it so embarrassing, had she worn the blasted thing?

He shifted his gaze to the earl. Fairborne looked decidedly

glum—the result, no doubt, of his visit that afternoon with Jacqueline Esquaré. He would have found no welcome at the little house on Tottenham Court Road unless he'd come bearing expensive gifts and, of course, that he could not do unless he got his hands on Miss Barton's fortune.

A rustling of the heavy drape behind Yves alerted him to the fact that he had company. Instinctively, his right hand whipped to his nape to grip the knife he always wore strapped to his back.

"No need for that, lad," a deep voice proclaimed. "I'm here at your request."

Yves released his hold on the knife and turned somewhat sheepishly to greet the tall, hawk-nosed man who had just entered the box. "Forgive me, Your Grace. Force of habit. I am pleased you could join me for tonight's performance." Smiling, he bowed to the only person he knew who would address a French nobleman of two-and-thirty years as "lad."

"Wouldn't have missed it for the world once Robert Castlereagh briefed me on what you were up to," the duke said. "Risky business, but then I've never known that to stop you in the past. I understand you've narrowed the list of suspects to three men."

Yves nodded. "Actually that was Lord Castlereagh's doing, but I concur with his thinking."

"As do I. Robert told me what you want of me, and I shall be happy to help in any way I can to bring the traitor to justice. But hopefully I can finish with my part of the show before the first intermission so I can adjourn to my club. I am no admirer of Will Shakespeare's famous prince. If I'd had as much trouble making up my mind as that fool Dane, the British army would still be choking on the dust of a Spanish plain."

"I'd not think of asking you to suffer through the second act, Your Grace," Yves said, struggling to keep a straight face. "But it might aid the cause if you would drop by Jacqueline Esquaré's box before you leave."

"You ask a great deal, lad. But I'll do it for king and country. Though I doubt anything Bonaparte had to offer will compare to the wrath of the delightful Miss Wilson when next I feel moved to pay her a visit."

He laid a hand on the hilt of his dress sword. "Very well then, let us get to it," he said, stepping forward to stand beside Yves at the front of the box. The newly installed gaslight glistened off the medals decorating his uniform—medals awarded him by his grateful country.

A cry immediately went up from the floor, "Wellington! It's the duke himself!" Every eye in the theater turned toward Yves's box and as one, the audience stood and cheered England's greatest hero.

The duke raised his arm in greeting, obviously enjoying the adulation accorded him. But Yves was only interested in the reactions of three people to his being singled out by the duke. The first was the tall, brown-haired woman who stared at him in wide-eyed disbelief, the next the grinning popinjay on her right, and lastly the golden-haired man on her left, whose handsome face registered a combination of hatred and fear that gave Yves yet another reason to believe the Earl of Fairborne might be the traitor he sought.

He gave himself a figurative pat on the back. Thanks to his clever maneuvering, all the players were in place, and what better setting for the drama to unfold than Drury Lane Theatre!

Chapter Five

Her mind in a turmoil, Rachel sat down once the applause and cheering for the Duke of Wellington had subsided. Now what was she to think? The Frenchman had to have been telling the truth about his association with the duke. She had seen with her own eyes the great man put a hand on the count's shoulder and smile as if saying to all who watched him, "This is my true and trusted friend."

But why would a wealthy French aristocrat, and trusted friend of England's beloved "Iron Duke," enter another man's house like a burglar in the night?

And why would such a man be so anxious to explain his bizarre behavior to a countrywoman from Yorkshire whose favor he sought to win with an expensive gift? To insure her silence, of course. There was no other logical explanation.

He had, in fact, all but begged her to keep quiet about that bewildering night until she had heard him out—and so she would until she knew the truth about the mysterious Frenchman. But Wellington or no, if the count's explanation lacked the ring of truth, she would confess all to the Earl of Fairborne.

Edgar was her friend and the one to whom she owed her loyalty—especially now, when the poor man was so worried about the "business" that had kept him in the city all day. He had, in fact, been so distracted he hadn't even commented on the colorful shawl that Mary had insisted she wear.

Her priorities firmly established, she sat back, folded her hands, and listened with half an ear to the conversation between the earl and their odd little host while she waited for the play to begin. Actually, it was more a monologue by the baron on the current scandals circulating in the *ton,* as Edgar said scarcely a word.

"Drury Lane is a truly magnificent theater," she said when the baron paused to catch his breath. She'd hoped that by introducing a new subject, she might draw Edgar into the conversation. To no avail; he appeared too lost in his own thoughts to acknowledge her effort.

Not so the baron. "Pleased you like it," he said, his narrow, gold-bedecked chest puffed out as if he were somehow responsible for the lavish decor. "I frankly admit the plethora of gold trim and rich colors speak to my flamboyant soul, and my friend, the Regent, has been gratifyingly vocal in his approval as well." He glanced at the earl, as if daring him to disagree.

"Of course there are those amongst us who find this latest version of the theater a bit too Frenchified for their taste." Thornton's narrow lips curled in a sly smile that gave Rachel the distinct impression he was enjoying himself at Edgar's expense. She sensed a spiteful streak in the prissy little dandy that instantly put her on her guard.

With a definite sense of relief she watched the first act curtain rise on the grim, gray battlements of Elsinore Castle. She had heard all she cared to from her garrulous host.

But Bernardo had scarcely finished issuing his opening challenge to Francisco than the baron tapped her on the arm with his chicken skin fan. "Now that, in my opinion, is a capital set. Painted by Whitmore, don't you know. Devilish clever fellow and authentic to the bone. Both Prinny and I heartily approve of his work. How does it strike you, Miss Barton, or is it too much to ask of a provincial to pass judgment on a London stage setting?"

"It is a spectacular set," Rachel said, "and exactly as I imagined a seventeenth century castle after reading Mr. Shakespeare's play. But, of course, you are right. I have nothing to judge it by since there are no theaters in the Yorkshire village where I live."

The baron's eyes widened. "Good heavens, I have to wonder how any civilized person can survive in such a barbaric place."

Rachel was tempted to tell the unpleasant fellow she wondered how anyone of moral substance could survive in the shallow atmosphere of London. But she held her counsel. She doubted her opinion would be of any interest to a self-styled arbiter of culture like the baron.

At first glance this friend and former coworker of Edgar's had appeared to be nothing more than an aging version of the three foolish young lordlings she had encountered on Bond Street. Now she was not so sure. She suspected the only foolish things about Baron Thornton were his outlandish manner of dress and his never-ending gibberish—both of which were as much an act as any performed on the stage. She glimpsed a cunning intelligence beneath his silly prattle and vacuous smile, and suspected the baron might become exceedingly vindictive if crossed. In short, there was something about the prissy little dandy that made her blood run cold.

"I am absolutely devoted to theater," Thornton continued in his bombastic monotone. "Never miss a performance here at Drury Lane. I've had a yearly subscription to this very box since the day Elliston took over."

He withdrew a lace-edged handkerchief from his cuff and dabbed at a bead of perspiration on his milk white brow. "Marvelous showman, Elliston, and another great friend of the Regent's. Discovered that delightful Italian chit, Vestris, don't you know. Exquisite young creature with legs that go up to her armpits. Prinny never misses a performance when she's on the boards. Mark my words, you'll see him pop into the royal box tonight once this dreary business with the Danish prince is over and the comedy begins."

"Ummmm," Rachel murmured, doing her best to watch the play and ignore the baron's chatter. To hear him tell it, he virtually lived in the Prince Regent's pocket.

"Now opera, that's a different story entirely," Thornton droned on. "Attended one once, but never again. The infernal caterwaulers sang so loud I couldn't hear myself talk."

Rachel had to wonder why someone who professed such devotion to the theater never glanced at the stage. But then most of the audience appeared more interested in carrying on their own conversations than in listening to what the actors had to say. She had to strain to catch a word here and there over the hubbub.

Not until the actor playing Hamlet stood alone on the stage bemoaning the death of his father did the noise abate somewhat, and then only because a stagehand held up a placard stating "Quiet Please. Important Speech." Rachel's opinion of Londoners had never been high, but it was rapidly plummeting to a new low.

The baron raised his opera glasses and she took heart. But he swept past the stage to survey the occupants of the private boxes on the opposite side of the theater. "I say, Fairborne, take a look at the first tier to the right of the stage. It appears that little tart,

Jacqueline Esquaré, has snared herself a protector rich enough to supply her with a theater box—and a prime one at that."

"The devil you say." The earl snatched up his glasses and trained them on the spot Thornton indicated.

The baron watched, a sly smile on his face. "Must be that Frenchie count she's been seen with lately. Birds of a feather and all that. Rumor has it the fellow is rich as a nabob. But then he'll have to be to keep that one in line, wouldn't you say, Fairborne?"

Edgar's only answer was a noncommittal grunt and an abrupt lowering of his glasses. But the look of rage that distorted his face sent shivers down Rachel's spine.

She studied her tightly clasped hands and acknowledged that she, too, was as tense as a tightly drawn fiddle string. The news that the Frenchman who'd been stalking her had taken a mistress should have come as no surprise. She had seen him with the woman at Vauxhall. Still inexplicably, she found tonight's tasteless public display of his liaison with a known courtesan particularly offensive.

But then what could one expect of an aristocrat? None of them were what they first appeared to be—not the baron nor the disturbing French count nor even the Duke of Wellington, if the rumors she'd heard about him were true.

Even her good friend, the Earl of Fairborne, had managed to shock her. For this angry, grim-faced man who sat beside her bore little resemblance to the mild-mannered fellow she had seriously considered marrying. In truth, until this moment, she would not have thought Edgar capable of such intense hatred as that he displayed for the Comte de Rochemont.

If she didn't know better, she might think there was an element of envy in his hatred. But, of course, that was impossible. A man as high in the instep as Edgar would have no reason to envy his enemy's dalliance with a woman he had termed "a French whore."

But what could have caused the bitter enmity between the two men? Had it been something as simple as a possession they had both coveted or a woman they had once both wished to marry? Whatever the reason, she found Edgar's sullen silence as disturbing as Baron Thornton's senseless gibble-gabble.

Neither man raised his glasses to survey the stage during the entire first act. But once the curtain came down to herald the first intermission, both sets of glasses were again trained on the first tier box. "Well, well, it appears the lovely Miss Esquaré has come up in the world. Amazing what a wealthy patron can do for a common trollop." The baron's voice dripped with sarcasm. "Do my eyes deceive me, Fairborne, or is that England's greatest hero kissing her dainty fingertips?" He leaned across Rachel to tap Edgar's shoulder with his fan. "What say you to that, my friend?"

Edgar's only answer was an incoherent snarl. He thrust her shawl to Rachel and grasping her arm, hauled her from her seat. "I have seen enough. We are leaving," he muttered, and promptly proceeded to do so, with Rachel in tow.

She followed without objection, but she did a little seething of her own. Not that she particularly cared to stay after witnessing the disgusting spectacle of the Duke of Wellington and the Comte de Rochemont paying court to a French courtesan. But she felt that at the very least, Edgar owed her the courtesy of asking her permission before he cut short her first, and probably only, evening of London theater.

She would never forget the look of unholy glee in Baron Thornton's eyes when he bade them good night or his rasp of laughter as they quit his presence. It was plain to see the spiteful fellow took joy in humiliating others, and she felt deeply humiliated for Edgar. She would not have expected a grown man to throw a temper tantrum because his enemy's new mistress was admired by the Duke of Wellington. But then neither had she expected that same man to go into a blue funk when a matter of business had not gone as he'd wanted. She had never allowed herself that luxury when there was trouble at the mill.

She told herself Edgar's childish behavior was but a temporary lapse—that he had one too many things on his plate at the moment. But in her heart she knew she would never feel the same about him again.

To Rachel's relief, the ride back to the townhouse was accomplished in absolute silence. She would have been hard put to come up with the kind of small talk Edgar usually favored.

She avoided his eyes as he handed her down from the carriage and escorted her up the steps, then waited silently while he raised the knocker and rapped sharply on the massive carved door. To her surprise, no one answered, and he rapped again . . . and again before a sleepy-eyed footman finally opened the door.

"What the devil is going on here?" the earl demanded. "Since when must I wait on the steps like a beggar until I am granted admittance into my own townhouse?"

"Beg pardon, milord, I didn't hear—"

"You were asleep! Don't bother to deny it. Well you'll not collect another penny from me for sleeping on duty. I'll give you ten minutes to take off that uniform and get out of my house."

"But, milord—"

The earl raised a threatening fist. "Out of my sight, you worthless lay-about."

Rachel stared at him, mouth agape. He had the same look of unmitigated rage that had twisted his features when he'd viewed the Comte de Rochemont introducing his mistress to the Duke of Wellington. Edgar was most definitely not himself this evening.

"It is close to midnight and he is only a boy," she said once the footman had disappeared down the shadowy hall that led to the kitchen and the servants' quarters. "Surely dozing off is not a serious enough offense to warrant his being sacked. Are you aware of how difficult it will be for him to secure another position without a good reference?"

Edgar cast her a frosty look. "Your cit background has never been more apparent than at this moment, my dear. You must strive to gain a better understanding of the proper order of things before you enter the ranks of the nobility as my countess."

He removed his hat and gloves and set them on the table just inside the door. "Servants exist for one purpose only—to attend to the needs of their betters. When one shows signs of laziness or ineptitude, he must be discharged immediately before such traits infect the entire household. Now if you will excuse me, I believe I shall adjourn to my bookroom for a brandy before retiring—unless you wish me to first escort you to your chamber."

Rachel tossed her head. "That will not be necessary, my lord. I am, as you pointed out, a commoner—thus perfectly capable of finding my own way." So saying, she marched up the stairs and into her chamber, locking the door behind her.

Bright moonlight poured through the window, and with a weary sigh, she opened it and leaned out to gaze at the backyard garden below. To no avail. The ugly scene in the entry hall played again and again in her confused mind—a fitting ending to an all-around dreadful day.

A movement in the shadows below and a click of the garden

gate told her the young footman had taken the earl at his word and was departing without the all-important reference—and all because his employer had had a bad day in the city and was in a foul mood.

Rachel had never before been privy to how Edgar interacted with his servants. She knew now, and the knowledge shocked her to the core. She told herself that he was a product of a spoiled upbringing and servants that had toadied to his every need from the time he was in leading strings. In short, he was a typical aristocrat. But that didn't change the fact that she could never trust the welfare of her mill workers and sheepherders to a despot with a callous disregard for those who served him.

It was time she faced the sad truth that her dream of a kindly husband and children of her own had been just that—a dream. It was time she woke up and returned to Yorkshire and reality.

Rachel had not yet finished her first cup of morning tea when Edgar strode into the breakfast room the next morning, apparently fully recovered from his childish pique. From his smiling face and jaunty air, she would never have guessed the previous evening had turned into such a dreadful debacle had she not been there to witness it.

"So, dear ladies, how shall we amuse ourselves today?" he asked as he took a seat and poured himself a cup of the black coffee he preferred to tea. His charming smile encompassed both Rachel and Verity. "I am at your command the entire day."

"You are too kind, my lord," Verity twittered. "I think we should go someplace where dear Rachel can show off the new bonnet and shawl she bought yesterday on Bond Street."

"Indeed we should," the earl agreed. "I am eager to see them myself."

Verity frowned at Rachel. "Don't tell me you wore that dreadful brown thing to the theater when you could have worn your beautiful new shawl. Really, my dear, what must one do to instill a sense of fashion in you?"

Rachel spread her piece of toast with strawberry jam before answering. "As a matter of fact, I did wear the new one," she said, and left it at that.

"Of course, the shawl your abigail brought you just as we were leaving the house. I cannot believe I failed to mention how lovely you looked."

Rachel shrugged. "As I remember it, my lord, your thoughts were elsewhere."

A flush suffused the earl's cheeks. "I was indeed remiss, but I shall endeavor to make it up to you today, dear lady. Now tell me where would you like to go? What would you like to do?"

Two pairs of eyes turned her way, and Rachel decided now was as good a time as any to make her announcement. She managed a stiff smile. "As a matter of fact, I am planning to spend the day packing my trunks. I have been away from Yorkshire, and my mill, much too long."

Verity stared at her in wide-eyed astonishment, and the earl's cup clattered onto his saucer, spreading a circle of brown coffee across the pristine table covering. "But I will not hear of your leaving London so soon!" he declared. "There is so much of interest you've yet to see."

"I sincerely appreciate the generous hospitality you have shown me and my companion all these weeks, my lord. But I for one have seen all I care to of London. I fear the life of the aristocracy is much too complicated for a simple countrywoman."

An odd, almost fearful, expression crossed the earl's face. "But what of our plans for the future? We need to discuss them, firm them up. If you do not care for London, we can reside in—"

"I agree we need to talk," Rachel interjected, casting a meaningful glance at Verity. The last thing she wished to do was air her personal linen in front of her nosy companion. "We can speak in private this evening after dinner, if you wish. But in the meantime, I would appreciate your alerting your coachman that I wish to leave at dawn tomorrow."

The color blanched from Lord Fairborne's face. "My dear, if either I or that fool Thornton did anything to offend you last evening—"

"I am not offended," Rachel said quickly. "I am simply tired of London and homesick for my small Yorkshire village and for the people who make up my life there."

"People?" Verity shrieked. "What people do you have in mind? That boring fellow who helps manage your mill? The colorless creature who teaches your mill workers' brats? The mill workers themselves? Have you failed to notice that you have no social life in Yorkshire. Indeed, you are considered too eccentric to be accepted by the local gentry and I, as your relative, am tarred by the same brush."

She turned to the earl. "Please try to talk some sense into her, my lord. It is not natural for a young woman to drudge away her days in a mill and spend her evenings scribbling numbers in dusty ledgers."

"I shall do my best, dear lady. Perhaps if you would leave us alone for a short while, I can persuade her to change her mind about leaving London."

"Well I certainly hope so. I would never think of abandoning my responsibilities, of course, but I swear I shall die of loneliness if forced to return to that miserable village in the back of beyond." Verity rose from her chair, dropped her serviette on the table, and hurried from the room.

"Now, my dear, what is this foolishness about returning to Yorkshire?" From Edgar's patient tone of voice, one would have thought he was addressing a particularly exasperating child.

Rachel felt her hackles rise, but before she could answer, O'Reilly, the butler, appeared in the doorway. He carried a small silver salver on which reposed a letter sealed with a thick blob of red sealing wax. "Beggin' your pardon, milord. This just came in the post for you, and I was thinking it might be of some importance."

"Devil take it, O'Reilly, can't you see I'm busy?" The earl snatched the letter from the salver, slit the seal with a table knife and quickly scanned the single sheet., The color instantly blanched from his face and as if he could not believe his eyes, he read the short message again.

"There is serious trouble at . . . at my estate in Surrey," he said, rising to his feet. "I have no choice but to leave at once to take care of it."

He gripped the back of his chair with both hands. "I shall be gone no more than three days at the most. Please promise me you'll not leave until I return."

"It is already September and winter can set in early in the north of Yorkshire—"

"Three days cannot make that much difference. Surely you can grant me that much for the sake of the friendship we have shared."

He looked so distraught, Rachel couldn't bring herself to add to his problems. Much as she hated the thought of even one more pointless day in London, she reluctantly gave him her promise. She even went so far as to stand on the steps of the townhouse and wave him on his way, then hurried to the sitting room off her bedchamber to avoid encountering Verity.

She glanced longingly out the window at the gorgeous day, but decided against venturing abroad in London. The Frenchman would undoubtedly track her down wherever she might go—if, she thought sourly, the blasted libertine could tear himself from the arms of his beautiful mistress.

Now that he had proved his connection to Wellington, she could safely leave the business about the bookroom an unsolved mystery. Better that than to endure his annoying presence and the embarrassment of acknowledging his gift of the shawl. For, of course, she couldn't return it now that she'd worn it.

She would, she decided, spend the morning packing everything—the shawl included—except the clothes she would wear in the next three days and those she would need for the trip to Yorkshire. Then she would devote the rest of the day—indeed the next three days—to reading the books she had purchased at Hatchard's.

It was a good plan, if she discounted the fact that by the end of the day her muscles were cramped from too much sitting and her eyes ached from too much reading. Then, of course, there was the unpleasant scene with Verity. If she heard one more complaint about returning to Yorkshire, Rachel vowed to pay the troublesome woman a year's wage and send her packing.

Still all that aside, the simple act of deciding to go home had revived Rachel's flagging appetite to where even the new chef's food seemed tasty. Furthermore, she slept like a babe the entire night for the first time since arriving in London.

Humming a cheerful tune, she descended to the breakfast room the next morning, filled her plate, and tucked into a hearty breakfast of greasy sausage, burned toast and coddled eggs as tough as shoe leather. With but two more days until she could shake the dust of London from her shoes, nothing could dampen her spirits.

"Beggin' your pardon, miss."

Rachel paused, fork in hand, to find the butler hovering in the doorway, an anxious look on his round, ruddy face. He cleared his throat. "There's a gentleman asking to see you, miss. A Mr. St. Armand. I've put him in the blue salon."

"A caller for me? At this early hour?" She had met no one by that name since arriving in London. Unless . . . there were half a dozen Threadneedle Street bankers who handled her London account. He must be one of them.

Abandoning the remains of her breakfast, she followed the butler to the small salon opening off the entrance hall and stepped through the doorway. One look at the tall, black-haired man standing at the window told her this was not one of her bankers.

"You!" she gasped, as O'Reilly closed the door behind her. "What are *you* doing here? And why did you give the butler a false name? If you thought I would refuse to receive you in the Earl of Fairborne's townhouse, you thought correctly, sir. It is plain to see there is no love lost between you."

The Frenchman raised an expressive eyebrow. "I see that your tongue is as sharp as ever, even at this early hour. But you accuse me wrongly, Miss Barton. The butler asked my name, which I gave him. He did not ask my title."

"Oh! I suppose that makes sense." Rachel frowned. "Still, I want to make one thing clear right now. It was most improper of you to send me that shawl, as you well know, and I had no intention of wearing it to the theater. I was forced into it by an unfortunate set of circumstances completely beyond my control."

The Frenchman chuckled. "I guessed as much from the look on your face when you took your seat in Baron Thornton's box. But I assure you I meant no disrespect in sending it to you. I purchased it on impulse because I could see you were much taken by it—in fact would have purchased it yourself had you not been discomposed by my presence. Have you never done anything on impulse, Miss Barton?"

"I am not an impetuous kind of person," Rachel said stiffly, and felt a flush heat her cheeks at that blatant untruth. She'd lost count of the number of times Jacob Zimmerman, her mill superintendent, had warned her to "think again" before she made another radical decision about the operation of the mill.

"To be entirely truthful," she amended, "I would have bought the shawl the minute I saw it if I hadn't spent all my money on a bonnet."

The Frenchman's lips quivered, and her cheeks grew hotter yet at the thought he might be laughing at her. "But what a delightful bonnet it is," he said with questionable solemnity. "A bargain at any price."

Rachel raised her chin defiantly. "My thought exactly, and the shawl matches it perfectly. Unfortunately, I cannot, in good conscience, accept such a gift from a man I scarcely know." She flushed, remembering it was already packed at the bottom of her trunk. "I shall simply have to pay you for it."

"It is only a shawl, Miss Barton. If the sight of it offends you, give it to your maid." This time the Frenchman made no attempt to disguise the spark of laughter in his eyes. "But rest assured, your virtue is safe. If I'd been attempting to seduce you, I'd have sent you a diamond bracelet."

Rachel gritted her teeth. A pox on the blasted Son of Gaul! How did he always manage to make her feel like the veriest country bumpkin?

"I assume you had a reason for calling on me at this unlikely hour," she said in her haughtiest voice.

"I did, mademoiselle. Since my spies inform me the earl is away from London, this seemed a propitious time for our talk."

"Very well. Say what you have to say, but pray make it brief. My companion is due to come down to breakfast at any moment, and she is a consummate busybody, as well as an ardent admirer of the earl's. If she should see you here, she would be certain to tell him."

"We have a problem then, for what I have to say cannot be covered in a few minutes. Name another time and place where we can safely meet, and I guarantee I will be there."

"Is that really necessary? I accept that you are a friend of the Duke of Wellington's and, therefore, pose no threat to my country."

"It is necessary, Miss Barton, and I will not leave here until we can make satisfactory arrangements for a meeting."

The last thing Rachel wanted was an assignation with the bewildering Frenchman, but he left her no choice. "My companion takes a nap each afternoon after her luncheon," she said after a moment's thought. "I could meet you at half past the hour of one o'clock at the Upper Grosvenor Street entrance to Hyde Park."

"An excellent choice." The laughter was back in the Frenchman's eyes. "It is private enough so we can carry on a discreet conversation, yet public enough so not even a dangerous fellow like myself would dare molest you."

Rachel elevated her chin another notch. "I am sorry if I offend you unfairly, sir. But not even your endorsement by the Duke of Wellington changes the fact that the circumstance of our first meeting was odd, to say the least."

"Very odd indeed, except for one delightful moment that is burned in my memory forever," he agreed with a grin that set Rachel's teeth on edge. "But you have made it plain you will think me no gentleman if I mention that."

"As if you cared what I think of you. You are a rogue, sir, as we both know, and I cannot imagine what you can say that will explain why a man as wealthy as you are reputed to be should turn to burglary. Still, for my peace of mind, I will hear you out."

His expression sobered. "There is more than your peace of mind involved here. Do not fail to meet me as arranged. Your future, even your life, could depend on what I have to tell you."

Chapter Six

A smoky heat haze had descended on the city by the time Rachel reached the entrance to Hyde Park. Still, it was good to be surrounded by trees and grass and open sky instead of the walls of the earl's townhouse—especially when she felt as troubled as she did at this moment.

The Frenchman's warning had set her teeth on edge. Too many momentous happenings had occurred in her life in the past month—and one way or another, they had all involved a certain black-haired Adonis who could raise goose bumps on a marble statue with his charming smile. She could scarcely believe she had agreed to meet alone with a total stranger, and a foreigner at that.

She didn't like the Comte de Rochemont; she certainly didn't trust him. True, though she would never admit it, his kiss had set her heart pounding and her senses reeling, but that only proved he was an accomplished rake. If she had ever doubted it, she doubted it no more after watching him fawn over his notorious mistress.

Yet unaccountably, his scornful judgment rankled her. She might not be as worldly as his friend, Jacqueline Esquaré, but neither was she the "babe in the wood" he had labeled her. A glance at her chatelaine watch told her she was twenty minutes early for her appointment with the annoying fellow. Too restless to sit idly on the bench beside the gate, she decided to take a short stroll down the bridle path.

This was not her first visit to the park. Once the earl had driven her through it in his curricle at the fashionable hour of five o'clock; once she had slipped out while the household was still asleep and walked along the Serpentine while the dew was still on the grass. But both times she had entered by the Stanhope gate. She found this less used section of the park more to her liking.

Birds chirped in the trees above her and flower beds ablaze with color bordered the paths. Marigolds, daisies, and cottage pinks threatened to spill from one bed; another boasted holly-hocks, snapdragons, and sweet williams—yet another a dozen colors of nasturtiums. Rachel's heart leapt with joy. Never in her wildest dreams had she expected to find an English country garden in the center of London.

Farther along the path she discovered a cluster of purple and yellow pansies in a weed-choked bed, their saucy faces tilted hopefully toward the smoky sun. The scraggly little blooms re-minded her of the bed of pansies in her garden in Yorkshire and she all but drowned in the wave of homesickness that engulfed her.

The other flower beds she'd viewed had been immaculate, and a nearby wheelbarrow and trowel proclaimed this one the gardener's next project. How she envied him his happy occu-pation. She ached to sink her fingers into the rich black loam and rip out the weeds that all but obscured the poor blooms.

Furtively, she glanced up and down the bridle path. Early in the morning the benches had been occupied by nannies watch-ing their charges chase their balls and roll their hoops; late in the afternoon the park had swarmed with the carriages of mem-bers of the *ton* striving to see and be seen. But now, at this mid-point in the day, she had this secluded section of the vast park all to herself.

She couldn't resist the temptation. She felt a particular affin-ity for pansies. The "commoners" in her garden, they were far less spectacular than her exotic roses or peonies. But those showy aristocrats required endless hours of care to keep them free of aphids and blight, while the sturdy pansy plants more or less survived on their own.

Dropping to her knees, she tore off her gloves, pulled a few of the largest weeds, and tossed them into the barrow. "There now, isn't that better?" she crooned—and imagined she glimpsed smiles on the faces of the brave little blooms she'd uncovered.

The soil was moist from a recent rain and the tangle of this-tles and dandelions and pale green chickweed yielded easily to her probing fingers. One by one she freed the pansy plants from the weeds that were suffocating them. It was the first produc-tive thing she had done since she'd left Yorkshire, and she found the simple act so satisfying, she lost all track of time.

*   *   *

Yves had arrived at the agreed meeting place ten minutes past the hour, expecting to find Rachel Barton waiting impatiently for him. She had the look of a woman who would be unfailingly punctual. To his surprise, she was nowhere in sight.

Illogically, he found her tardiness unspeakably annoying. How dare the irritating female be late for their appointment when he had made it clear he had information vital to her welfare.

For another ten minutes, he paced back and forth beneath the giant oak tree just inside the park entrance—growing more incensed with each step he took. Cursing under his breath, he stopped to look at his pocket watch and for the first time noticed what appeared to be a large, brown dog crouched beside a flower bed a few hundred feet ahead.

He looked again. *Sacré bleu!* That was no dog! It was a woman who looked very much like the one from whom he had taken his leave less than two hours earlier.

Heart pounding, he sprinted down the path toward the shocking sight. Memories of another woman collapsed on the terrace outside his house in Paris raced through his brain. Amalie, too, had been on her knees when he'd found her on that fateful day, doubled over in agony, with her arms clasped across the blood-soaked bodice of her gown. She had lived just long enough to whisper the warning that had saved his life.

In the few seconds it took him to reach Rachel Barton's crumpled body, he tortured himself with frightening speculation, shocked to realize how protective he felt toward the naive stranger whose life had briefly touched his. Was Fairborne the traitor, as Lord Castlereagh suspected? Had he returned to London unexpectedly, learned the heiress planned to meet with his enemy, and followed her here to the park to dispose of her as he'd disposed of others who had posed a threat to him?

Rachel had just pulled a particularly large clump of chickweed when she heard what sounded like feet pounding down the hard-packed gravel path. Startled, she glanced up to find the Frenchman barreling toward her—his black hair streaming behind him, his face as gray as the ashes on a cold hearth.

Clutching the clump of chickweed, she sat back on her heels and regarded him warily as he came to a grinding stop just inches away from her. "Good heavens, what is wrong?" she asked.

For an interminable minute he remained silent, his steely gaze riveted on a spot somewhere between her waist and her bosom. She glanced down, fearful she'd find a giant spider or some other creature crawling up the front of her gown. She could see nothing.

"What is wrong?" she asked again, alarmed by his strange pallor. Did she just imagine it or were his hands actually trembling?

He ignored her question. "What the devil are you doing?" he demanded in an oddly hollow voice. "Why were you slumped over as if in pain?"

Slumped over indeed! She squared her shoulders, refusing to be put on the defensive by the Frenchman's strange question, though it did make her realize how ridiculous she must look. "Anyone with eyes in his head can see I am weeding a pansy bed," she said defiantly, and tossed the clump of chickweed into the harrow.

His black brows drew together in a fierce frown. "But why?"

"Because it needed doing." Rachel felt her cheeks flame. "And because I sorely miss my garden in Yorkshire."

"Ahhh!" His voice softened and a relieved smile brightened his handsome face. "You are weeding Hyde Park because you are homesick. That I can understand. I, too, often long to dig my fingers into the warm earth again."

To Rachel's surprise, he hunkered down beside her and stripped off his fine kidskin gloves, as if he intended to pull weeds alongside her. "Don't even consider it," she said, scrambling to her feet. "It would be most unseemly and you would ruin your breeches if you knelt on the ground."

He laughed. "It would not be the first pair of breeches I have ruined in such a way, though I admit the others were made of sturdy homespun."

Rachel stared at his long, elegant fingers with their neatly manicured nails and ornate signet ring, his coat of dark gray superfine, his silver-gray waistcoat and pale gray breeches. "You jest, sir. When have you ever weeded a bed of pansies?"

"Never," he admitted, standing up. "But I pulled my share of weeds from hills of potatoes and rows of beans when I was a lad. The process is, I believe, much the same."

Rachel eyed him with frank skepticism. "I understood you were a French count. Did you come by the title just recently?"

"No, Miss Barton. Mine is a very old and respected title which has been passed down through the St. Armand family for many generations. I am the eighth Comte de Rochemont."

"Then, sir, your story about your childhood chores does not ring true. Since when have the children of French aristocrats worn homespun and weeded vegetables?"

"Since our nurse hid my sister and me at her brother's farm the night our parents and grandparents were dragged from their beds and executed by the sansculotte." His eyes turned as bleak and wintry as a Yorkshire January. "Luckily Monsieur and Madame Durand had twelve black-haired children of their own. The local authorities never noticed when the number mysteriously increased to fourteen. I lived as a farmer's son from my sixth year until I was old enough to make my own way in the world, and had it not been for a kindly village priest, who was a staunch Royalist, I would be as uneducated as one."

Speechless with shock, Rachel pictured the horror of that night—the terror and despair of a six-year-old boy made an orphan by a mob of bloodthirsty revolutionaries. She had read about the infamous Reign of Terror, of course, but she had never before met one of its victims. Yet somehow she knew instinctively the horrifying story she had just heard was a true one.

"Was this terrible thing that happened to you the reason you acted as the Duke of Wellington's agent and spied against France?" she asked softly.

"I did not spy against France, Miss Barton. I love France." Rage darkened his beautiful silver eyes. "I worked to overthrow the bloodthirsty peasants who murdered my family, and my king, and held my beloved country captive."

"Forgive me. I spoke without thinking," she said, and realized she accepted without question the truth of the Frenchman's heartbreaking story. Forgetting her recent antagonism toward him, she laid a comforting hand on his arm.

Yves stared at her dirt-encrusted fingers and remembered another woman who had stirred him with her touch. But Amalie's fingers had been slender and elegantly tapered. This woman's looked strong and capable of hard work. Amalie's hands and arms had been as white and soft as the petals of a water lily. A sprinkling of freckles decorated this woman's sun-bronzed skin. In truth, she bore no resemblance to his elegant love.

Still, he felt strangely drawn to the tall, plain Englishwoman.

There was an unusual gentleness in her touch and a look of compassion in her warm brown eyes for a stranger she had every reason to distrust. He sensed she was one of those rare individuals whose generous heart transcended her unremarkable features and drab mode of dress.

"My name is Yves . . . Yves St. Armand," he said impulsively. "I would be honored if you would address me by my given name. I would be even more honored if I might be allowed to address you by yours."

She couldn't have looked more surprised if he had told her he was Genghis Khan, and he realized how bizarre his request must have sounded under the circumstances. He couldn't imagine what had possessed him. He was not normally given to impulse. He waited, expecting to be sternly put in his place. But to his surprise, she said, "My name is Rachel," in that firm, no-nonsense way she had of speaking. "You may address me as such if you so desire."

"Thank you, Rachel," Yves said, raising her fingers to his lips. Despite all the odds against it, he sensed a fragile bond forming between this very proper Englishwoman and himself. He found the idea oddly appealing. Most of the women he knew were boringly predictable; Rachel Barton constantly surprised him.

He wished he could wait until she knew him well enough to trust him before he risked destroying that bond by revealing his suspicions about the nobleman who was courting her. But time was running out. If Fairborne was as desperate to get his hands on her fortune as Yves suspected, the blackguard might convince her to elope with him to Scotland—a possibility that must be avoided at all cost.

There was nothing for it but to get on with the task of convincing the Yorkshire heiress to keep a tight hold on her fortune, maybe even lend her cooperation to his investigation of Fairborne. Sadly, the only way he could accomplish this was to make her face the truth of why the Earl of Fairborne was courting a woman so far beneath him on the social ladder. Yves was loath to wound any woman's pride in such a way—and he felt particularly guilty when the woman was Rachel Barton.

It seemed the more he learned about her, the more protective he felt toward her. Perhaps this was because her honest, rather naive outlook on life provided a welcome contrast to the devious women in his own social circle—perhaps because he saw something in her that reminded him of the sturdy French farm wife who had taken a frightened six-year-old into her home and heart.

Whatever it was, he must guard against feeling too much empathy for Rachel Barton. A man bent on vengeance could ill afford such tender sentiments.

"Shall we walk farther into the park while we have our long-overdue talk?" he asked, offering her his arm.

She blushed as if his simple request had somehow been improper. "I—I do not think I should," she stammered, and he recalled the dressing-down he had given her for walking the streets of London alone. How ironic that she should choose this particular time to heed his advice.

"It is already half past the hour," she said, glancing nervously at the gold watch pinned to her gown, as if that were the only reason for her refusal to walk with him, "My companion will be unbearably inquisitive if I am away from the townhouse when she wakes from her nap."

She surveyed him through narrowed eyes, once again every inch the starchy spinster. "However, as long as we have met this way, I should like to hear your explanation of why you were searching the Earl of Fairborne's desk. But I warn you, despite your apparent connection to the Duke of Wellington, I still feel obliged to report the odd incident to the earl. I should have told him a fortnight ago."

Yves caught her upper arms in a vicelike grip. "That would be most unwise, Rachel. Fairborne could be a dangerous man."

She stared at him with wide, startled eyes. "Edgar dangerous? You cannot be serious. He is the most mild-mannered of men—well, most of the time." She frowned and Yves suspected she was recalling the rage the "most mild-mannered of men" had exhibited last night at the theater. Unless she was a greater fool than she appeared to be, the lady must have some inkling that her suitor was not the saintly fellow he pretended to be.

Rachel brushed at a fly buzzing around her head. "Edgar is a typical aristocrat. He assumes his noble birth ensures he will always get his own way. When it does not, he shows his temper, as you are doing now. But that does not make him dangerous . . . except to those who rely on him for their living."

Yves frowned. "For your information, I am not showing my temper. But I repeat, Fairborne could be a dangerous man," he said grimly, his frustration mounting over her stubbornness. In one breath Lord Castlereagh had forbidden him to openly accuse any man of treason and cold-blooded murder unless he had absolute proof of guilt. In the next breath the Foreign Secretary had agreed the heiress should be warned to stay on her guard around her would-be suitor. Unfortunately, he'd offered no clue as to how both of these directives should be accomplished.

Yves took a deep breath and began again. "It is vitally important to the welfare of England that what I have to tell you remains a secret. Unless you can give me your word that you will repeat it to no one, our conversation must end right now."

"Damn and blast!" Rachel stamped her foot. "You know very well no woman could resist the lure of such a secret." She raised her right hand. "Very well, I swear that not one word of what you have to say will pass my lips."

"Very well, I came to London to seek out the English nobleman who sold military secrets to Bonaparte—"

"An English nobleman a traitor to his country?" Rachel shook her head. "I have no great love for the nobility, but I find that very difficult to believe."

"Nevertheless, it is true. Information was passed to Bonaparte in the spring of 1812 that nearly turned the tide of battle at Salamanca. The same informant betrayed the names of two French aristocrats working to bring about Bonaparte's downfall. The Marquis de la Basse was murdered by Fouchet's minions and I escaped a similar fate only because I was warned in time." He paused to draw a deep breath. "The friend who brought that warning died in my arms."

"Dear God!" Rachel pressed trembling fingers to her lips. "But what has that to do with the Earl of Fairborne? Surely you cannot suspect him—"

"Aside from Lord Castlereagh, the British Foreign Secretary, only four men in Whitehall, indeed in all of England, were privy to the information in question," Yves continued. "There can be little doubt that one of the four is the traitor. I am determined to find out which one is guilty and bring him to justice if it is the last thing I ever do."

Shock darkened Rachel's expressive eyes to a deep, unfathomable brown. "And the Earl of Fairborne is one of those four?"

"He is—which, of course is why I was searching his desk a fortnight ago."

"But that is the most ridiculous thing I have ever heard. Edgar has his faults. But nothing he has ever said or done would lead me to believe he is anything but a loyal British citizen." She paused as if in thought. "But even if he were not, which I do not for a minute believe, why would a man with his wealth and title betray the country in which he enjoys such privileges?"

Yves shrugged. "A man can be driven to desperate measures for many reasons. He can have acquired expensive tastes that drive him into debt—or be fool enough to have lost his fortune at the gaming tables. Such a man might well be tempted by the vast amount of money Bonaparte was willing to pay for the right information."

"If you think that, sir, I fear your years at the emperor's court have made you so jaded you have a twisted view of your fellow man. But be that as it may, you cannot hang Edgar on those hooks. I know for a fact he is not a gamester, for he has told me so himself—and as for his expensive tastes, he can well afford to support them."

Yves gave a vicious kick to a stone lying in the middle of the path. It wreaked havoc with his boot, but frustration made him need to kick something. Rachel Barton was living proof that any woman could be blinded by the charms of a clever man.

Bow Street had ascertained the Earl of Fairborne was in debt to his eyebrows and not only to London's merchants. Every gaming hell in the East End held his unclaimed vowels. It might well be true that he was not the traitor. Still, at the very least he was a crass opportunist angling to marry an heiress to support his extravagant way of life and his lust for a French trollop.

Yves gritted his teeth. It was all he could do to keep from grabbing the stubborn woman and shaking her until she came down off her comfortable cloud.

She stopped beneath a large oak tree bordering the path and turned to face him. "You said there were four men privy to the information. Are you planning to investigate the other three as well?"

"I am, with the help of Bow Street. Well, actually two other than Fairborne. One man has already been cleared of suspicion."

Rachel blinked. "Good heavens! Never say the Bow Street runners are involved in this!"

"Of course they are. Did you think it was something I had drummed up on my own?" Yves cursed softly. "Don't bother to answer that. I can see you did."

Rachel ignored his angry gibe and resumed walking. Yves immediately fell into step beside her. "If only one man has been eliminated from your list, the earl must be your second suspect," she said after a moment's thought. "How close are you to finishing that investigation and going on to the third?"

Yves braced himself. This was the moment for which he had been waiting. "Not close enough. As you may recall, I was interrupted during a crucial part of it. Naturally, I have proceeded along other investigative lines, but I need to finish that phase of the search before I can assure those who need to know that the Earl of Fairborne is cleared of suspicion."

That, Yves decided, was a nicely ambiguous statement if ever he had heard one. A sound behind him caught his attention, and he drew Rachel to the side of the bridle path to let a lone horseman trot past while he waited impatiently for her reaction.

"Are you saying you feel compelled to finish your search of the earl's bookroom before you can move on to the next suspect? I believe I mentioned before that breaking and entering is a hanging offense in England. Or will Lord Castlereagh and the other officials at Whitehall speak for you if you are caught?"

"I fear not. But what good is an investigation if it is not thorough? I am determined to ferret out the murderous traitor. If I must risk my neck to do so, so be it."

They had reached the Upper Grosvenor Street entrance to the park. Weary from the strain of the last few minutes, Rachel sank onto the bench just inside the gate and folded her hands in her lap. It occurred to her that Edgar must have discovered the Frenchman had been prying into his affairs. That would explain his unnatural rage.

But he could not know the whole of it. Edgar was a proud aristocrat and a staunch Englishman. If he were aware he was suspected of treason, he would undoubtedly demand satisfaction from his accuser, and something told her he would be no match for the Frenchman.

She felt obliged to do her best to bring about a peaceful settlement of the unhappy affair. Edgar might no longer be a man she would consider marrying, but she owed him that much.

She raised her head and met the watchful silver gaze of the man who stood before her. "Tell me, Yves St. Armand," she said softly, "why do I have the feeling my silence is not the only thing you want from me?"

Chapter Seven

Yves sat down on the bench beside Rachel and covered her hand with his. "Do you believe the Earl of Fairborne is innocent of the charge of treason?"

"Of course." She snatched her hand away as if burned by his touch. "The very idea is so ridiculous, I cannot believe anyone would give it credence, not even . . ."

"Not even a Frenchman." Yves finished her sentence for her. So much for that "fragile bond" he had sensed just moments ago. But he wasted no time on regret. He needed to get into the earl's townhouse, and it had been locked as tightly as a castle under siege during the past fortnight.

"If you truly believe in Fairborne's innocence, then help me to prove it," he said quietly. "Unlock the bookroom window for me when he is away from home. Help me search for the evidence I seek."

"Help you? I most certainly will not. Whatever his faults, Edgar has been a good friend to me—and you have no interest in clearing his name. You only want to find someone you can send to the gallows so you can congratulate yourself on a job well done."

Yves shrugged. "I admit there is some truth in your accusation, but the same search that can prove the earl's guilt can prove his innocence as well."

Rachel studied his face with troubled eyes. "If the search you suggest does not turn up the proof you seek, will you give up this madness and convince Bow Street and Whitehall to do so as well?"

Yves gave careful thought to the wording of his answer. "If I fail to find the evidence I need in the bookroom, I promise I will adjust my thinking accordingly."

The glow of righteous triumph shone in the lady's eyes. "In

that case, sir, I will help you and tonight would be a good time since the earl is not due back from his estate in Surrey until tomorrow or the next day."

"Tonight it is then, Rachel. I shall be outside the window at the stroke of midnight. The servants should all be abed by that hour." He ignored the twinge of guilt he felt at the ease with which he had gained her cooperation. It was in a good cause, and it was no fault of his that innocent zealots were so easy to gull.

But what was this nonsense about an estate in Surrey? If the earl did own such an estate, it was never mentioned in the report Whitehall had compiled on him. Furthermore, according to the message relayed from the Bow Street runner shadowing him, the Earl of Fairborne had been spotted galloping hell-bent-for-leather on the high road to Dover.

Rachel waited until the clock on the mantel chimed the hour of midnight before she slipped from her bedchamber, candle in hand, and made her way to the bookroom. No sooner had she placed her candle on the desk and opened the heavy velvet drape, than a shadowy figure appeared at the French window.

Her pulse quickened. It had seemed so logical—so right—when Yves St. Armand had claimed that the same search that could prove Edgar's guilt could prove his innocence as well. But she had listened to those persuasive words in the bright light of day; now in the dark of midnight she had the uncomfortable feeling she had let herself be talked into betraying a friend. With grave misgivings, she lifted the latch and stepped aside to let the Frenchman enter the Earl of Fairborne's bookroom.

Swiftly, without a word, he removed his high-crowned beaver and gloves and placed them on the desk. Then using the candle she'd brought with her, he lighted two more tapers. "There that is better. Now we can see what we're doing." So saying, he pulled open the top, right-hand drawer, searched its contents, then ran his hand beneath it, apparently to make certain nothing was affixed to the bottom.

"What exactly are you looking for?" she whispered.

"Something—anything that will tie Fairborne to Bonaparte— a pass through the French lines, a letter signed by Fouché or even the emperor himself."

"Do you plan to search Baron Thornton's desk in this same manner?"

He paused in his search. "How did you know the baron was one of the suspects?"

"It seemed logical since Edgar told me they had worked together at Whitehall during the war." Rachel paused a moment before adding, "I probably should not say this, but the other night at the theater I gained the impression that there is more to the baron than the frivolous facade he shows to the world. It was as if something unspeakably evil were coiled inside him, ready to spring out at a moment's notice."

Yves nodded his agreement, surprised at her astute analysis of the man. "What I've learned of Thornton so far would indicate he leads two lives—one in the environs of the *ton,* the other in London's infamous East End, where he is reputed to have explored every perversion known to man."

"I knew it. The mere touch of his fingers on my arm made my skin crawl. Then you are going to investigate him?"

"I am. As a matter of fact, he is next on my list, and yes, I will find a way to search his desk."

Rachel shook her head. "Then, sir, you will be embarked on a fool's errand twice over."

"Why the devil do you say that?" Yves asked, impatience sharpening his hoarse whisper.

"It stands to reason if either the earl or the baron were guilty of treason, neither would be so foolish as to keep the evidence of the crime lying about in desk drawers. No sane man would."

Yves closed the top drawer, opened the second one, and followed the same procedure. "That is most likely true. But what if the traitor believes in the old adage 'the best hiding spot is the one in plain sight'? I dare not overlook any place where the proof I need might be."

"Proof you are not even certain exists," Rachel pointed out.

"Oh, I am certain—as certain as if I held it in my hand. Intuition tells me that whoever the traitor may be, he is so taken with his own consequence, he will not be able to resist keeping a memento of how he outsmarted the best minds in Whitehall."

Rachel couldn't argue with that. It was, in fact, exactly the sort of thing she could imagine Baron Thornton doing. What she couldn't understand was why Yves hadn't made the suspicious fellow the first target of his investigation. Chances were he would have saved himself a great deal of time and trouble.

She watched him open the last drawer in the desk and feel beneath it before checking its contents. "Well now, isn't this interesting," he remarked, lifting out a stack of papers and depositing them on the desk.

Rachel's heart skipped a beat. "Wha—what did you find?"

"Statements of account. From green grocers, butchers, haberdashers, carriage makers—some of them more than a year old. Here is one from that renowned London tailor, Mr. Weston, which is just slightly less than England's war debt. Apparently the rumors are true that Fairborne is, as you English say, 'Sailing the River Tick.'"

Rachel stared at the monstrous collection of unpaid bills, her eyes wide with shock, and Yves felt sickened by his own cruelty. He could just as easily have stuffed the invoices back into the drawer before she saw them. But, of course, it suited his plans to have her realize her noble suitor was hopelessly in debt. If she was the practical lady he judged her to be, she would think twice before she let him run through her fortune in the same reckless manner he had squandered his own.

He watched her leaf through the stack and waited for her to explode with anger or dissolve into tears as he would expect any woman who discovered she'd been played for a fool to do. To his surprise, she did neither. Except for her extreme pallor and the grim line of her mouth, she showed no sign that this disclosure about the earl affected her in any way. Once again, he found himself admiring the lady's fortitude under stress.

He wished he could assure her that just because one man had courted her to get his hands on her fortune, not all men looked at her bank account with greedy eyes. But the proud tilt of her chin invited no such sympathetic comments.

Instead, he said, "It would appear you were right. If Fairborne has anything to hide other than his unpaid bills, he has opted for a safer place than his desk drawers. I believe we can rule out his bedchamber as well. No man is fool enough to think he can keep anything sacred from his valet."

Raising his head, he made a speculative study of the wall of books behind Rachel. "Now if I were intent on hiding something like a letter or written pass . . ." .

Rachel blinked. "Surely you cannot be thinking of hunting

through the pages of every book in the earl's library. It would take all night."

"Not if two of us worked at it."

He treated her to one of the seductive smiles that had gained him anything he wanted from the ladies at the French court. It merely earned him an angry scowl from Rachel.

"I hate being a part of this ugly business," she declared vehemently. "The fact that the earl lives beyond his means may explain his willingness to marry a commoner, but it is not a valid reason to suspect him of treason. If it were, half the *ton* would be under suspicion."

"I have leveled no accusation," Yves argued. "But until I have explored every possibility, how can I, or his superiors at Whitehall, be certain of his guilt or innocence?"

To Rachel's surprise, he reached out an elegant hand and tucked a stray lock of hair behind her ear, sending a hum of wicked sensation pulsing through her veins. "What is wrong, Rachel?" he asked softly. "Are you afraid I will find proof that you have been even more mistaken in a man to whom you have given your trust and affection?"

"No." She closed her eyes against his hypnotic silver gaze. "God knows Edgar has his faults. I can believe he would betray a woman. I doubt there are few of your gender who have not been guilty of that sin at one time or another. But I cannot believe he would betray his country."

Yves slid his fingers across her cheek and cupped her chin gently but firmly. "What hold does Fairborne have over you that you are willing to forgive his greed and deception?" he demanded.

"I forgive him nothing," she said bitterly. "But I am not so vindictive I would wish him falsely accused of treason."

"Then help me prove him innocent of the charge."

Rachel's eyes popped open. "Damn you, Frenchman. All right! If there is no other way to rid myself of your annoying presence, I will help you turn every book in this room upside down."

Twisting out of his hold, she strode to the bookcase. "I will take the bottom row; you take the second. We'll work our way to the top."

A little over two hours later, they had examined every book on the first six shelves and found nothing that even bordered on suspicious. But Yves took note of one interesting fact. All the volumes were bound in the finest leather with the title and author's name stamped in gold, but inside the elegant covers, most of the pages were uncut.

It was all too obvious that the earl had spent a fortune stocking his library with handsomely bound classics he never read so he could pose as a man of letters. From the bleak look on Rachel's face, Yves deduced that she found this proof that her noble suitor was more show than substance every bit as appalling as the proof of his indebtedness.

He found himself wanting to lay his hand on her arm—to comfort her as she had comforted him in the park. But all things considered, he felt certain he was the last person on earth whose touch she would welcome at that moment.

He stared at the four additional rows of leather-bound books between him and the high ceiling and cursed his stupidity. Had he been thinking straight, he would have realized he could have saved time by working from the top down while she worked from the bottom up. Now he would need the rolling library ladder to reach the books on the upper shelves, which meant it was a task for one person only. It would be close to dawn by the time he finished the tedious task.

With a groan, he stepped onto the first rung of the ladder and reached for the volume on the far left of the sixth shelf—a copy of *Plato's Republic*. To his astonishment he found it was not a book, but a two-inch thick rectangular block of wood with a strip of gold stamped leather on the end facing the front of the shelf.

"What is this?" he mused, running his fingers along the tops of the other "books" on the shelf, only to find they, too, were fakes. He climbed another rung, made a quick check of the next shelf, and discovered the same thing.

"I'll say one thing for Fairborne," he said, choking back the laughter that rumbled in his throat. "He may be a spendthrift on one hand, but on the other he is a very practical fellow. It appears there were limits to what he was willing to spend to pose as a student of the classics."

Rachel frowned up at him. "Why do you say that?"

He descended the ladder. "We can forget about checking the rest of the books. They are all like this," he said, passing the block of wood to Rachel.

With wide, shock-filled eyes, she stared at the object in her hand as if it were a snake about to bite her. Yves made a lunge to catch it as it slipped from her fingers and succeeded instead in sending a small, silver tray holding the earl's pens and sealing wax crashing to the floor. The clatter reverberated through the room like the boom of a cannon.

With a curse, he retrieved the "book," while Rachel returned the tray of writing materials to the desk. Then touching his finger to his lips to insure her silence, he held his breath and waited to see if the noise had awakened any of the servants. As he'd feared, he soon heard footsteps in the hall outside the library door.

"Get behind the drape," Rachel whispered and because there was no time to do anything else, he obeyed her with just seconds to spare before the door burst open.

"Beggin' your pardon, mistress, but I was woke from me sleep by a queer, rattlin' kind of sound."

Yves recognized the voice as that of the Irishman who had accompanied the earl into the library a fortnight earlier—the same Irishman who was his source of information about Rachel's and Fairborne's activities.

"I'm afraid it was I, Mr. O'Reilly." Rachel's voice sounded apologetic and amazingly steady. "Clumsy thing that I am, I dropped a book. Please forgive me for disturbing your slumber."

"'Twas only a book that made such a racket?" The Irishman sounded a bit dubious. "Is it all right you are then, mistress?"

"I am perfectly fine—just restless and unable to sleep."

Yves marveled at Rachel's calm demeanor under such circumstances. But then he should have expected no less from the remarkable lady from Yorkshire.

"'Tis well after midnight and the stairwell dark as Satan's soul. Would you be wantin' me to see you to your chamber, mistress?"

"No thank you, Mr. O'Reilly. I'll not keep you from your bed. It will take me a while to choose a book and then I can find my own way. I've a lighted candle, you see." Rachel paused. "Well actually I have three at the moment so I can read the titles of the books."

"That you have, mistress. I'll be sayin' good night to you then."

"Good night to you, too, Mr. O'Reilly."

Yves waited until he heard the click of the door before he stepped from behind the concealing drape. Rachel collapsed onto the chair facing the earl's desk, her head in her hands. "That was cutting it a bit close," she whispered. "It was only pure luck that I noticed your hat and gloves on the desk and stepped in front of them before the earl's butler saw them."

"Luck indeed," Yves agreed, tongue in cheek.

She studied him with deeply shadowed eyes. "You've made your search of the earl's bookroom; now you can be certain there is no evidence proving him the traitor you seek."

"I can be certain there is no such evidence in this bookroom at any rate."

Rachel's dark brows drew together in a frown. "Surely you cannot mean to pursue this investigation of Lord Fairborne further."

"I cannot give it up unless I find evidence that one of the other two suspects is the traitor," he snapped, his patience grown thin. Considering all they had learned of the earl's shortcomings in the past three hours, he could not believe she still defended him.

"Well you'll not find what you seek here," she declared, "so please leave before we both end up in serious trouble."

"As you wish. But first, please be good enough to answer a question that has me completely baffled." Yves raked his fingers through his hair in an unconscious gesture of frustration. "How can such a forthright, intelligent woman remain loyal to a man like Fairborne? Granted, he may not be the traitor I seek, but surely you must see he is a shameless profligate and a pompous ass who goes to great lengths to pose as something he is not."

Rachel's eyes flashed with anger. "I am not defending his spendthrift ways nor his pitiful attempt to represent himself as an intellectual. But I am not so quick as you to condemn human frailty. If I were, I would not have lent my assistance to a man so lost to decency as to publicly flaunt his relationship with a common whore."

Yves felt his mouth drop open at the note of disgust he heard in her voice. He had a sudden vision of how he must have appeared in her eyes when he staged that scenario at the theater, and he felt heat flooding into his cheeks. Chalk another one up to the Yorkshire heiress. No woman had brought him to the blush since he was a green lad fresh from the farm.

"Touché, Rachel," he said dryly. "If you were as adept with a sword as with that sharp tongue of yours, I should fear for my life. But my moral character, or lack thereof, is not the subject currently under discussion."

He clasped her shoulders and swung her around to face him. "Surely after what you have learned this night, you cannot be so eager to wear a coronet that you would still consider marrying a fool like Fairborne."

Rachel blinked. "Why should you care one way or another whom I choose to marry?"

Yves shook his head. "I have asked myself that very question, and the only answer I can come up with is that I like you and would be sorry to see you ruin your life."

"You *like* me?" Rachel stared at him, intrigued in spite of herself.

"I do. I admire your honesty and intelligence, your stubborn, albeit senseless, loyalty to a friend and your unexpected compassion for a total stranger. In short, I think you are one of the most unique women I have ever met."

Yves searched her face with grave eyes. "Ironically, while I despise Fairborne, I envy him as well. Few men can claim a friend as loyal as you, Rachel Barton. I wish I might have the right to call you *my* friend."

Rachel stared at him, too astounded to utter a word. She had heard the French described as impulsive, unpredictable, and excessively demonstrative. Evidently the rumor was true. With not the slightest hint of embarrassment, this French nobleman had declared he liked her and wanted her to be his friend. It was too bizarre to be creditable.

Still, there would be one very definite advantage to having a French friend. They did have a way with words. Madame Francine had called her "willowy," which was ever so much nicer than "skinny." Now Yves found her "unique"—a decided improvement over "odd duck."

Unfortunately, nothing in her staid Yorkshire background had prepared her to deal with such exuberant people—nor with the bewildering feelings this particular Frenchman aroused in her.

"So, what say you, Rachel? Will you be my friend?" Yves interrupted her musings and held out his hand.

Against her better judgment, Rachel placed her hand in his. "I will—as long as you keep your promise to refrain from making any accusations of treason against Edgar, or any other Englishman, unless you have certain proof of guilt."

"I always keep my promises, Rachel." Yves traced tiny circles on the back of her hand with his thumb and sent waves of sensation swirling to parts of her body she had never before realized were so sensitive.

"But one promise between friends deserves another," he said, tracing an ever-widening circle. "For your own sake, as well as my peace of mind, promise me you will not let that generous heart of yours be taken in by Fairborne."

"Give me some credit," Rachel said bitterly. "I may be naive, but I am not a fool."

"You will refuse his suit then?"

"Of course I will. I have always wondered why a man so high in the instep would offer for a commoner who dealt in trade."

Yves's thumb traced a wider circle. "You do not seem too heartbroken by his deceit, my friend."

Rachel shook her head. "My pride is wounded, but my heart is whole." She withdrew her hand from his. One more circle and she might not, in all honesty, be able to make such a statement.

"Then I am glad we discovered the earl's guilty secrets in time to save you from a disastrous marriage."

Yves looked so pleased with himself, she hadn't the heart to tell him she had already made up her mind to reject Edgar's offer—not because he was under investigation, nor even because she had learned that he was an irresponsible spendthrift and fraud. She doubted one aristocrat would understand that another had irreparably blotted his copybook by sacking a footman.

Yves relinquished her hand, only to grasp her upper arms in his strong fingers and draw her to him. "Shall we seal our pact with a friendly kiss?" he asked, a devilish twinkle in his silver eyes. "It would be a pleasant way to end these clandestine hours we have spent together."

Rachel's gaze automatically flew to his sensuous mouth. She could think of nothing she would rather do than kiss the firm lips so close to hers—lips that had haunted her dreams for a fortnight. But she would only make a fool of herself if she admitted that.

"If you are thinking to repair my damaged self-respect with your offer, I thank you kindly," she said, wriggling from his grasp. "And admittedly a kiss would be pleasant. But as you so wisely pointed out, I am 'a babe in the woods' where men are concerned—and you, my friend, are most definitely a man, and a Frenchman at that."

She sighed. "In short, you are out of my league. Kisses such as yours would be wasted on a plain-faced country spinster; you should save them for your beautiful French mistress."

Yves's mouth dropped so far open, Rachel feared his jaw had become unhinged. She ducked her head to hide her smile. Apparently the charming fellow was not accustomed to having his kisses refused.

However, he quickly recovered and reaching for her hand, raised it to his lips. "A pity you are such a proper Yorkshire lady, Rachel. You do not know what you're missing."

Ah but she did! She remembered all too well the pleasure of his kiss—and never doubted the heartbreak she would be inviting if she allowed herself to become accustomed to such pleasure.

Snatching her hand from his, she picked up his high-crowned beaver and gloves and handed them to him. "I bid you good night, sir. I am tired and long for my bed."

Yves promptly perched his hat at a jaunty angle on his glossy black hair, drew on his gloves, and swung a long, muscular leg over the windowsill. "Good night it is then, Rachel," he said with a wicked grin. "Never let it be said that Yves St. Armand kept a lady from her bed."

He stepped onto the terrace, but turned back before he disappeared into the night. "Remember this, my newfound friend," he said in a voice scarcely above a whisper. "If ever you need my help, you can always reach me at the Pulteney Hotel."

Rachel leaned on the windowsill and gazed into the shadowy garden long after she heard the quiet click of the gate latch. Her fingers still tingled from the warm male lips that had brushed them, and she was struck by the irony of the situation in which she found herself.

This strange new friend of hers seemed intent on keeping the Earl of Fairborne from gaining control of her fortune. But, in truth, Yves St. Armand posed a much greater danger to her than Edgar Hanley ever could. For she could only lose her money to Edgar—but unless she was very careful, she could lose her heart to the charming Frenchman.

Chapter Eight

Yves whistled the tune of a bawdy ditty he'd learned from a Parisian courtesan as he made his way to the Pulteney Hotel through the dark streets of predawn London. He might not have found the evidence he sought, but his late night search of Fairborne's bookroom had not been a loss.

From his discovery of the stack of unpaid invoices and the fake books to the moment Rachel vowed to refuse Fairborne's offer, Yves had sensed luck was with him all the way. He still felt a little guilty about how easy it had been to extract that promise from her, but he salved his conscience with the thought that it was as much to her benefit as his.

He had not lied to her when he'd told her he liked her and would hate to see her ruin her life by such a misalliance. But neither had he been entirely truthful. He'd somehow neglected to mention that her welfare was not his only concern.

With the pack of creditors nipping at his heels, Fairborne had to be getting panicky, and nothing would be more apt to drive him to do something rash than to have the heiress he was stalking refuse his suit.

Yves entered the spacious walnut-paneled lobby of the Pulteney Hotel still whistling the same tune, but stopped short as a familiar figure rose from one of the high-backed chairs grouped near the fireplace.

"You keep late hours," Philippe de Maret, Amalie's twin brother, said in French. "I was afraid that stiff-necked clerk behind the desk would throw me into the street if you didn't make an appearance soon."

With arms outstretched, Yves advanced toward the slender dark-haired Frenchman. "What the devil are you doing in London?" he asked, giving Philippe a boisterous hug. "Last I heard, you had sworn to never again leave Paris."

"Situations change and one must change with them," Philippe said in French and saluted Yves with the traditional Gallic greeting of a kiss on the left cheek, then the right.

Out of the corner of his eye, Yves glimpsed the look of horrified disapproval on the desk clerk's face. "Never mind the clerk," he said quietly. "He lost his only son at Waterloo and hates all Frenchmen. I doubt he'd be civil to me if I were not paying such an exorbitant price for my suite."

"Ahhh. Perhaps that is why he flatly refused to let me into your rooms to wait for you, even though I assured him I was your best friend and third cousin once removed."

"I rather think it had something to do with the fact that you look as if you've slept in your clothes for the past week." Yves sniffed. "And smell like it as well."

"As a matter of fact, I have." Philippe shrugged. "I was in something of a hurry when I left France and didn't have time to pack any clothes. To be truthful, I scarcely had time to pull on my trousers and boots. The husband of the lady I was visiting returned unexpectedly and since he was a rather important member of Fat King Louie's court, I felt it wise to put the Channel between us as soon as possible."

Yves shook his head. "How often have I warned you that your fascination with other men's wives would get you in trouble?"

"Other men's wives never badger me to make them *my* wife." Philippe's infectious grin made him look so much like his sister, Yves instinctively braced himself for the stab of pain he felt whenever he thought of Amalie. It came, but for the first time in the three years since her death, the agony had softened to where he could tolerate it without breaking into a cold sweat.

"Well, are you or are you not going to invite me to share your suite—and lend me the money to replenish my wardrobe?" Philippe asked with a hint of the impatience that was so much a part of the volatile de Maret nature. "Unless you do, I am in serious trouble, for I haven't a franc to my name."

"You've never had a franc to your name in all the years I've known you," Yves said as he escorted Philippe toward the stairwell at the opposite end of the lobby. "Both you and Amalie were born with a total disregard for the value of money."

"True. But luckily we had you to look after us."

"And who will look after you when I finish my business here in London and sail for the Americas?"

Before Philippe could answer, Yves looked up to find a soberly garbed, gray-haired man walking across the lobby toward him. "What now?" he exclaimed, coming to an instant stop with one foot on the first stair. "That is Neville Bittner, Lord Castlereagh's assistant. There must be news of the traitor I seek—important news, if Bittner seeks me out at this hour."

"You have learned the identity of the Englishman who caused Amalie's death?" Philippe instantly discarded his mask of sophisticated insouciance and studied the man who approached them with the shrewd eyes of the coldly efficient agent with whom Yves had served during the war.

"We have narrowed it down to three men, one of whom I find particularly interesting. But as yet, I lack the proof Whitehall demands."

"Since when have you begun listening to Whitehall's demands?"

"It is a long story," Yves said. "One I will tell you once we hear what news Bittner brings."

After the briefest of greetings, Yves led the way to his suite and poured three large brandies. "Speak freely," he said to the stocky middle-aged Englishman. "Philippe de Maret was one of Wellington's most trusted agents and has a personal reason for wanting the traitor apprehended."

Bittner's impassive gaze lingered a second on Philippe as if judging the accuracy of Yves's statement before he said, "Lord Castlereagh sends two pieces of news. First, we have learned that Viscount Blevins's windfall was a legacy from another Oxford professor, and Baron Thornton's fortune came from an uncle in Jamaica who died without issue."

"The devil you say." Yves scowled. "Well that eliminates them as suspects. Too bad about Thornton. As Miss Barton pointed out, there is something about the odd little fellow that makes one's skin crawl."

Bittner raised an expressive gray brow. "I think you will find my second piece of news more interesting." He took a healthy drink of brandy. "You knew, of course, that Bow Street had assigned a runner to shadow the Earl of Fairborne."

"I did."

"And that he had followed his quarry to Dover."

"He sent me a note to that effect just before he left London."

"His body was found early last evening in the alley behind

the Blue Whale, a notorious dockside tavern. There was a bullet hole between his eyes."

"Sacré bleu!"

"He was stripped of all identification, but luckily the tavern owner recognized him as the runner who had investigated a series of thefts in Dover last fall and sent word to Bow Street."

Bittner paused to take another drink of brandy. "According to the innkeeper's note, there were two other bodies in the alley— one a local whore, the other a well-dressed gentleman of French derivation, who had arrived in Dover three days earlier. That is all the information we have at the moment. However, it seems an unlikely coincidence that Lord Fairborne made a hurried trip to Dover just hours before the murders occurred."

Yves took a white-knuckled grip on his glass. "If I ever doubted that he is the traitor, I doubt it no more. I would hazard a guess that the Frenchman was a former official in Bonaparte's government who threatened to expose Fairborne unless he was paid off."

"His lordship's thinking exactly," Bittner agreed. He finished his brandy and set the glass on the small pie-shaped table beside his chair. "Lord Castlereagh feels you should take a close look at the murder scene as soon as possible in the hope you may find something that will prove the killer's identity. But beware. The death of the runner serves as a warning that the traitor you seek to unmask is deadly dangerous. Kevin Monahan was one of Bow Street's most capable operatives. One would expect such a man to prevail in a back alley skirmish."

Yves took a healthy swallow of brandy, but not even France's finest could warm the chill that gripped him. "Please convey my thanks to his lordship for the information and the warning. I will leave for Dover immediately and be assured I will tread carefully. I have every intention of living to see the black-hearted devil pay for his sins."

"Then God bless you, sir, and good hunting," Bittner said, and with a stiff bow took his leave.

"Now I would like to hear that long story you have to tell me," Philippe said, switching to French as soon as the door closed behind the Foreign Secretary's assistant. "But first the reason, if you please, why you look as if you have just been struck on the head with a particularly heavy hammer."

"I believe I have," Yves said, automatically answering in his native tongue. Moving to the window, he watched the first pale fingers of dawn creep down the street fronting the hotel. With a groan, he slammed his clenched fist against the sash. "God in heaven, what could have possessed me to do such a stupid thing? I knew the traitor was a cold-blooded killer—and Fairborne has been my prime suspect all along."

Philippe stared at him, eyes wide with amazement. "What the devil is the matter with you?" he demanded. "You have dealt with killers in the past. They have never terrified you before."

Yves turned to face his friend. "I am not terrified for myself. Fairborne has been courting an heiress from Yorkshire—a simple countrywoman who is far too trusting for her own good."

Philippe smiled wryly. "Ah, I see. And you have formed a romantic attachment to the lady."

"Nothing of the sort," Yves snapped, steadfastly ignoring the memory of Rachel's warm, golden brown eyes and gentle touch. "The woman is a tall beanpole and plain as an old shoe—not at all the sort of female I find attractive. But she is the most compassionate, generous-hearted . . . Damn it, I should not like to see her harmed."

"No gentleman would." Philippe frowned. "But why do I feel there is more to this than you are telling me?"

Yves clenched his fists so tightly his nails bit into his palms. "I knew Fairborne was desperate to get his hands on Rachel's fortune and hoped he would be driven to do something foolish if she turned him down."

"So—"

"So I proved to her, among other things, that he was so deeply in debt he would be willing to marry any woman with a sizable fortune."

Philippe whistled softly. "Which is tantamount to building a bonfire next to a keg of gunpowder."

"Exactly. I realize that now. But I wish to God it had occurred to me sooner." Yves paced the floor like a caged tiger. "In the name of friendship, I encouraged her to refuse his offer, never thinking what he might do if she crossed him. A fine friend I am. I have been so obsessed with avenging one woman's death, I have unwittingly put another's life in jeopardy."

Philippe walked to the cabinet that stood against one wall and poured himself another brandy. "What's done is done and there is no point in agonizing over something you cannot control. Your first objective is to flush out the traitor, and you cannot be in Dover and London at the same time."

"True, but I have a contact within the earl's household. The least I can do is send a lad with a five-pound note and instructions that O'Reilly should watch out for her until I return."

"Then by all means do so if it will ease your mind," Philippe said, tossing back his brandy. "In the meantime, I shall have a wash and raid your wardrobe so we can leave for Dover within the hour."

"We?" Yves smiled, feeling better already. He could think of no man he would rather have guarding his back than Philippe de Maret—and no one better equipped to protect Rachel from that devil, Fairborne, than his wily Irish butler.

Rachel was awakened from a long nap by Mary, the abigail, who announced the earl had returned to London and would be joining her for dinner.

Damn and blast! Throwing off the quilt that covered her, she sat up and dangled her legs over the side of the bed.

She had not expected him back so soon. Furthermore, she was not accustomed to staying up all night, then napping during the day. She felt cranky, disoriented, and not at all rested—hardly the ideal mood in which to tell a peer of the realm she had decided she couldn't marry him. But tell him she must and the sooner the better.

With Mary's help, she changed her dress, tidied her hair and made her way to the small salon adjoining the dining room where Edgar and Verity sat together on a small sofa, enjoying a predinner sherry. Edgar leapt to his feet at Rachel's entrance.

"I trust you found no serious problem at your estate in Surrey," she said, offering him her hand.

"None I could not handle." With an enigmatic smile, he raised her fingers to his lips and Rachel found herself wondering why she felt no response to his touch, when Yves had set every nerve in her body tingling with the same gesture.

"Forgive my travel dirt," the earl apologized as Rachel took a chair opposite the sofa. "I did not want to take time to bathe and change as it would mean putting dinner back another hour or two, and I am hungry as a bear in spring."

"That is quite all right, my lord," Rachel said, smiling at his apt simile. For, in truth, he did look rather like a large, scruffy bear with his honey gold hair rumpled by the wind and his usually immaculate clothing wrinkled and dusty.

He was even missing one of the ornate silver buttons from his handsome watered silk waistcoat. Too bad, for they were quite unique. The green-eyed, split-tailed dragon decorating each of them was a miniature of the dragon in the Fairborne coat of arms that hung in the townhouse entry hall, and the eyes were tiny emeralds.

"Did you miss me?" he asked, reclaiming his seat on the sofa.

"Miss you?" Verity gave his arm a playful tap with her fan. "Rachel will never admit it, but the truth is she was utterly lost without you."

"Indeed. I am gratified to hear it." The odd, almost triumphant, note in Edgar's voice set Rachel's teeth on edge, as did the smile he bestowed on her. A se'nnight ago she would have thought the smile sincere; now she knew better.

"The dear girl never left the townhouse—just moped about like a lost soul." Verity sighed behind her fan. "Something I never thought to see."

Rachel groaned. Every word the annoying busybody uttered made the task of rejecting the earl's proposal that much harder. "I was not moping about," she muttered. "I packed my trunk and spent the rest of the time reading my new books."

"Nevertheless, I am overjoyed to know you were as lonely for me as I was for you, my darling girl," Edgar declared, blithely ignoring her reference to packing her trunk. He set his half-empty glass on a table next to the sofa and leaning forward, clasped both of Rachel's hands in a crushing grip. "My happiness knows no bounds. I have been waiting forever for a sign that you returned my tender feelings."

Rachel opened her mouth to point out that the "sign" had come from Verity, not her, but the earl cut her off before she could speak. "At long last the uncertainty is past and I am assured I acted wisely in choosing you to be my countess."

"Yes, well we need to talk about that, my lord. But in private if you please."

"What is there to talk about, my dear one? You have demonstrated how you feel about me, and you are already aware of my regard for you."

The rasp of impatience in Edgar's voice startled Rachel. Again, it bore a shocking resemblance to the tone he had used when he'd dressed down the unfortunate footman. "I think it would be best if we waited until you are rested from your journey to discuss the matter," she said quietly.

"I do not need rest; I need to have my affairs properly settled. Simply name the day, Rachel, and I will obtain a special license."

"How romantic," Verity twittered.

Rachel stared at him, aghast. "You presume too much, my lord. I am not ready to name the day." She tried to extricate her hands from his, but the earl only gripped them harder.

"Why delay the inevitable?" he asked, his twitching right eyelid betraying his agitation. "We both know we are destined to marry sooner or later."

Verity nodded her head in agreement. "The earl is absolutely right, Rachel. My dear Wilfred always said stubbornness in a woman is not an attractive trait."

"I acknowledge no destiny that obliges me to marry any man," Rachel declared, struggling to check her rising temper. She had vowed the day she buried her father she would never again let anyone run roughshod over her. It was a vow she intended to keep for the balance of her life.

For one brief instant, she caught a glint of something very like rage in the earl's eyes. But in the space of a heartbeat, his usual genial expression returned. Dropping her hands, he said, "Forgive me for pressing you, my dear. I am in love—and as everyone knows, love makes a man impatient."

He sounded sincere. So much so, she might have believed him if she hadn't seen the drawer full of tradesmen's bills he must pay before his creditors hounded him into bankruptcy. She shuddered, remembering how close she had come to succumbing to the lure he had offered of a loving husband and children.

"Tease me no longer, dear Rachel," he purred. "Name the day and put me out of my misery."

His misery indeed. She sensed a desperation in him today that had never before been evident—a desperation only thinly disguised by his tight smile and unconvincing portrayal of a lovesick swain.

The problem at his estate must be more serious than he was willing to admit. Between that and his other pressing financial problems, the spendthrift earl was drowning in a sea of his own making and apparently looked to her to throw him a lifeline.

Enough of his Spanish coin. It was high time she set him straight about his chances of marrying her. She had hoped to do so without Verity looking on, but if the earl didn't mind an audience, why should she. Her initial anger over his deceit had cooled and she felt nothing but disgust and pity for this man she had once called friend. Though he did not deserve it, she would give him a chance to bow out of his pretended affair of the heart with dignity.

She smiled sweetly. "I promise I will consider your offer very carefully, my lord. But a woman with my responsibilities cannot rush into something as serious as marriage. I will give you my answer in six months' time."

"Six months!" The words exploded from his mouth as if they had been shot from a cannon. "But that is intolerable. You cannot expect me to hang in limbo for half a year."

She sighed. "No, I don't suppose I can. I shall certainly understand if you turn your attention elsewhere. Perhaps you should consider another heiress—a woman of your own class. Luckily you have only wasted a few weeks on me."

"What a dreadful thing to say!" Verity's horrified gaze leapt from Rachel to the earl and back again. "She must be out of her head with fever, my lord. I should have known she had taken sick when she spent the entire afternoon in bed."

"I am not out of my head and the only sickness I suffer from is homesickness," Rachel snapped. "I have my trunk packed and I want to go home to Yorkshire immediately."

The earl paled. "You cannot mean that, my dear. You are peeved because I have left you alone so much recently, aren't you? Yes, I can see that's it. But that is no reason to make a hasty decision based solely on emotion. The very rashness of it tells me you need a man to do your thinking for you."

Rachel gritted her teeth. "The last thing I need is a man to think for me," she declared in a tone of voice icy enough to freeze milk in August. "My decision to return to Yorkshire is not based on emotion. I simply do not like the idea of leaving my mill in the hands of my superintendent." If the truth be known, she would trust Jacob Zimmerman with her life, but the earl need not know that.

Fairborne rearranged his handsome features into a sympathetic mask, but Rachel found the result more alarming than reassuring. "I understand your concern for your mill," he said. "But again I say you need a husband to take care of such details for you."

Verity sniffed. "Exactly what I have been telling her for the past three years."

Rachel tossed her head. "What balderdash!"

"Tell me, my dear," he said softly, "how do you propose to travel from London to Yorkshire?"

"Why, the same way I traveled from Yorkshire to London," she declared, then remembered she had made the trip as the earl's guest.

He raised his glass to his lips and took a sip of his sherry. Rachel held her breath, suddenly and inexplicably uneasy about what he was about to say.

"Alas, I find I am not in a position to offer you the use of my travel coach." His smile looked decidedly smug. "It is currently being repaired—and my town coach is not equipped to make such a long journey."

Rachel slowly released her breath "And how long will these repairs take?"

Fairborne shrugged. "Who knows? A se'night—possibly longer. Workmen are so unreliable these days."

"Then I shall simply have to hire a carriage," she said, grateful she had thought to stuff a fair amount of money in the toe of one of the half boots she'd brought to London.

"With the roads between here and Yorkshire swarming with thieves and highwaymen? I think not, my dear. As your host, I am responsible for your welfare and I couldn't think of allowing you to undertake such a journey in a hired carriage. I fear you really do need a husband to save you from your own womanly foolishness. The distressing news I received this afternoon only bears out that truth."

"Distressing news?" Rachel and Verity echoed in unison.

"I stopped by my club when first I returned to London and to my distress learned that rumors are running rampant about an unmarried woman residing in my townhouse without a proper chaperone."

"What nonsense. I am chaperoned by my father's cousin, a very proper widow."

The earl inclined his head toward Verity in an elegant bow that had the plump little lady twittering like a flustered canary.

"You know and I know that Mrs. Dalrymple is a proper chaperone. But unfortunately, she is not known to the *ton*."

Rachel sniffed. "I don't care a fig what the *ton* thinks of me."

"But I care what they think of me, my dear. I will not have my reputation impugned by salacious gossip."

Rachel had to bite her tongue to keep from pointing out that failing to pay one's bills was the surest way she knew to "impugn" one's reputation.

"Under the circumstances," Fairborne continued, "I have no recourse but to publish a notice of our betrothal in tomorrow's *Times*."

"You must be mad!"

Verity emitted a horrified gasp and clamped her fingers around Rachel's arm. "What are you thinking of to speak to his lordship in such a manner? Listen to him. He is a man and a peer of the realm. He knows whereof he speaks." She sighed. "My dear Wilfred always said, 'A woman who attaches too much consequence to her own opinion is a danger to herself and everyone around her.'"

"A wise man, your Wilfred," the earl declared, "as I'm certain Rachel will agree once she has time to think things over." Fairborne's voice was silky and with a matching smile he rose and offered one arm to Rachel, the other to Verity. "Shall we partake of dinner, ladies? I for one am famished."

The very thought of sharing a meal with the overbearing fellow turned Rachel's stomach. "Please excuse me," she said stiffly. "I believe I shall retire to my chamber; I find I have quite lost my appetite."

"What a shame. If you find you are hungry later, you have only to notify the footman stationed outside your chamber door."

Rachel couldn't believe what she was hearing. "Since when have you stationed a footman outside my door?"

"Since I decided you are the most important person in my life, dear heart, and must be under my protection at all times."

Verity wiped a sentimental tear from her eye. "What a considerate fellow you are, my lord. Just like my dear Wilfred. I hope Rachel appreciates how lucky she is to have you."

"Oh, I am certain she does, dear, lady." Fairborne's smile was positively beatific. "She herself once referred to me as 'the kindest man she had ever known.'"

Rachel had heard enough. Without another word, she spun on

her heel, stalked into the hall and mounted the stairs to her bed-chamber—determined to gather her wits and decide how best to extract herself from the web in which the earl seemed determined to ensnare her.

Chapter Nine

One hour passed, then another, and Rachel was no closer to solving her problem than she had been when she'd fled the earl's presence. A sliver of fear slid down her spine when she realized how completely at Fairborne's mercy she had put herself.

What a fool she had been. How could she have failed to see that he was exactly what Yves had claimed—a man in such desperate financial straits he would stop at nothing to get his hands on her fortune.

Her stomach cramped with hunger; she had missed both lunch and dinner. But pride kept her from requesting food of the footman outside her door. She wondered where Verity was. After the woman's tirade against Yorkshire, she had no choice but to write her a note releasing her from her position of companion. That done, she sat back and waited—for what she didn't know. Then just when she'd decided that pride made a poor dish to fill an empty stomach, she heard a knock on her door.

"Who is it?" she asked, ready to shove a bureau in front of it if the earl demanded entry.

"'Tis me, mistress." Mary's voice sounded muffled and a bit shaky. "I've brought you some supper and come to turn down your bed and lay out your night rail."

Rachel breathed a sigh of relief. "Are you alone?"

"Yes, mistress, except for the footman sitting here in the hall. Please let me in. Mrs. Tibbs, the housekeeper, will sack me if I fail to do my proper job."

Rachel believed the little maid. After the incident with the footman, nothing that occurred in this household would surprise her. Opening the door a crack, she verified that Mary was indeed alone before she let her in.

The girl was even more pale than usual and her eyes looked

too large for her face. "Are you all right, mistress?" she whispered, setting the tray of food on the nightstand. "I was listening outside the door and heard what the earl said to you, and heard him order Mr. O'Reilly to station a footman to guard you as well."

Though the night was hot and humid, Mary shivered and clasped her arms about herself as if she were chilled. "I've come to warn you to leave this place tonight. Go home to Yorkshire before the earl traps you into wedding him."

Rachel managed a stiff smile. "I thank you for your concern, but there's not a man alive who can make me wed him if I don't want to. This is the nineteenth century—not the Dark Ages."

"Begging your pardon, mistress, but 'tis plain to see you know nothing about the wicked ways of men—especially men as desperate for money as the earl is. The servants have not been paid a penny this quarter, nor the last. 'Tis why the chef took a position elsewhere."

"Somehow that doesn't surprise me," Rachel said, recalling the drawerful of unpaid bills.

Mary searched her face with troubled eyes. "Oh, I don't doubt you're as smart as he is—probably smarter. But trust me, if a man as big and strong as his nibs should decide to have his way with you, there would be little you could do about it. Think, mistress. If he got you with child, would you let your babe be born a bastard?"

Rachel sat down on the edge of the bed before her knees collapsed beneath her. Such a thing had never occurred to her. But remembering Edgar's bruising grip on her hands, she knew Mary made a point well worth considering.

"I would leave this instant if I knew how to get past that blasted footman," she said, embarrassed by the quaver she heard in her own voice.

"I could help you with that, mistress. I know the fellow well. He can be easily flummoxed. But where would you go in the middle of the night in London?"

"I have a friend who currently resides at the Pulteney Hotel," Rachel said after a moment's thought. "I think he would help me find a way to get back to Yorkshire—at least I hope he would. Can you tell me how to find the hotel?"

"Of course, mistress. Every Londoner knows the direction of a grand place like the Pulteney. But you'll be hard put to find a hackney in Mayfair late at night and 'tis not safe for a woman to be walking alone on the streets after dark." She hesitated. "But I could go with you—all the way to Yorkshire if you'd like."

"That is very kind of you, Mary, but I would feel guilty asking you to disrupt your life in such a way for me."

Two bright spots of color flared in the girl's pale cheeks.

"But I'd do you no greater favor than you'd do me, mistress. I need to get out from under Mrs. Tibbs's heavy thumb." She took a quivery breath. "I also need to put some miles between me and a certain footman who has not been honest about his intentions."

"Ah, I see. Well then, we have a bargain, for I am sorely in need of an abigail with your talents." Rachel searched the young maid's flushed face. "Is this unscrupulous footman by any chance the same one who is guarding my door?"

"The very same," Mary whispered, ducking her head as if ashamed to make such an admission.

"Then I'll not worry if he loses his position because I manage to escape the equally unscrupulous earl."

"If I had my way, the bounder would lose more than his position," Mary said bitterly. "But that's neither here nor there. I'll come by a little before midnight and keep him occupied whilst you sneak out your chamber door. The servants' stairwell is at the far end of the hall. If you take that, you can slip out through the kitchen door into the walled garden and wait for me there. Can you do that, mistress?"

"Of course I can." Rachel smiled at the brave young woman who had come to her rescue. "But I hope you realize you are taking a great risk in helping me this way. If we fail to get away, you will be discharged without references and there will be little I can do to help you."

"We dare not fail, mistress—so we will not." With a final whispered, "Midnight it is," Mary opened the door and stepped into the hall.

Midnight. The very word made Rachel's heart beat faster. For the second night in a row she would sit in her chamber and count the minutes until the witching hour. Only this time she would not wait for Yves to come to her. She would go to him and with what her father would have surely termed a "stupid blind faith" place her life and her future in his hands.

*　　　*　　　*

Dawn was breaking over the grime-encrusted buildings of London when Yves and Philippe stabled their weary horses and walked into the lobby of the Pulteney Hotel. The vast room was as starkly impersonal as ever—the paneling as dark and gloomy, the elegant upholstered chairs and settees as uncomfortable and the clerk behind the desk as unfriendly. But Yves was so glad to see it, he could have fallen to his knees and kissed the roses in the Axminster carpet.

The trip to Dover had been long and fruitless. He'd had such high hopes that the dead Frenchman's room at the inn would yield some clue to his connection with Fairborne. It had yielded nothing more exciting than a soiled linen shirt, a change of smallclothes, and an ivory-backed hairbrush.

The alley in which he, his dockside whore, and one of Bow Street's finest men had met their gruesome fate had yielded little more. Yves reached into his pocket and fingered the small, shiny object that was his only memento of the frustrating trip—one slightly tarnished silver button that could have lain in the alley a day, a week, or a year before he'd spied it in the dust and garbage.

He was aware the button could have decorated the waistcoat of any one of a hundred men traveling through Dover. The Blue Whale Inn was a popular stopping place and the men frequenting the taproom often stepped into the alley to relieve themselves or negotiate a price with a local harlot.

He had kept the button because he could imagine a dandy like Fairborne wearing a waistcoat with uniquely elegant buttons in the shape of a two-tailed dragon with tiny emerald chips for eyes. Also, for some reason he could not begin to explain, he had felt an odd, tingling sensation in his fingertips whenever he touched it.

Still, he could not logically consider it a clue. If by chance it had been torn from Fairborne's waistcoat by one of the people he had murdered, he would surely have disposed of the garment and remaining buttons.

He stopped at the desk before he and Philippe mounted the stairs to his suite to fall into bed and sleep away the day. "Have any messages been left for me while I was away from London?" he asked the clerk.

The clerk stared at him with hostile gray eyes set in a gray, pinched face. "No messages."

Yves breathed a sigh of relief. His greatest fear had been that a message from Rachel requesting his help would arrive while he was out of town. He'd had no choice but to ask O'Reilly to watch out for her, but he had not felt entirely comfortable leaving her in the care of the enterprising Irishman.

After he'd had an hour or two of sleep, he would find a way to contact her and warn her she would be wise to wait awhile before flatly rejecting Fairborne's offer of marriage. Not that she would listen to him. Rachel Barton was the most stubborn, opinionated woman he had ever had the misfortune to meet.

He had started up the stairs when he heard the clerk's surly voice. "In case you're interested, Frenchman, some woman came looking for you well after midnight. But, like I said, she left no message."

Yves whipped around and strode to the desk with Philippe close behind him. "A woman? What was her name?"

"She didn't say."

"Was she small, dark-haired, with a French accent?" Jacqueline Esquaré was the only woman he knew who was bold enough to visit a man at his hotel in the middle of the night.

The clerk's grudging no was barely audible.

Yves's heart plunged to his boots. "What did she look like?"

"Like any other woman, far as I could tell."

Yves gripped the edge of the counter with white-knuckled fingers. "I would like a little more explicit description, if you please."

The clerk ducked his head as if loath to look him in the eyes. "Tall, plain kind of woman. Had her maid with her. Leastwise, I think the young one was her maid."

Yves cursed softly but explicitly in French. "What did she say?"

"I already told you she left no message." A spiteful gleam lighted the clerk's pale eyes. "But she looked mighty upset when I told her you were out of town."

"*Sacré bleu!* Where did she go?"

"How should I know?"

Yves leaned across the counter, caught the little man by the lapels of his jacket, and lifted him off the floor. "Think, damn you! It could be a matter of life or death!"

The clerk's eyes protruded from his head and a gurgling sound emanated from his throat, but not a word crossed his lips. Yves was about to give the annoying fellow a good shake when he felt a sharp tap on his shoulder. "I suggest you let the English bullfrog loose before he swallows his tongue," Philippe said in French. "Then you'll never hear what he has to say."

Yves emitted another string of colorful curses, but he dropped the clerk, who collapsed across the desk, limp as a rag. "Speak up," he ordered, his fingers still twisted in the fabric of the fellow's jacket.

The clerk raised his head to stare at Yves with bloodshot eyes. "She asked the direction of the nearest coaching station," he gasped, and slithered to the floor in a formless heap.

Yves scarcely noticed him. Turning on his heel, he sprinted toward the doorway through which he'd entered a few minutes earlier.

"We are going out again, I see," Philippe called after him.

Yves glanced over his shoulder. "I know this coaching station. I have passed it many times on my way to the hotel. If I am lucky, Rachel will still be there."

Philippe lengthened his stride and caught up with him just as he dodged a milk wagon pulled by two mammoth Percherons. "This Rachel to whom we are rushing with such haste, despite the fact that we are both dead on our feet—she is the plain English countrywoman for whom you feel no attraction?"

"As I told you, she is a friend. Nothing more. I feel responsible for her because in my zeal to catch the traitor, I put her in danger." Yves unconsciously slipped into the guttural French of the farming area where he had been raised. "For certain something is seriously wrong if she came to the hotel in search of me. She is not the kind of woman to visit a gentleman's place of residence without a very good reason."

Moments later they reached their destination. Not a coach was in sight and the only person on the staging platform was a stoop-shouldered man in a rusty black coat and stained gray breeches.

Yves approached him. "Are you by any chance the night station manager?"

The old fellow looked up from the copy of the *London Times* he was reading and shaded his eyes against the bright sunrise.

"I am that, young sir."

"I was to meet a friend here and I am afraid I may have missed her—a tall lady probably dressed in brown and accompanied by her maid."

"There was a tall lady in a pretty shawl and bonnet, if that's the one ye mean. Her and her young maid boarded the coach for Northampton a good two hour ago."

"Northampton? Is that by any chance a stop on the way to Yorkshire?"

The old man wagged his head. "It is. One of many. As I told the Irishman who was trailing close behind them, they have a long ride ahead of them afore they reach Skipton and the Dales."

Yves exchanged a telling glance with Philippe before thanking the old man for his information. "She is gone. I failed to help her as I promised," he said bleakly once they were out of earshot of the stationmaster, and felt as if every word were a stone lodged in his chest.

"How can you say that? Thanks to you, the earl's butler saw your friend safely through the dark streets of London and aboard the coach."

"He should have cornered her and insisted she wait at the hotel until I returned."

"I doubt the clerk would have let her into your rooms."

"Devil take the clerk. I would like to wring the annoying fellow's neck. The very thought of a gently bred woman like Rachel traveling such a distance in a public coach with naught but her maid to accompany her is beyond bearing."

"I was afraid you would say that." Philippe surveyed Yves through heavy lidded eyes. "We are not, I hope, going to tear after her. She appears to have successfully escaped the villain's clutches."

"And rendered herself fair game for any highwayman or disgruntled ex-soldier who takes a notion to rob a public coach. I have no choice but to catch up with her and see her safely delivered to her home in Yorkshire." He pondered the problem a moment before adding, "I'll borrow a travel coach from my friend, the Earl of Stratham. He will be staying close to London for the next month or two since his wife is heavy with child. But you may feel free to use my suite, and my wardrobe, while I am gone."

Philippe shrugged. "Your trousers are too long for me and your boots too large. Since I cannot cut a fashionable swath across London society until you pay for my new wardrobe, I may as well tag along as a second knight errant. Besides, I have always wanted to try my hand at driving a coach and four."

"As have I." Yves grinned. "Very well, my friend. I shall

borrow Stratham's coach and cattle, but not his coachman—and we'll turn our rescue of the Yorkshire heiress into a true adventure."

They walked in silence back to the hotel. But before they reached the entrance, Philippe placed a hand on Yves's shoulder. "I cannot help but think this woman, Rachel, means more to you than you are admitting—even to yourself. If you think I shall be offended that you have come to care for someone other than Amalie, abuse yourself of that notion."

"I told you Rachel is just a—"

"I know—a friend. But nevertheless, I will say what I have to say." Philippe tightened his grip on Yves's shoulder. "I loved my sister dearly and I would have cut your heart out if you had betrayed her while she lived. But Amalie has been dead three years and you are a man who needs a woman."

"I have not lived as a monk since her death."

"No. You have bedded many women and each one looked more like Amalie than the last. It is time you let go of the past and looked to your future. Perhaps this tall Englishwoman, who is nothing at all like Amalie, is that future."

Yves shook his head. "Rachel Barton is not the kind of woman to whom I am attracted."

"Because she is plain of countenance?"

"No. Because she is too stubborn, too opinionated, too independent. Once you meet her, you will realize why I say she can never be more to me than a friend."

Philippe grinned. "Then I envy your 'friendship' with this woman, as I envied your 'friendship' with my sister. I cannot remember ever having had a friend for whom I felt true kinship—except perhaps you. But unfortunately you are not a woman."

Yves gave an angry shrug that dislodged Philippe's hand from his shoulder. "Damn you for the rake you are. I suppose you think it is impossible for a man to respect and admire a woman and not want to take her to bed."

"On the contrary, it is entirely possible if the woman is eighty years old." Philippe chuckled. "Tell me, cousin, how old is this plain-faced spinster for whom you feel such respect and admiration?"

It was Rachel's first experience with a public coach, and she soon discovered this mode of travel was nothing like traveling in a luxurious, well-sprung private carriage. The squabs were stained and foul-smelling, the windows grimy, and every bump in the road rattled her teeth and jarred her bones.

She dreaded the thought of what the overnight accommodations would be for the passengers of such a vehicle. Come to think of it, she had never seen a public coach at one of the well-appointed inns she had stayed at when traveling with her father, or the Earl of Fairborne.

To make matters worse, Mary turned out to be a poor traveler. Within thirty minutes of their setting out from London, the little maid's complexion turned a bilious green and she curled up in a pathetic heap on the seat opposite Rachel. Luckily, they were the only two people in the coach and by the time they stopped at the coaching inn where the driver made his first change of horses, Mary's discomfort had eased somewhat.

They just had time to visit the convenience and have a quick cup of strong tea. Then back to the coach they went, but this time they were not alone.

The first new passenger to climb aboard was a plump, apple-cheeked farm wife. She settled her broad hips on the seat next to Mary, removed her knitting from a drawstring bag, and announced, "Mrs. Sarah Cuddle's me name and I've just come from visiting me first grandbabe, and a fine, strapping lad he is."

Rachel smiled. "What a happy trip that must have been."

"Aye, 'twas that for sure. For there be nothing on God's green earth feels as good as holding a new babe." Her blue eyes twinkled. "When someone else has the care of it."

She glanced up from her knitting as the next passenger squeezed through the door and lowered himself onto the far end of the seat Rachel occupied. He was an immense, barrel-shaped fellow with small, pale eyes and thinning gray hair. Planting his dusty boots firmly on the floorboard, he removed his hat and gloves and regarded his fellow passengers with a scowl that plainly said he had no interest in socializing with them.

Mrs. Cuddle accorded him no more than a quick glance before chatting on. "Had twelve babes of me own, I did, and all but two alive and well to this day, praise God. I've done me share of changing nappies and washing the smelly things as well. Still, I must say, it don't seem natural not having a babe suckling at me breast."

The old man's eyes fairly popped from his head and even

Mary looked a bit taken aback by the woman's statement, but Rachel chuckled to herself. After the philistines she had dealt with in London, she found such earthiness refreshing.

Next two earnest-looking young men with books under their arms approached the coach. University students, Rachel deduced, and deep in what looked to be a heated discussion on ancient history, since she heard words like Babylon and Gilgamesh when they stopped by the open door. The subject had always fascinated her and the tedious hours ahead would pass more quickly while listening to the two scholars debate it. She gathered her precious shawl about her shoulders, slid over, and pressed herself against the wall of the coach to allow them room on the seat.

"La, dearie, don't be worrying yourself about them," Mrs. Cuddle said. "It's turnips to toenails they're half-price fares what sits up top; students always are. And a good thing too. I've nothing against a bit of learning, but lads as has some are like to talk your arm right out of your sleeve. There'd be no getting a word in edgewise for the rest of us with such as them riding inside."

To Rachel's disappointment, the students did indeed climb onto the roof. A moment later the coachman shouted to his team and the coach lurched out of the inn yard.

Mrs. Cuddle's work-roughened fingers again set the knitting needles to clicking rhythmically. "Now where was I?" she asked, and promptly answered herself with, "Ah yes, as I was saying, there'll be no more babes for me with my good old husband turning up his toes last winter." She laid down the sweater she was knitting long enough to wipe a tear from her eye. "Never thought a putrid throat could take a man his size in less than a fortnight."

Rachel murmured appropriate words of sympathy. Mary and the old man remained silent. In truth they both appeared to be dropping off to sleep as Mary's head was nodding against Mrs. Cuddle's shoulder and the old fellow's chin bobbed on his chest with each vibration of the coach.

"'Tis a lucky thing I've three grown sons to work me farm and three more near old enough to help." Mrs. Cuddle continued. Then without so much as a pause for breath, she launched into a detailed description of all six of her sons and her four daughters as well.

Rachel gave serious thought to joining the students on the roof at the next stop, but for the sake of common courtesy, she made an effort to stay awake during the old woman's boring recital.

To no avail. The last thing she heard as she gave up the struggle and closed her eyes was Mrs. Cuddle's voice, "And then there's me son-in-law, bless his soul, and a fine catch me daughter made, if I do say so meself . . ."

What seemed but moments later, she was awakened by a strange sound she could not at first identify. Stifling a yawn, she rolled her head to the right and found herself staring at Mary's backside. Sleepy as she was, she could see the poor girl was hanging out the window and casting up her accounts.

She watched Mrs. Cuddle pat the little maid on the back. "Poor thing," the kindly farm wife sympathized. "'Tis the dry heaves she has and well I know how she feels. I was that way with my first babe too. Afraid to close me eyes, for each time I woke me stomach made me pay for every minute I'd slept."

Her babe! Shock drove the haze of sleep from Rachel's brain and she sat bolt upright. No wonder the poor girl had been so anxious to leave London.

Finally Mary ceased her violent retching and fell back against the seat, limp as the handkerchief with which Mrs. Cuddle wiped her face. "There, there, missus," the old woman crooned. "Ye'll feel better now that ye're done with that nasty business and I've just the thing to set ye up right."

Loosening the drawstring on her capacious bag, she drew forth a small, green bottle. "'Tis a mint tisane of me own making. Brewed fresh each spring when the leaves are young and tender. The village witch-woman taught me to make it when I carried me second babe, and 'tis the best thing I know for the kind of sour stomach ye have."

She eyed Mary speculatively as the girl took a sip from the bottle and leaned back against the faded squab, utterly exhausted. "How far along are ye then, dearie?"

Mary's terrified eyes sought Rachel's and her quivering chin said she knew there was no use denying the obvious. "Three months by my reckoning," she said with quiet resignation.

"And what kind of husband have ye to be letting a wee thing like yerself travel across the country when ye're breeding?"

Tears welled in the little maid's eyes. "I . . . I'm not—"

"Mrs. Tucker is newly widowed," Rachel interjected, silencing Mary with a quelling look. "Her husband was killed in . . . in a carriage accident in London a fortnight ago. I am taking her home to Yorkshire to birth her babe."

"Bless ye then for the good friend ye be. With all the widows and orphans the war has left scattered about England, there'd be none in a coldhearted place like Lunnon town to pay her mind."

"True," Rachel said; her gaze locked with Mary's. "But I guarantee in Yorkshire both she and her child will have all the care and affection they need."

Mary's head still rested against the squab; her hands still lay slack in her lap and her eyes still looked dull and listless. But even as a tear trailed down her pale cheek, the corners of her mouth curved upward. It was, Rachel realized, the first time she had seen the girl smile.

Chapter Ten

It had been a long, exhausting day and it was not over yet. By the time the sun dipped low on the horizon, Rachel was so stiff and sore from the jouncing of the coach, she felt as if she had been pummeled, mauled and pelted with rocks. She had to wonder how long Mary could survive this kind of physical punishment without losing her babe.

Luckily the coaching inns along the way had never been more than two hours apart and at each, they had been granted a brief respite, as well as a change of travel companions. Invariably passengers they had come to know departed the coach; strangers came aboard.

The talkative Mrs. Cuddle was replaced by a taciturn solicitor's clerk delivering documents to a client in Luton; a ruddy-faced farmer with mud caking his boots supplanted the surly, barrel-shaped man. These, in turn, were replaced by a young mother and two small children with runny noses and hacking coughs, a hawk-faced old man in a threadbare cutaway coat and knee breeches, and a scrawny, black-garbed fellow who introduced himself as Orville Stebbins, a vicar's assistant. A motley collection of humanity to be sure, but they seemed harmless enough traveling companions.

Not so the man who joined them at what the coachman announced was the last stop before the Green Parrot, the inn at which they would spend the night. To begin with, he was huge—so huge he seemed to fill every inch of the coach the minute he climbed aboard. Inexplicably unnerved by his presence, Rachel took a deep, calming breath and promptly gagged. He was obviously long overdue for a wash.

Surreptitiously, she studied his pockmarked face and stringy black hair, his dirty fingernails and dark, hooded gaze. Everything about the scruffy-looking fellow set her teeth on edge.

Mary sidled closer to her and stared at him with wide, frightened eyes—an expression echoed on the face of the young vicar's assistant, who was the only other passenger at the moment. The timid fellow pressed himself against the side of the coach, leaving as much space as possible between him and his new travel companion.

Rachel fixed her gaze on the window, hoping to discourage any conversation on the stranger's part. To no avail. "Where are you ladies bound?" he asked in a voice that sounded as if it had been dredged up from the bowels of the earth.

"Yorkshire," Rachel murmured reluctantly. She might not want to chat with him, but neither did she want to antagonize him. She had never been the missish sort, but there was something about the man that made him appear—there was no other word for it—menacing.

"Yorkshire, is it? Then we'll have a long ride together, for that be where I'm going as well."

Mary pressed even closer and Rachel could feel her trembling. She gave the little abigail a tentative smile, hoping to allay her fears. Though if the truth be known, she felt a bit jittery herself. She wondered if the new passenger could be one of the thieves or highwaymen Edgar had claimed haunted the highways between London and Yorkshire. Or had fate unfairly saddled an innocent man with a countenance that appeared the embodiment of evil?

Just in case, she took a firmer grip on the reticule that contained all the money she had with her. A mistake she realized instantly, as an undeniable gleam of avarice appeared in the obsidian eyes watching her. She had been planning to nap this last leg of the day's journey, but nothing could induce her to close her eyes or relax her hold on her reticule now. She would be in serious trouble if she found herself stranded and without funds so far from her destination—especially with a pregnant woman on her hands. Much as she hated to, she had to admit that Edgar might have been justified in claiming it unsafe for a gently bred woman to travel by public conveyance.

The next two hours seemed endless. Absolute silence reigned in the coach as the stranger made no more attempts at conversation, and his disturbing presence had put paid to the easy exchange Rachel had shared with Orville Stebbins earlier. In fact, she was so aware of the stranger's unflinching perusal, she scarcely registered the tooth-rattling jolts and joggles that had bothered her so much earlier.

But at long last they pulled into the inn yard of the Green Parrot. Orville Stebbins bolted from the coach like a rabbit from its burrow. Then as if rethinking his course of action, he returned and rather sheepishly handed Rachel and Mary down.

"I'll be leaving the coach now because the church I serve is in a village five miles east of here," he said in a hoarse whisper as the three of them walked toward the inn. "But I've something to tell you before that monster in the coach catches up with us."

He swallowed hard and his Adam's apple bobbed up and down like a cork riding a wave. "There have been countless robberies hereabouts recently and"—his gaunt cheeks turned scarlet—"a farmer's daughter was dragged from her cart and brutally assaulted last week."

"Good Lord!"

"If the rumors be true, a thief who goes by the name of Wolf Walton is the culprit, and our fellow passenger fits his description to a gnat's eyebrow."

Rachel scowled. "I cannot say that surprises me. I shall bring him to the attention of the innkeeper immediately."

"I wouldn't advise it, ma'am. The owner of the Green Parrot may well be in league with the thief. 'Tis a known fact that all the riffraff for miles around gather in his taproom every evening."

"But that is outrageous! Why, then, would the public coaches stop here?"

"They have no choice. The regular coaching inn for this district burned to the ground six months ago under rather mysterious circumstances." He scowled. "I tell you all this, not to frighten you, but to alert you to keep your chamber door securely bolted."

Stebbins regarded Rachel with round, sorrowful eyes. "I wish I could render you more assistance, ma'am. But a warning is all I have to offer."

"For that I sincerely thank you, sir. As the saying goes, 'Forewarned is forearmed.' Be assured I shall vigilantly guard the safety of my maid and myself—and my ready cash as well."

Brave words, but Rachel entered the inn with serious reservations. The noise inside the building was deafening—most of it emanating from the taproom to the right of the entry. For though the evening was still young, it was already overflowing with patrons, and most of them appeared to be well into their cups.

"I'd like a bedchamber for myself and my maid," she directed the innkeeper's wife, a plump, white-haired woman in a dingy mobcap and stained apron.

"One room or two?" the woman asked. "But I'll tell ye right off, we've no trundle beds so ye'll have to pay for two rooms or share a bed."

"One room will do and I'd like our suppers served in our chamber as soon as possible," Rachel said briskly. Ordinarily she would never consider sharing her bed, but under the circumstances, it seemed prudent to keep Mary as close as possible.

She counted out the necessary coins and grasping her portmanteau with one hand, her reticule with the other, followed the old woman up the stairs. With Mary tagging close behind, they made their way along a shadowy hallway to a dingy little room containing a narrow bed, a chair and a table on which sat a fat, tallow candle.

Remembering Orville Stebbins's advice, she threw the bolt on the door as soon as she and Mary were alone. "There now," she said with forced cheer, "the chamber is somewhat stark, and admittedly rather noisy, with the taproom directly below us. But once our supper is delivered, we'll be set for the night and I, for one, am tired enough to sleep through cannon fire."

Mary gave a weary sigh. "As am I, mistress." Out of habit, she began to turn down the bed as she'd done every night at the earl's townhouse. But no sooner had she folded back the blanket and sheet, than she pressed her hands to her cheeks and gave a shriek of dismay. "God in heaven, we cannot sleep in this bed," she cried. "It looks as if pigs have rooted in it."

From where she stood, Rachel could see the sheets were grimy and stained. Furthermore, once the bed was opened, the stench of human sweat, and something else she didn't care to identify, permeated the small room.

Her temper flared. "How dare that slovenly creature take my money and consign us to sleep in the accumulated filth of everyone who has occupied the bed before us! I will find her and demand clean bedding—even pay extra for it if I must." Fists clenched, she stalked to the door and reached for the bolt.

"Stop, mistress!" Mary rushed forward and caught her arm. "'Tis not safe to step into that dark hall. Wait until our supper is delivered to complain about the bedding."

Rachel shook her head. The girl was right, of course. What

could she have been thinking to let anger and frustration rob her of her common sense. Anyone could be lurking outside that door. She shuddered to think what might happen to her if she encountered one of the drunks from the taproom or, God forbid, her evil-looking travel companion. She doubted a cry for help would be heard over the din of the revelers below—or for that matter, heeded in a place like the Green Parrot.

More shaken by her loss of control than she cared to admit, she moved to the window and stared at the inn yard below while she gathered her wits. She had always believed herself to be a strong, levelheaded woman. But the bewildering happenings of the past few days had forced her to admit that when it came to judging men, she was as foolish and gullible as a feather-headed young female fresh from the schoolroom. It was a sobering admission.

Now this! She made herself a solemn vow that if she survived this hellish journey, she would never again leave Yorkshire—and would live the rest of her life as a contented spinster.

A knock on the door interrupted her unhappy musings. "Who is there?" she called.

"Do ye or do ye not want this supper?" The voice sounded surly, but definitely feminine. Rachel opened the door to find the innkeeper's wife balancing a tray containing a loaf of bread, a wedge of cheese and a pitcher of ale, as well as a knife and two mugs.

Rachel waited until she had set the tray on the bedside table before directing her attention to the disreputable condition of the bed. "I will require clean sheets, blankets and pillow covers," she said briskly. "If you are short of chambermaids, as I assume you must be, my maid and I will make up our own bed."

The woman regarded her sourly. "In case ye've forgot where ye be, ye crazy woman, this is the Green Parrot—a common coaching inn meant to serve common folk. If it's clean sheets and fine food ye're after, ye should've stopped at the Hare and Hound like the rest of the gentry." So saying, she turned on her heel and shuffled out of the room.

Rachel had no choice but to close the door behind her. When she did, she caught a glimpse of the gigantic man lounging in the open doorway across the hall. For one heart-stopping instant, his gaze locked with hers. Then she slammed the door and shot the bolt before Mary could see him.

"A lot I accomplished with my demands," she said bitterly.

"It could be worse, mistress. With the night so warm, we can spread our pelisses atop the bed and sleep in our clothes—and bread, cheese, and ale will make us a fine meal."

"You're right, of course," Rachel agreed, shamed by Mary's determined cheerfulness. She managed a weak smile. "At least nothing more can go wrong before morning."

Nothing except that the bread was moldy and crawling with weevils and the cheese was as dry and hard as a chunk of rock.

With a resigned shrug, Mary declared the cheese hopeless. But she cut a thick slice of bread and holding it firmly between her thumb and forefinger, whacked it two or three times on the table-top.

Rachel frowned. "Whatever are you doing?"

"Banging out the weevils. There's many a time I'd have gone hungry when I was growing up if I'd let the little buggers ruin my appetite." She took a healthy bite of the bread and washed it down with a mug of ale.

"Can't say I care much for the taste of moldy bread," she said with a grimace, "and the ale's not near as good as what Mr. O'Reilly keeps on hand." She wiped the foam from her lips and poured another mug. "But they'll do to fill my belly so I can sleep. "

Rachel silently applauded her maid's ability to adjust to their unhappy circumstances. Still, nothing could induce her to eat weevil-infested bread—which left the ale the only thing fit for human consumption. She had never been an ale drinker—nor indeed a drinker of any kind. Her father's frequent bouts of drunkenness had abused her of any desire to indulge in strong spirits. But her stomach rumbled with hunger and since there was nothing else to fill it . . .

She poured a mug and drank it slowly while she watched Mary spread the pelisses on the bed. After the first few sips, she decided the rather bitter brew was not all that unpleasant to the taste. She poured a second mug and drank it down as well.

"If you're not accustomed to ale, mistress, you'd best not drink a third one," Mary cautioned. "For you'll find yourself foxed if you do."

Rachel nodded her agreement. "I do believe you're right," she said gravely. "But I fear your warning has come too late. For the room appears to be spinning like a top and there is an odd knocking sound in my ears."

Mary stared at her with huge, frightened eyes. "'Tis not your ears, mistress. 'Tis someone banging on the door." She pressed her hand to her bosom. "Dear God, it must be him come to rob and ravish us like the fiend he is."

Rachel's brain was fuzzy, but not so fuzzy she couldn't figure out which "him" Mary had in mind. "Shhh," she whispered. "Maybe he'll go away if we ignore him."

"I doubt it, mistress. I've seen his kind before. They don't go away; they just get meaner."

Rachel pondered what Mary had said, or at least came as close to pondering it as her addled brain would allow. "Then we should be prepared in case he breaks down the door," she said, and hiccoughed softly. "I will arm myself with the bread knife; you take the fireplace poker."

"Oh, mistress, 'twould be no use my doing that," Mary wailed. "My hands are shaking too much to hold on to it."

"Pull yourself together, Mary," Rachel ordered sternly. "You have been so brave up till now, and this is no time to give in to your fears." She cocked her head. "Listen—the knocking has stopped. I do believe he has given up."

But no sooner had the words left her mouth than the knocking began anew, louder and more forceful than before. "Open the door, ye silly bitches, if ye knows what's good for ye." There was no mistaking the deep bass voice, and Rachel took a firmer grip on her knife, more convinced than ever that the great, hulking creature was intent on tearing the door off its hinges.

Then just when she thought all hope was lost, the pounding abruptly ceased and in its place she heard voices—loud, angry voices turning the air blue with vile curses. She had to assume they belonged to patrons of the taproom.

Next came a dull thud, as if someone had stumbled into the wall. She had never felt such heart-pounding terror as she felt at that moment. She and Mary would have had little enough chance of prevailing against the malevolent giant; they would have none at all against him and a gaggle of drunks.

After a long moment of silence, the knocking began again, as determined as ever, and a new voice demanded, "Open the door, damn it!"

Thump, thump, thump. The door quivered in its frame. "Devil take it, Rachel, open up."

Thump, thump, thump. Over the noise of the pounding, she heard the poker clatter onto the wooden floor, and turned to find Mary frozen with fear, her eyes glazed and the color blanched from her face. Rachel could offer the poor girl no solace. In truth, she could do nothing but stare at the quaking door and pray it was stronger than it looked.

Thump, thump, thump. "Devil take it, I know you're in there, Rachel. Open this door or so help me, I'll break it down." The voice was louder and seemed even more menacing because it spoke directly to her.

She shook her head in dismay. But how could that be? Somewhere in the foggy recesses of her mind, it occurred to her that there was no way her would-be attackers could have learned her name.

Unless . . . all at once she knew why the voice had a ring of familiarity.

"Yves!" she cried and pushing past Mary, she flew to the door, unbolted it and threw it open.

"Yves!" she repeated as her eyes feasted on the miracle before her—and with a strangled sob, she flung herself into the Frenchman's strong arms.

There was nothing quiet or ladylike about the way Rachel wept. She made loud, gulping noises. She snorted and hiccoughed and gasped for breath. Her face turned blotchy, her breast heaved and her shoulders shook with great, wracking sobs.

Before Yves could manage to hand her a handkerchief, she'd drenched his jacket and shirt with buckets of salty tears. He found the sight of a proud woman reduced to such a state hard to bear, particularly when he'd had a hand in bringing her to it.

"It h-has been s-such a d-dreadful day," she wailed.

"I know," he commiserated, awkwardly patting her back. "I can imagine what that blasted public coach must have been like." He glanced toward Philippe, keenly aware that his friend was enjoying every minute of the emotional melodrama.

"And this is s-such a d-dreadful place."

"A den of thieves," he agreed. "But we'll soon have you out of here and safely settled in a reputable inn."

"And that d-dreadful man—"

"I promise you, he will never bother you again."

For some reason he could not begin to fathom, his words of assurance triggered yet another spate of convulsive sobs. There was nothing he could do except hold her close and murmur soothing words in her ear while she cried out her distress. Unconsciously, he slipped into French and found himself echoing the words Madame Durand had used to comfort him when he'd sobbed in her arms so long ago.

Finally Rachel's shoulders ceased their shaking; her eyes gave up their watering. She raised her head and searched his face with grave, brown eyes framed by tear-spiked lashes. "I have never, in my entire life, been so glad to see anyone," she whispered. "But I have to wonder how you found me . . . indeed why you even made the search."

"It is a long story, but essentially I found you by following the route of the coach I'd been told you'd taken." He brushed a lock of tear-drenched hair off her cheek. "My reasons for searching for you are a bit more complicated. Suffice it to say, you are my friend and I knew you must be in serious trouble if you called at my hotel in the middle of the night."

Tears welled in her eyes again. "I cannot thank you enough for coming to my rescue," she said softly. "You give new meaning to the word 'friendship.' "

"And you give new meaning to the word 'foolhardy,' " he scolded to cover his chagrin over her undeserved praise. True, he had followed her to make certain she arrived safely in Yorkshire, but he had another reason as well. Fairborne was certain to pursue her and make another try at securing her fortune. Desperation was making him careless and Yves was betting he would make a fatal mistake that would tip his hand.

"What did Fairborne do that impelled you to set out on such a journey without proper escort?" he asked. "And in a public coach, for God's sake?"

"He declared he was madly in love with me and insisted we marry immediately. When I refused, he stationed a footman outside my chamber door to prevent my leaving the house."

"The devil you say!"

"With Mary's help, I escaped and we walked to the Pulteney."

"And found me gone. Why in heaven's name didn't you wait in my suite until I returned?"

"I asked to, but the desk clerk got very insulting—"

Yves spat out a string of expletives in Parisian gutter French. "I should have throttled the little weasel while I had the chance."

Rachel ignored his outburst. "I had no idea when you would return and I was desperate to get away from London. A public coach seemed my only solution. I had never ridden in one, you see, so I had no idea what they were like—or what dangers one might face when traveling in them."

She hung her head. "You have already done so much for me. I hesitate to impose further. But before you return to London, could you help me purchase a carriage and team, and hire a coachman who would see me home to Yorkshire? I would be ever so grateful because I've had no experience with conveyances other than my pony cart."

Damn the annoying woman. How could he dress her down when she already looked so contrite. This meek and mild Rachel threw him all off-kilter.

"You will have no need of a carriage and team," he said. "I brought a carriage with me and intend to see you safely home. I could not rest easily otherwise."

"You are planning to take me all the way to Yorkshire? Oh Yves, what a wonderfully thoughtful thing to do." She sounded a little breathless and the glow in her soft, brown eyes turned them a deep, lustrous gold. For one whimsical moment, he felt as if he were sinking into their luminous depths.

"Ahem."

Yves nearly leapt out of his boots at the sound of Philippe's voice. He read the sudden panic in Rachel's eyes when the young marquis stepped out of the shadows. She obviously thought him one of her attackers. Slipping a protective arm about her shoulders, he said, "Miss Barton, may I present my friend, Philippe de Maret, the Marquis de Brune, who has driven up from London with me."

Rachel's cheeks flamed, but she made no apology for the emotional outburst Philippe had witnessed. "It seems I have two Frenchmen to thank for my rescue," she said simply, and held out her hand.

"My pleasure, mademoiselle." Philippe raised her fingers to his lips in a lingering caress that made Yves long to rearrange the lecherous fellow's handsome features.

"Gather your belongings and your maid so we may quit this

miserable place," he said brusquely and watched Rachel hurry to do his bidding.

"So that is the stubborn, sharp-tongued, impossibly independent woman for whom you can never feel more than friendship," Philippe murmured in French once she was beyond hearing. "I think, my friend, you must be stark-raving mad."

Yves scowled. "Rachel is not herself at the moment," he replied, also in French.

"Well whoever she is, I find her completely charming. I sense she is one of those delightful creatures who is sincerely grateful when a man goes out of his way to please her."

"Rachel is not one of your 'delightful creatures,' you blasted libertine," Yves snarled. "'Nor is she about to become one, if I have anything to say about it. My God, man, she is a plain-faced country spinster and furthermore, she towers over you. Carry on your foolishness with someone more your type . . . and size."

Philippe gave a noncommittal shrug. "Have you never heard that variety is the spice of life."

Yves clenched his fists, tempted to lay the little coxcomb out beside the giant he had already felled in defense of Rachel's virtue. He should have known better than to accept Philippe's offer of help. The marquis might be the first man he would choose to have at his side in a fight—but he was the last one he would trust with a woman.

He glanced up to find Rachel approaching with her maid at her side. "May I introduce my dear friend, Mary Tucker," she said smiling brightly. "Mary, these two gentlemen are the Comte de Rochemont and the Marquis de Brune."

The young maid bobbed a curtsy, and out of the corner of his eye, Yves saw Philippe's mouth drop open—a first for the jaded French aristocrat. But then it was not every day that a count and a marquis were formally introduced to a lady's maid.

Yves picked up Rachel's portmanteau with one hand, cupped her elbow with the other, and proceeded to guide her down the shadowy hall. They had taken but a few steps when she stopped in her tracks. "Good heavens, is that who I think it is?" she asked, peering at the man who was slumped against the wall.

Philippe stepped over the unconscious giant's outstretched legs. "Behold your evil molester vanquished, mademoiselle, and I never so much as broke a fingernail in the process."

"Nor raised a finger," Yves mumbled to himself, thinking of his bruised knuckles.

Rachel regarded Philippe with wide, shocked eyes. "He isn't . . . I mean you didn't . . ."

"*Mais non, mademoiselle.* Though I was sorely tempted, I did not take the blackguard's life. But he will have fewer teeth with which to chew his mutton from this day on." Even in the dim light from the single wall sconce on the stairwell, Yves could see the impish grin Philippe turned on him.

He groaned. Something told him that before the trip to Yorkshire was completed, he and his humorous friend were going to come to blows.

Chapter Eleven

Traveling with Yves St. Armand was like nothing Rachel had ever before experienced. The charming Frenchman was, to say the least, shockingly unconventional. He provided her with a luxurious, well-sprung carriage that, oddly enough, had no coachman—then vied with his friend, the marquis, for the privilege of handling the reins.

He arranged their first night's lodging at an inn which obviously catered to the most proper of clientele—even asked that a trundle bed be set up for Mary in Rachel's bedchamber so there could be no hint of impropriety. Then in the next breath he ordered supper served to him and "his lady" in a private parlor, while Mary dined in Rachel's room and the marquis chatted up the barmaid.

Rachel suspected the highly improper intimate supper was all part of his plan to help her heal her damaged self-esteem. But it was the closest she had ever come to a romantic liaison, and it appealed to that wanton side of her nature that only Yves awakened.

Supper over and the covers removed, he sat back in his chair and bestowed one of his earthshaking smiles on her. "So tell me about yourself, my friend. You already know a great deal about me; I know next to nothing about you."

He startled her. No one had ever asked such a thing of her before. "There is little to tell. I lead a very quiet life. I read and work in my garden. But most of my time is devoted to managing my mill."

His right eyebrow shot upward. "Are you saying you manage it yourself?"

"Of course. I have a capable superintendent, but any major decisions made in the past three years have been mine." She smiled. "I suppose that shocks you. It does most people."

"On the contrary. I find it fascinating. But I have to wonder how a woman would have gained the knowledge to manage a textile mill. If I may be so bold, just what were these decisions you made?"

To Rachel's surprise, he looked genuinely interested, and she couldn't resist the temptation to launch into her favorite topic. "When I took over the mill, my workers were still living in cottages built by my grandfather—cottages with damp dirt floors and leaky roofs. Two babes and a three-year-old died that first winter and I lost my best weaver to lung fever in the spring.

"I had new cottages built the next summer—which, of course, angered a great many of my fellow mill owners. I was told I had set a dangerous precedent. I imagine I set an even more dangerous one when I established a school for my mill workers' children and decreed no child under thirteen would ever again work in Barton Mill. One owner became so incensed, he tried to have a law passed forbidding any woman to own a mill."

Yves frowned. "I'd heard rumors that very young children were made to labor in the textile mills of both France and England. Apparently those rumors were true."

"I cannot speak for other parts of England, or for France, but I can tell you five- and six-year-olds are made to perform the most dangerous tasks imaginable in virtually every mill in Yorkshire except mine," Rachel said. "But I cannot take credit for being the first to denounce the vicious practice. That belongs to a mill owner in Scotland, whose name escapes me."

"But you have done something about your convictions and as the saying goes, 'actions speak louder than words.'" Yves wondered if she realized how her eyes glowed when she spoke of her school. It was obviously very dear to her heart.

"So, in addition to all your other dangerous precedents, you are educating your workers' children. Have you not heard that is asking for trouble?"

"I have," Rachel said solemnly. "In fact, I have it on good authority that once they learn to read and write, they will turn on me like a pack of wild dogs."

"But still you have built a schoolhouse, hired a teacher, and provided books and whatever else it takes to keep a school operating. I fear you are indeed a dangerous woman, Miss Barton."

"I have provided a teacher, one willing to work for barely

enough to keep body and soul together until I can afford to pay her a decent wage," Rachel protested. "But the schoolhouse is merely a dream for the future. Right now, the classes are held in one section of the Barton House stable."

"Still, I suppose you had to find a way to compensate the parents of the students for the loss of income to the family."

Rachel flushed. "It was a negligible amount, hardly worth mentioning."

"I fear your detractors may have a point, Miss Barton," he teased. "It would appear you are more inclined toward philanthropy than profit."

"That is not true," Rachel protested. "I am an excellent businesswoman. The fabric woven at Barton Mills is in demand in every major city in England, and I can drive as hard a bargain as any man. I have never failed to show a substantial profit in the three years I've owned the mill." She frowned. "Well, maybe not exactly substantial, but I have always operated free of debt."

"Indeed, Madame Philanthropist. But surely you are not going to stop there. What further shocks are in store for the British textile industry?"

Rachel leaned forward, elbows on the table. "You may think me mad, but I have made exhaustive studies that prove beyond a doubt that the efficiency of even my best weavers rapidly decreases after twelve hours at the loom. As soon as I can see my way clear, I intend to cut the hours of all my workers from fourteen a day to twelve."

"Good God, woman, you will be stoned as a heretic!" Yves shook his head. "Let us hope those studies of yours prove to be correct."

Rachel raised her chin defiantly. "I can see you think me a softhearted fool, which is what Jacob Zimmerman, my mill superintendent, calls me."

"No, Rachel, I think you are the most remarkable woman I have ever met."

Rachel stared at him, dumbfounded. "Remarkable" sounded even better than "unique." Having a Frenchman for a friend was most definitely a boost to one's self-regard.

Yves studied her with grave eyes. "You still have not satisfied my curiosity as to how you became so knowledgeable about the management of a textile mill."

She shrugged. "I have my father to thank for that. He put me to work sweeping the carding room floor on my sixth birthday. By the time I was fourteen, I could card, spin, and weave as well as the most skilled workers in the mill."

A look akin to horror crossed Yves's face. "But that is monstrous! What kind of man would consign his own daughter to such drudgery when she was barely out of leading strings? Surely your mother had something to say about that."

"My mother died when I was three—and in defense of my father, he knew I would someday inherit the mill and felt I should learn all I could before that happened.

"It was not as bad as it sounds," she added quickly. "I was never made to crawl inside a working machine to clean out lint or retrieve a lost shuttle." She refrained from adding that she still had nightmares about the mangled body of a boy her age who had attempted to perform the dreaded task.

"Furthermore, I only worked half a day—seven hours to be exact. The rest of my time was spent with a tutor—a wonderful old man who taught me to read, write, cipher, and above all, to love books."

Then since her conscience pricked her because she had cared deeply about her tutor and cared nothing for her father, she added, "I quite enjoyed learning about the mill as well."

Yves was not fooled. "No wonder you are so opposed to child labor. You've had firsthand experience," he said, reaching across the table to cover her hand with his. As always, his touch triggered an odd, quivery feeling somewhere in the region of her stomach. She knew she was gaping at him like an awestruck schoolgirl. She couldn't help it, any more than she could help entwining her fingers with his.

Yves saw the longing and confusion in her eyes and felt shamed that he was the cause of it. In truth, he felt shamed by Rachel herself. In many ways her childhood had been even more desolate than his own. He had had his sister and the twelve young Durands as companions, and Madame Durand's motherly arms to hold him when he woke from his nightmares. He wondered who had been Rachel's childhood companions other than her father's mill workers and a kindly old tutor. Who had held her and rocked her when she was frightened?

Yet she appeared to harbor none of the bitterness that had driven him to spend his entire adult life seeking revenge against those who had wronged him. Rachel had put her ugly memories behind her and devoted her efforts to building a decent future for those who could not build it for themselves. The contrast was less than flattering.

"It is late and we have another long day ahead of us tomorrow," he said, rising abruptly to his feet. "I will see you to your chamber."

Rachel looked a little startled by his sudden move, but made no demur. Together they walked up the stairs and down the candlelit hall toward their rooms. "Thank you for my lovely evening," she said as they stopped before her door. "It is a gift I'll not soon forget." She smiled and touched her fingers to his cheek. "You are a good listener, Yves St. Armand, and a caring friend."

Yves felt humbled by the tremor of emotion he heard in her voice. Staring into her earnest, trusting eyes, he was struck with an earth-shaking realization. He might never feel the fiery, all-consuming passion for Rachel that he had felt for Amalie, but he sincerely cared about her and wanted to see her happy. An overpowering tenderness welled within him, and gripping her slender shoulders with both hands he drew her to him.

Rachel went willingly into his arms. She could not imagine what had prompted his sudden show of affection; she didn't care. She would simply snatch this one wondrous moment from the endless tedium of her life and savor it again and again in the long, dull years ahead.

Yves lowered his head and his mouth brushed hers with melting gentleness. Then amazingly, his arms tightened about her and groaning deep in his throat, he raked his tongue across her lips until she opened them to his sensuous exploration. Instantly, she was awash with the same dark, bewildering longings his first kiss had evoked.

She felt as if she were on the edge of a great cliff and once she tumbled off, nothing in her life would ever again be the same. But the longer the kiss went on, the more tantalizing she found the thought of soaring into space. Then just as her toes slipped over the edge, he raised his head and stared at her with eyes glazed with shock.

"*Sacré bleu,*" he muttered between clenched teeth. He had meant the kiss to be one of understanding and compassion for a friend whose past was as painful as his own. But the minute his lips touched hers, his wits had gone a-begging. He had kissed her, not as a friend, but with the lusty abandon of a lover, and she had responded with an unbridled passion that sent waves of pleasure washing through him.

The scent of her hair lingered in his nostrils, the taste of her mouth was on his tongue. He was painfully aware that his blood ran hot in his veins and he ached with unfulfilled need.

He stepped back, needing to put her at arm's length. "Well that was a surprise," he said, and immediately felt a complete fool for saying it.

"Not to me. I have known since the first time you kissed me that you had the power to make me feel things no other man could."

He stared at her, dumbfounded. Would he ever become accustomed to this woman's uncompromising frankness?

"I—I apologize for letting my desire for you get out of control," he stammered once he had recovered sufficiently to do so.

She gulped. "Are you saying you desire me?"

"Of course I do. I am not made of stone." He avoided her eyes, fixing his gaze instead on a spot just beyond her right shoulder. "But desire is not enough to offer a woman like you and I am not ready to love again," he said softly. He had, in fact, sworn on Amalie's grave that he never would. Every woman he had ever loved had been taken from him—his mother, his grandmother, Amalie, even kindly Madame Durand. He had good reason to be reticent about once again baring his naked heart to the cruel sword of life's uncertainties.

Rachel couldn't believe what she was hearing. Not even in her wildest flights of fancy had it occurred to her that Yves felt anything for her but a warm and caring friendship. It had been enough until now. His admission that he desired her changed everything. The idea both thrilled and terrified her.

How quickly his words had given wings to her earthbound dreams; how high those dreams were soaring at this moment. For the first time, she faced the bewildering truth—she was falling in love with the charming Frenchman, and there was nothing she could do to stop herself.

She wondered what manner of woman had claimed his heart in the past. She felt certain it had not been Jacqueline Esquaré, or any other woman of her ilk. But whoever she had been, she must have hurt him deeply to render him so leery of loving again. Rachel wondered how any woman could be so foolish as to betray the trust of a man like Yves St. Armand?

She sighed. As for his admission that he desired her, it was all too plain he regretted making it, and regretted the kiss that had motivated it. The look in his beautiful silver eyes was like that of a wild animal with its paw caught in a trap. She had no choice but to set him free.

"It was only a kiss," she said, gently cupping his face in her two hands. "An enjoyable experience to be sure. But I am a practical woman and did not read more into it than you intended. We are still the best of friends, Yves, but nothing more."

They were the most difficult words she had ever uttered.

Moonlight streamed through the open window of Yves's room at the inn, bathing the faded carpet and dusty bed hangings in a silver radiance that obviated the need to light the tallow bedside candle. He lay, stripped of his clothing, atop the counterpane of the narrow bed, staring at the shadows dancing between the ceiling beams.

Sleep eluded him. Try as he might, he could not stop thinking about what Rachel had revealed of her childhood. Nor could he forget the look in her eyes when she'd dismissed the kiss they'd shared as a simple expression of friendship. He had known too many women to mistake that look. But the very thought that Rachel might have come to care for him in *that* way struck terror in his heart.

He liked her too much to want to hurt her. But hurt her he would if she made the mistake of falling in love with him. She was not the kind of woman who appealed to him in *that* way. How could she be when she was the direct opposite of Amalie?

Then why had his pulse raced and his body become embarrassingly aroused the minute his lips touched hers?

Because, devil take it, he had never claimed to be a saint. He was a man in whom lust was an ever-present hunger and he sensed an innocent sensuality in the strong-willed countrywoman that spoke to that hunger.

If he were not a man of honor he would be tempted to take advantage of her innocence. But a brief affair was not enough to offer Rachel. She deserved a man who could give her a home and children—a man who could love her with every fiber of his being.

He was not that man. His body might still feel lust, but his heart lay buried in a graveyard in Paris.

The morning of the fifth, and last, day of the trek from London to Yorkshire began with Yves riding one of the two mounts they kept tethered to the back of the carriage while Philippe took his turn as coachman. The sky overhead was a vivid blue, the sun was warm on his face and Yves was at peace with his conscience, at least for the moment.

After that fateful kiss he and Rachel had shared, he had vowed that for the balance of the journey he would keep his lust under control and his conversation impersonal. He had adhered religiously to both vows, though admittedly he had found the second one considerably easier to keep than the first.

Rachel had a razor-sharp mind and she was obviously starved for a chance to share her thoughts with someone who could match her in intelligence. She'd pounced on every subject he'd raised as eagerly as a puppy might pounce on a fresh bone.

One evening he'd inquired about the books she'd read and he'd literally opened the floodgates. Before he could catch his breath, he'd found himself trading quotes with her from Robert Burns's "My Luve Is Like a Red, Red Rose." From that they progressed to Wordsworth's and Coleridge's *Lyrical Ballads* and thence to arguing the merits of *Waverly,* Scott's controversial novel published two years earlier.

That subject exhausted, they'd moved on to Alexander Pope, whom Yves cited as his favorite English satirist. Rachel promptly declared the revered poet a malicious neoclassic dictator, and the lines were drawn. That heated argument had lasted until well after midnight and Yves had retired to his bed worn to the nub, but certain he had never enjoyed a mental sparring match more.

Another evening, to his regret, Philippe had joined them for supper and stayed on to keep Rachel entertained with his witty, and wicked, tales of the decadence and intrigue of the French court. The marquis had been at his flirtatious best and he'd soon had her laughing and blushing like a silly young girl fresh from the schoolroom. Yves had not been amused. He'd cut the evening short by declaring they had a long day ahead of them and were all in need of an early night. He'd fallen asleep that night with Philippe's mocking laughter ringing in his ears.

Luckily at the inn north of Skipton, where they'd stopped their last night on the road, the innkeeper's daughter had been a buxom wench with a come-hither smile. Philippe had quaffed one glass of the dark, Yorkshire ale she was serving, happily passed up supper, and followed her into the nether regions of the inn to satisfy his more pressing hunger.

At another time, in another place, Yves might have challenged him for the comely trollop's favor, and won. But, oddly enough, he'd not been in the mood for casual dalliance. In fact, as Jacqueline Esquaré had complained, he'd lived much like a monk for the past few weeks—a state of mind and body heretofore foreign to him.

Last night had been no exception. With Philippe otherwise occupied, he'd had Rachel to himself and he'd had no desire to trade places with his randy friend. "Tell me about this Yorkshire of yours," he'd suggested over dinner—and so she had. With glowing eyes and eager lips, she'd talked far into the night about wild moors and gentle pastureland, ancient monasteries and modern textile mills, large cities like York and villages so small only the inhabitants knew their names.

Yves had found himself intrigued and now, with the morning still young, he was beginning to recognize some of the things she had described.

He had already spied a monastery and what looked to be a turreted castle atop distant hills—and stopped to examine some mysterious ruins that reminded him that both Romans and Norsemen had once roamed the north of England.

They had also ridden past three of Yorkshire's famed textile mills, and the narrow-windowed red brick buildings had all looked so much alike, he felt certain he could have passed the same mill twice and never known the difference. The workers' cottages adjoining the mills had been amazingly similar as well, with their sparsely thatched roofs, walls of rotting wood, and sagging porches.

Grimy, hollow-cheeked toddlers had regarded the passing carriage with solemn eyes. It occurred to him that none of the children looked to be above the age of five, and the only adults in evidence were white-haired ancients. Apparently everyone from six to sixty labored in the mills.

He was beginning to appreciate the challenge Rachel had faced when she'd inherited Barton Mill, and to understand why she could not bring herself to view the miserable hovels surrounding her competitors' mills. From what he'd seen so far, he had to conclude that the rats in the sewers of Paris lived better than most Yorkshire mill workers.

"How far are we from our destination?" he asked her when next they stopped to water the horses and give them a much-needed rest.

"The foothills are just ahead. Beyond them is the pass through the mountains that leads to my valley. With any luck we should reach Barton House just about dusk." Rachel frowned. "A good thing, too, because poor Mary is not at all well. She does not fare well in a moving carriage. I shudder to think what would have happened to her if we'd had to stay with the public coach."

As Rachel had indicated, the road stretched northward past two more mills similar to the ones they had already passed. Then leaving the lowlands behind, it wound through gentle foothills and onto a steep, rocky slope better suited to mountain goats than carriage horses. It was Yves's turn at the reins, and it took all of his skill and strength to keep the team under control.

The air grew noticeably cooler as they climbed upward, and the pungent scent of pine drifted on a brisk breeze. After what seemed an interminable ascent, he guided the horses around a jut of black granite and found himself in a narrow, wooded ravine rimmed by tall cliffs of sheer rock, from which a dozen small waterfalls tumbled into a rushing river. He gazed about him, awed by the beauty and peace of his surroundings.

"This is more like it," Philippe declared as they stopped beside the river to again water the horses. With a weary sigh, he dismounted, cupped his hands and drank deeply of the clear, cold water.

"A beautiful spot," Yves agreed as he climbed down from the coachman's bench. "But I suspect winter sets in early in these mountains."

"It does indeed." Rachel joined them beside the river. "The locals call this 'the roof of northern England' and once it snows, this steep, twisting road can be very treacherous, as a great many travelers have learned. My mother was killed in a carriage accident one Christmas Eve just around the next bend."

"My deepest sympathy, *cherie*," Philippe's voice was gentle. "I know what it is to lose one's parents when a child."

Yves murmured his sympathy as well, and added, "We shall remember your warning about the pass and not delay our return to London overlong." But he found himself wondering if there was more to the story than Rachel was telling. He wondered if his wife's tragic death had played a part in turning Rachel's father into a man so lacking in compassion he would rob his only daughter of her childhood.

The sun was setting on the far horizon when Yves guided the carriage around the sharp bend that had claimed the life of Rachel's mother. He brought it to a halt at the edge of a promontory overlooking a high valley that stretched as far as the eye could see.

A good half of it was covered with a patchwork of small farms bounded by low rock walls, reminiscent of the farm in Normandy where he had spent most of his childhood. Interspersed among these stood a few structures too large to be farmhouses, yet too small to be the manor houses of the aristocracy. These, he assumed, were the dwelling places of that uniquely British entity, the country squire.

Directly below the plateau on which he stood, lay a small village dominated by a steepled church, and beyond the village stood what had to be the Barton Mill.

Evening shadows had already crept over the valley, but he could see it was the same kind of narrow-windowed, red brick building as the other Yorkshire mills, but with one unique difference. Rachel's mill was surrounded by sturdy cottages with newly thatched roofs, fresh coats of paint and small, fenced gardens. He smiled to himself. His philanthropic friend had indeed improved the lives of the people who worked for her.

A moment later, Rachel stepped from the coach. "We've reached my valley," she said, smiling up at him. "And that is Barton House." She pointed to a rambling two-story stone and timber house with four tall chimneys. It was separated from the mill by a row of beech trees and surrounded by lush green lawns, colorful flower beds, and a low stone wall similar to those surrounding the valley farms.

"It looks like you—comfortable and unassuming," Yves said as he climbed down from the coachman's bench.

Rachel blinked, and he realized that was not the sort of thing a lady would take as a compliment. But he had meant it as such. For with his first view of the gracious old house, he had gained the odd feeling that he had visited it before and would feel at home within its solid walls in the same way he felt at ease with its owner.

"So tell me, who owns all the sheep?" he asked surveying the vast grassy meadow that covered more than half of the valley. "There must be hundreds of them."

"I do," Rachel said, "and the meadow on which they graze as well."

"All that land and none of it devoted to crops? Surely the sheep could graze on a quarter of it."

"I suppose they could." Rachel shrugged. "But I have no interest in farming my land. As long as I produce the wool I need for my mill, I am content."

Yves shook his head. "Still it seems a terrible waste."

"Everything north of London has been a waste as far as I am concerned," Philippe declared, as he joined them to gaze at the scene below. "And this is surely the back of beyond."

Rachel laughed. "I think you are a city person, sir."

Philippe nodded. "That I am, mademoiselle. Amalie and I were both happiest when surrounded by cobbled streets and tall buildings. Paris was the center of our world. We could never understand why Yves had such an aversion to it."

"Amalie?" Rachel's puzzled gaze encompassed both men. "I do not believe Yves has ever mentioned her."

Philippe glanced at Yves as if to say he had made a slip of the tongue. Yves knew better. The Marquis de Brune was much more shrewd than he appeared at first glance. He always had a good reason for everything he said or did.

"Amalie de Maret was my twin sister; she died three years ago," Philippe said quietly.

"So young!" Rachel murmured, and echoed the words of sympathy he had spoken to her a few minutes earlier.

Philippe hesitated, but only for a moment before he added, "Her betrothed was a British agent at Bonaparte's court. She was killed trying to warn him that he had been betrayed."

Shock widened Rachel's eyes and blanched the color from her cheeks. Yves could see her quick mind had instantly grasped the full truth of Philippe's terse statement.

"So that is why Yves is so obsessed with finding the traitor," she murmured, pressing her fingers to her temples as if suddenly gripped by blinding pain.

Yves gritted his teeth. *Damn Philippe for a meddlesome pest, and damn Rachel for a sentimental fool.* The subject of Amalie de Maret was his own private hell and he was not about to discuss it with anyone.

"It is time we were on our way," he said coldly. "I have no desire to maneuver the rest of this tortuous road after dark, and we should bespeak rooms at the inn before night is upon us."

Rachel shook her head, as if waking from a nightmare. "I will not hear of such a thing," she protested in a voice that held only a trace of the distress still lingering in her eyes. "After you have come so far on my account, the least I can do is offer you the hospitality of Barton House."

"And leave your reputation in shreds when we depart for London? I think not. We must observe the proprieties."

She shrugged. "I have no reputation except that of an eccentric spinster, and I quit worrying about what people thought of me long ago."

"Still, I think it best Philippe and I stay at the inn."

Yves winced at the wounded look in her eyes, and quickly softened his rejection by adding, "I doubt we will tarnish your good name if we dine at Barton House, and I should like to spend one day touring your mill before I return to London."

"You would?" Rachel sounded surprised. "I should be happy to show it to you, but I would never have thought to offer. I was given to understand that aristocrats have an aversion to anything that smacks of trade."

"Most aristocrats do," Philippe said dryly. "But I am convinced there is a peasant somewhere in Yves's background. It is the only explanation for some of his odd tastes."

Yves refrained from comment. He knew Philippe referred as much to his refusal of Rachel's hospitality as to his request to tour her mill. The marquis liked his comfort and Barton House sounded infinitely more comfortable than a coaching inn.

However, Yves had good reason to choose the inn. He felt certain Fairborne would pursue Rachel to Yorkshire and attempt to mend his fences. Yves intended to be as inconspicuous as possible when the blackguard made his appearance—something he could not manage as Rachel's houseguest.

For Whitehall be hanged. If he could not find the written proof Lord Castlereagh demanded, he would be forced to dispose of the murderous traitor in his own way, and he would have a better chance of escaping the hangman's noose in Yorkshire than in London. Once the deed was done, he would simply slip across the border into Scotland and board a ship bound for America out of Glasgow.

Chapter Twelve

With Rachel and her maid safely delivered to Barton House and the Earl of Stratham's carriage in the hands of the ostler at the Black Sheep Inn, Yves was ready to retire for the night. Not so Philippe. The innkeeper's oldest daughter was a plump, black-haired beauty whose shy smile had sparked a rakish gleam in the eyes of the Marquis de Brune the minute he'd spied her.

Yves left him to his conquest without a backward glance. He was still so angry with the annoying fellow, he could not trust himself to be civil. He had just dozed off when a loud knocking sound shocked him into instant wakefulness. Habit made him grasp the knife he'd stashed beneath his pillow, until he recalled where he was and who his intruder must be.

"Go away, Philippe. I am sleeping," he shouted in French. "You are the last person on earth I wish to see right now."

"Let me in," Philippe shouted back. "Or I will pound on this door until you do."

Yves knew his tempestuous friend would do as he threatened. Neither he nor Amalie had ever been shy about demanding their own ways. Reluctantly, he rose from the bed, pulled on his breeches, and opened the door.

Philippe stood on the threshold, his dark hair awry, his shirttail dangling. In one hand he held a bottle, in the other two glasses. "I did not come to apologize for apprising your friend, Rachel, about Amalie," he declared in slightly slurred French.

"I didn't imagine you had," Yves said dryly. "I have never known you, or your sister, to apologize for anything."

Philippe pushed past him, crossed to the bedside table, and poured two glasses. "I am here to tell you I have been thinking."

Yves raised an eyebrow. "To be more accurate, you have been drinking."

"So I have. But that is when I have my most profound thoughts." He raised his glass. "To the Yorkshire heiress, who is yours for the taking. Or has it escaped your attention that the lady's heart is in her eyes every time she looks at you."

Yves swallowed hard. "I think of Rachel as a friend—nothing more. I did not realize until you put on your little show this afternoon that she might possibly have tender feelings for me. She gave me no reason to believe so in London."

"Perhaps your chasing her down and escorting her across the length of England gave her hope her feelings were reciprocated."

"Are you saying you brought up that business about Amalie because you thought Rachel believed I was courting her?"

Philippe shrugged. "It would be a logical conclusion for a proper English spinster—even for one with as many self-doubts as Mademoiselle Barton. I fear she will be crushed when she learns you are not attracted to her—particularly now that she knows Fairborne was only interested in her money."

"I did not say that . . . exactly."

"Aha! Then you are attracted to her."

"How I feel about Rachel, or any other woman, is none of your business," Yves snapped. He had been more than patient with the annoying fellow's meddling, but enough was enough.

"Ah, but I am making it my business." Philippe poured himself another glass of cognac. "You are the closest thing to a brother I shall ever have and I would never consider poaching your private preserves. But if you have no plans for the heiress's future, I believe I shall try my hand at her."

Yves laughed. "As I recall you already did that two evenings ago with no apparent success."

"I was simply testing the water. My heart was not yet in the chase. But now that I think on it, Mademoiselle Barton may be the perfect woman for me—and I am most certainly the perfect man for her."

Yves's glass slipped from his fingers and a trickle of brown cognac spread across the white bedcover. "You must be mad. Name me one thing a Parisian dandy like you has in common with an English countrywoman."

"Money," Philippe said without a moment's hesitation. "She has more than she needs and I have none at all, since my grandfather did not think to hide a fortune in gold and jewels from the sans culotte as yours did."

Philippe's sensuous mouth curved in an infuriating smile. "I am just what the lady needs. It is obvious something or someone in her past has led her to believe she is unattractive and unlovable. There is no man on earth more qualified to change her mind on that score than I. The Yorkshire heiress will get her money's worth if she shares her marriage bed with me."

Yves leapt to his feet, pulse racing. "Damn your eyes! Try your hand with Rachel and you will face me at dawn over a brace of pistols."

"I'll do no such thing. You could shoot out both my eyes with your own closed, and well you know it." Philippe chuckled. "Listen to yourself. You are ready to kill your best friend over a woman you claim has no hold on your heart."

Yves sat back down on the bed and stared at his fists, which were so tightly clenched his nails bit into his palms.

"I was baiting you," Philippe said, "and you swallowed my bait as heedlessly as a fish swallows a fat worm." He leaned back in his chair and crossed one ankle over the other. "Perhaps you should take the lady to bed. Then you would know if it is love or friendship you feel for her."

"I cannot do that. Rachel is not some care-for-nothing trollop with whom I could carry on a casual liaison, which is all I have to offer her."

"Nonsense. The two of you were meant for each other. I poked my head in the door that night when you were arguing over some book you'd both read. You were so engrossed in each other, you never knew I was there."

"Granted, we share a delight in books—"

"And, though I cannot imagine why, a delight in the simple country life as well. I saw your face when you gazed down on her house in her valley. You had the look of a man who, after a lifetime of wandering, had finally come home."

Philippe's acute perception startled Yves. Still, he stubbornly shook his head. "What I feel for Rachel is friendship, combined with a profound respect and admiration . . . but it is not love."

Love had been the lightning bolt that had struck him when he'd first glimpsed Amalie de Maret across a crowded ballroom— the all-consuming passion that had made him remain in Paris long after he'd known it was time to run for cover. This tender emotion he felt for Rachel had crept upon him much too slowly to be love.

He shrugged. "Even if I were inclined to offer for the lady, which I am not, I am the last man on earth she should wed."

"How so?" Philippe sounded genuinely perplexed. "Yours is an old and honorable name and you are a wealthy man by any standard. You would not be coming to her hat-in-hand."

"The London *ton* might accept a wealthy French aristocrat. Commoners are less inclined to do so, as the clerk at the Pulteney proved. There must be many families in Yorkshire who have lost sons in the war. Once my identity became known, I would be shunned, and Rachel with me if she were my wife."

"A paltry excuse at best. Mademoiselle Barton does not strike me as someone who is overly concerned with what others think of her." Philippe surveyed Yves through narrowed eyes. "But, of course, we both know that is not the real reason you are afraid to admit your true feelings for her."

"I have no idea what that obtuse statement might mean," Yves said wearily. "But I feel certain you are about to tell me."

Philippe drained the last of the cognac in his glass. "You asked what Mademoiselle Barton and I had in common. I ask you now what did Amalie and you have in common?"

Shock propelled Yves to his feet. "Damn your eyes, you insolent pup!" He slammed his glass down on the bedside table. "I loved your sister with all my heart and she returned my love in full measure."

"No one who saw you together could deny the passion you shared," Philippe agreed. "The emperor himself voiced the fear that you would set Versailles afire with your smoldering looks. But what interests did you have in common other than what went on between the bed sheets? You hated every minute you spent in Paris; she despised every inch of the countryside that was your natural milieu. Tell me, my friend, where would the two of you have lived once you married?"

"How can I say? She was taken from me before we had time to make that decision." In truth, they had quarreled about that very thing just hours before she'd died and Yves had cursed himself ever since for the ugly words he had hurled at her.

Weary beyond belief, he walked to the window and stood gazing out at the moonlit night. "Why are you doing this?" he asked. "I thought you loved your sister."

"I did love her. She was my twin—the other half of me—and

I shall always grieve for her. But Amalie has been dead for three years and you are alive and the brother of my heart."

"What exactly is your point?"

"My point is that you are but two-and-thirty years and a man who sorely needs a wife and a nursery full of sons and daughters to gladden your days. Parodying the bard so revered by the English, 'I think you protest too much' that you feel nothing but friendship for this Englishwoman. Are you afraid that if you let yourself care deeply for someone so different from Amalie, you will be admitting she would not have made you a good wife?"

Philippe's probing question twisted the knife already buried deep in Yves's heart. "Damn you for the viper you are," he said, gripping the windowsill with white-knuckled fingers. "Leave me this instant. Spew your poison elsewhere or so help me, I will toss you out this window as I would any other piece of refuse."

Behind him footsteps crossed the floor. The door opened, then closed. Philippe had evidently taken his threat to heart. A blessing, since the miserable fellow could drive a saint to violence.

As could Amalie.

He turned from the window and searched the shadowy room, though he knew full well the voice that had spoken those traitorous words belonged to the same imp inside his head who had begun to torment him long before Amalie had died.

Shaken to the core, he poured himself another glass of cognac to dull his brain and lure the sleep that eluded him. A useless gesture, since it would take far more than was left in the bottle to close the lid on the Pandora's box that evil little imp had opened.

For in truth, the resemblance between Amalie and Philippe de Maret had extended far beyond their raven hair and mischievous dark eyes. Amalie, too, had been a bewildering combination of blatant narcissism and unexpected sensitivity. One minute she had been a warmhearted woman who had fulfilled his most erotic sexual fantasies—the next an annoying, self-centered child.

At the beginning of their tempestuous affair he had found her mercurial moods wildly exciting. But long before its tragic end, he had begun to lose patience with the childish half of his lover's dual personality. So much so, he had found himself wondering . . .

He stopped short, horrified by the admission he had almost made. Could Philippe be right? Would he have found it impossible to live with Amalie?

But what was he thinking? She had never been anything but enchanting. Even their most bitter quarrels had evaporated like mist in a ray of sunshine once he had taken her in his arms. She had been his one true love, and she had sacrificed her bright, young life to save him. No other woman could take her place in his heart.

From his waistcoat pocket he withdrew the bizarre silver button that for some inexplicable reason, he had kept on his person since the day he had found it in that alley in Dover. The dragon's emerald eye gleamed maliciously in the pale light of the waning moon and, as always, he felt an odd, tingling sensation when his fingers touched the evil-looking talisman.

Once again, he was reminded that the villain he sought was both a traitor to his country and a cold-blooded murderer.

Once again, he acknowledged that, as a man of honor, he was obligated to avenge the past before he could think about the future.

Rachel awoke her first morning back at Barton House to bright sunshine streaming through the window of her bedchamber and a persistent chiming of the mantel clock. She sat up and rubbed her eyes, shocked that she was still in bed at the hour of nine. But then what could she expect? She'd spent the night curled up on the window seat watching the moon make its lonely trek across the sky, and only crawled into bed when the first rays of dawn colored the horizon.

She had little to show for her night of rumination except a beastly headache. For nothing she had learned about Yves from his garrulous friend had changed how she felt about him. If anything, his capacity to care deeply about a woman only made her love him more.

But she had attained a certain sense of liberation when in the early hours of the morning she had faced the painful truth that Yves's confession that he desired her had not been as meaningful as she'd first believed. He could apparently feel desire for any woman, even one he considered a friend; but he had only loved once.

The wonder was that she had talked herself into daydreaming about something she'd known in her heart could never be. She was not the kind of woman who stirred a man's deepest passions or inspired his undying devotion—unless, as in the Earl of

Fairborne's case, he was passionately devoted to getting his hands on her fortune.

But all that did not change the fact that Yves had said he wanted to tour her mill, and she owed it to him to be up and ready when he arrived. Quickly, she completed her morning ablutions, scraped back her hair into its usual knot and donned a long-sleeved brown dress with white collar and cuffs.

Moments later she made her way down the stairs and into the kitchen for the cup of strong, hot tea she hoped would ease her headache. Her housekeeper, Mrs. Partridge, was busy preparing the noonday meal and the rich aroma of roasting mutton filled the low-ceilinged room. She looked up from the bread dough she was kneading and studied Rachel with worried eyes. "So, tha's finally left thy bed, Miss Rachel. I was that worried there be summat wrong wi' thee. Well, get sat down. I've a bit of home-cured in the pan."

"Tea will do fine. I've no appetite as I slept poorly," Rachel said, pouring a cup from the teapot on the counter next to the Robinson range. It was not as hot as she might have wished but like all proper Yorkshire tea, it was strong enough to make her eyes water.

Mrs. Partridge divided the smooth, white dough, shaped it into loaves and placed it in two long bread pans, which she set in the warming oven. "Thy fancy new maid claimed she heard thee crying in the night."

"Mary was imagining things," Rachel said firmly, hoping her eyes looked less puffy than they felt.

"Humpf!" Mrs. Partridge busied herself scouring the bread board with a stiff brush. "Quare goings-on around here if tha asks me. Since when has tha needed a lady's maid?"

"Mary can do more than attend to my needs," Rachel said defensively. "You've complained often enough that you need help keeping up the house."

"A girl from the village would have done fine; thy London maid will be naught but trouble."

"How could Mary be trouble?"

"Has tha not taken a good look at her? 'Tis for certain Jacob Zimmerman did when he come calling on thee this morning. Ogled her like he'd ne'er seen yellow curls and blue eyes afore. 'Tis not proper with her a common servant and him the mill superintendent with a wife dead scarce two years."

Rachel scowled at her nosy housekeeper, tempted to ask how she came by her snobbish attitude toward one of her own class. But out of deference to the old woman's long years of faithful service to her and her father, she confined her comment to, "I am certain Jacob meant no harm. Mary is such a pretty girl, she cannot help but attract the admiration of any man who sees her."

"Pretty is as pretty does," Mrs. Partridge said sourly. "The chit be too easy with her smiles for my taste, considerin' she be a new widow, and unless me eyes deceive me, one with a bun in the oven to boot."

Rachel had heard enough. Mrs. Partridge was a good woman, but she had turned bitter when her husband ran off with a local farmer's daughter half his age. Ordinarily, Rachel understood her need to hide her vulnerable heart beneath a caustic tongue. But not this morning.

"Leave it be," she spit out between clenched teeth. "Mary Tucker is a fine young woman to whom I am deeply indebted, and she has problems enough. I'll not tolerate your adding to them."

The old woman's mouth dropped open and her eyes glazed with shock. Rachel immediately regretted her angry words. Mrs. Partridge was more than a housekeeper; she was, in fact, the closest thing to a mother Rachel had ever known.

"I am sorry I snapped at you," she said contritely. "My head is throbbing and my nerves are frayed from my sleepless night."

The old woman flushed hotly. "'Tis I who should be beggin' your pardon, mistress. I forgot me place." She sighed. "In truth, I've turned into such a spiteful old woman, I scarce know meself anymore. I hated Mary Tucker the minute she walked through the door, and for no reason but that she reminded me . . ."

"I know," Rachel sympathized. She wished she could tell the truth about Mary's situation, but it was not her story to tell.

"Servant or no, your Mary's a bonnie lass." Mrs. Partridge took a deep breath. "If Jacob Zimmerman don't think her beneath his touch, I've no call to say different. Might be he'd welcome another man's get, with his own babe dead afore it seen the light of day."

"Good heavens, they just met this morning. Don't read more into it than is there."

Mrs. Partridge shook her head. "I know what I seen. Any man

that fuddlepated by his first look at a woman be ripe for the plucking."

Rachel held her counsel. But she could not imagine a prosaic fellow like Jacob Zimmerman being so swept away by his emotions he'd abandon the rigid protocol to which he normally adhered. Despite all the years they had worked side by side, she had never been able to convince him to address her by anything less formal than "Miss Barton."

She rose from the table, crossed to the range, and poured herself another cup of tea. "Speaking of Jacob," she said, "I assume he came to bring me up-to-date on the current production schedule. So where is he?"

"Back at the mill. Leastwise that was where him and that cheeky black-haired Londoner said they was going."

"Yves was here? So early? He and Jacob have met?"

"Aye. Sat at that very table, eatin' my scones and drinkin' my tea, cozy as two pups in the same litter. Then off they traipsed to solve some problem with the number four loom, as if a Londoner would know anything about that."

Rachel bolted down the last of her tea and stood up. Number four was the newest and best of her power looms. If something was amiss with it, she had best get to the mill as fast as possible. But what was Jacob thinking of to involve Yves in their problems? It was not the sort of thing that would interest a French aristocrat. She suspected Yves had expressed a desire to see her mill more out of courtesy than curiosity.

Some ten minutes later, after a brisk walk through the beech grove, Rachel arrived at Barton Mill. Since the sparse little office she and Jacob shared was empty, she pushed open the heavy oak door that separated it from the mill itself and stepped into the deafening cacophony of the carding room. Here gigantic machines combed and paralleled the fibers of raw wool destined to be spun into yarn.

"Good morning, Timothy," she shouted to the man operating the nearest machine.

"Good morning to thee, mistress," the stocky young fellow shouted back, never taking his eyes off the wool he was feeding into the machine. "'Tis good thee is back. Number four loom be down."

"So I heard." Dodging the dozen or more baskets of wool

surrounding him, she headed for the partition that separated the carding machines from the vast, steam-driven spinning wheels her father had purchased a decade before.

"Halloo, Maggie Robinson," she called to a stout, middle-aged woman manning one of the wheels that controlled the drawing, twisting, and winding that turned the carded wool into the yarn.

"Halloo, mistress," the woman called back. "If tha be looking for Jacob, tha'll find him and that handsome black-haired Londoner at number four. Jacob is fit to be tied with his best loom down."

Rachel smiled. Word spread fast through the mill if there was trouble. She tarried for a few minutes, watching Maggie's deft fingers make the necessary adjustments to the spindle as it received the newly spun yarn. She had known she missed the mill when she was in London. Until this moment, she hadn't known how much. This was her world—a world in which she felt competent and needed and accepted by the people who inhabited it.

With a final smile for the woman who had taught her all she knew about the art of spinning, she circled one of the vast dye vats and headed toward the weaving room. Here was the heart of the mill—the room that housed the amazing power looms that had been her father's pride and joy. Rightly so, for it was the uniquely beautiful fabric woven on these looms that had made Benjamin Barton the wealthiest mill owner in all of Yorkshire.

Rachel stopped just inside the door to listen to the rhythmic cadence of the shuttles. The "music of the looms" had called to her all her life. She had listened to it so often, she could distinguish the sound of one shuttle from another, and she instantly recognized that number four loom was silent.

Carefully, she picked her way around the dozen or more operating looms that stood between her and the silent one she sought. The first person she saw as she approached number four was the weaver sitting idly on a tall stool.

Beside him stood Jacob Zimmerman, holding a familiar blue jacket. "Good morning, ma'am," he said, sounding amazingly cheerful considering one of his precious looms was down.

She stared at the jacket. "Where is Yves?"

Jacob pointed to a pair of dusty leather boots protruding from beneath the massive framework of the loom.

Rachel gasped. "What in heaven's name—"

"Nothing to fret about." A grin spread across Jacob's lean,

craggy face and his eyes twinkled behind his spectacles. "Your friend from London wagered a quid the trouble with number four was not a worn shuttle as I suggested, but lint in the shed snubbing the shuttle's passage. This, of course, made no sense whatsoever, and so I told him."

Jacob had been the assistant superintendent of the largest mill in Lancashire before he came to work for her father and Rachel trusted his judgment implicitly. Still anyone could be wrong, and Yves did not appear to be a man who made claims he could not substantiate. But she could not begin to imagine how a French aristocrat came to know enough about a loom to even argue the point.

"What made you think the shuttle was worn?" she asked. "It shouldn't be. As I recall, it was one of those most recently replaced."

Jacob shrugged. "It was off rhythm. It sounded as if it had worn unevenly and was wobbling when it passed the weft through the shed. Furthermore, the loom was free of lint when I made my inspection five days ago."

Rachel nodded. "Then it has to be the shuttle. With the quality of wool we use, it is not possible for enough lint to have accumulated since then to impede the shuttle action."

"You know that and so do I, Miss Barton; Yves is about to learn it."

Yves? The two men had met but a couple of hours ago and already they were on a first-name basis?

Rachel's brows drew together in a frown. "I can see you are having the time of your life watching the poor fellow make a fool of himself."

Jacob laughed. "Indeed I am—and teaching him a thing or two about power looms while I'm at it."

"Damn and blast," she hissed. "Yves is a good friend who escorted me all the way from London out of the kindness of his heart. I do not like your making game of him."

Jacob looked surprised. "He strikes me as a good sport. I doubt he'll take it to heart, and it will do the cocky fellow good to be taken down a peg."

"I heard that." The object of their discussion slid out from beneath the loom. His forehead and cheek, as well as the front of his shirt, were streaked with grease, but he appeared not the least bit embarrassed by his disheveled appearance. He was, in fact, sporting a self-satisfied smile.

"You look uncommonly pleased with yourself for a man who has just lost a wager," Jacob remarked. "Are you so rich you can drop a quid and never miss it?"

"Rich enough, dear fellow, and richer now than I was a few minutes ago, thanks to you." Yves's grin widened. "I hope whoever does your cooking is a dab hand at preparing crow. For there are two things I neglected to mention when we were discussing our wager. Firstly, the farmer's wife who raised me was a weaver by trade and it fell to me to keep her loom in repair—and secondly, I never make a wager unless I'm fairly certain I cannot lose." So saying, he held up a wad of grease-soaked lint large enough to stuff a small pillow.

Rachel heard the weaver's gasp of astonishment even as her own breath caught in her throat.

"Where the devil did you find that?" Jacob demanded.

Yves laughed. "It was not a conjurer's trick. I simply recognized a problem I'd dealt with before. My surrogate mother had been a weaver before she married a farmer, and supplemented the farm income by plying her trade on the long winter evenings. True, Madame Durand's was a handloom, but the principle governing the shuttle action is the same. The minute I listened to your loom, I knew the shed was clogged with lint. It happened time and again when Madame Durand was forced to work with inferior wool."

"But it cannot be," Rachel protested. "We use only the finest wool in the weaving of our fabrics. Blue Faced Leicester, Suffolk, Shetland, Teeswater and, of course, my own prize Wensleydales. Not a one of those wools would cast off the kind of lint you have in hand."

"Unless . . ." Jacob glanced her way. "Are you forgetting that odd lot of wool you bought from the farmer from Karlsborough?"

Jacob glanced toward Yves, who had risen to his feet. "Miss Barton is as shrewd a bargainer as any man . . . unless her heart gets in the way. But let some down-at-the-heels fellow show up at her door with a hungry babe in his wagon and she'll buy whatever he has for sale and at twice the price as well."

Rachel gasped. "But I gave strict orders that wool was to be destroyed."

"Well it looks to me as if it got into the carding baskets instead."

"I didn't know, mistress. I swear I didn't," the stocky, brown-haired weaver wailed.

"Of course you didn't. Jacob was not attaching blame to anyone. He was simply offering a suggestion as to what might have caused the problem," Rachel smiled at the weaver. "But we will sort it out and in the meantime, I give you leave to take your dinner pail home and share the noon meal with your wife and babes."

"But, mistress—"

"Your wages will not be docked, if that's what is worrying you—providing you keep to yourself what you've seen this morning."

"Thee has my word on it, mistress. I'll go to my grave with my lips sealed." Eyes fairly popping from his head, the weaver grabbed his dinner pail and promptly scurried out of sight.

Rachel watched Jacob pull a roll of pound notes from his pocket, peel one off, and hand it to Yves. "Much as I hate to lose a wager, especially one where I have been made to look a fool, I am deeply grateful to you for pointing out our problem before we lost any more precious time. We can ill afford to do so with all the orders we've received this past month."

Rachel studied the wad of lint Yves had retrieved from the loom. "You are certain, then, that it is the Karlsborough wool that is causing the problem?" she asked Jacob.

"I am certain. Now that I think on it, I am not surprised it ended up in the carding baskets. For you and I are the only ones who would have recognized it was inferior wool. To anyone else—except maybe your crafty London gentleman-friend—wool is wool."

He handed Yves his jacket, then turned to Rachel. "I'll leave it to you to locate any fabric already woven with it, as yours are the most sensitive fingers for that task. I'll search out any of the blasted stuff left in the carding and spinning rooms."

With that pronouncement, Jacob took his leave of Rachel and Yves, but not before he murmured, "Don't let this one get away, Miss Barton. He is worth twenty of that other Londoner who was courting you."

Chapter Thirteen

Yves took note of Rachel's flaming cheeks and found himself torn between pretending he had gone stone deaf in the past few minutes, or treating Jacob Zimmerman's provocative remark as something so preposterous it merited only a passing comment. He chose the latter. He had always found it better to air a problem with a friend than to let it fester between them.

"Jacob is a good man and he is obviously fanatically loyal to you—which does you great credit," he said quietly. "I am honored that he finds me . . . worthy."

"So you should be," Rachel said with a puzzled frown. "He does not make friends easily and he has little use for aristocrats, to say nothing of French aristocrats."

"I am afraid he may think me an Englishman and a commoner. For reasons I cannot explain, I have always had a knack for learning languages. Germans think me a German; Spaniards think me Spanish. I have even, on occasion, been mistaken for a Russian. I did not mean to deceive him. I will tell him exactly who and what I am when next I see him."

"No. Please don't. What is the point of creating an unpleasant situation when you will be here such a short time?" Rachel's voice had an unusually sharp edge to it. "Jacob took an instant dislike to the Earl of Fairborne, and made little effort to hide his feelings whenever they met. It was most unpleasant."

Yves's opinion of the mill superintendent instantly went up a notch. If the need arose, he might consider taking Jacob into his confidence and enlisting his aid in trapping the traitor.

Out of curiosity, he asked, "What did Jacob mean when he said your fingers were best suited for the task of locating the fabric with the inferior wool woven into it?"

"It is a skill I have developed over the years—one I needed

if I aimed to produce a superior fabric. If you are really interested, I'll demonstrate."

"I am interested," he said. Then because she looked skeptical, he crossed his fingers and added, "I am not as opposed to dabbling in trade as most men of title. Who knows? I might even want to invest in a textile mill someday."

She apparently took him at his word, as she directed him to watch closely, and promptly began skimming her fingers along the surface of the fabric, as if she could feel where the strands of inferior yarn were interlaced with the warp.

He frowned. "What are you doing? I see no flaws in either the texture or color of the cloth."

"The flaw I seek is not discernible to the eye—only to the touch. Here, I will show you. Let your fingers glide across the fabric as mine do and think with your fingertips." She searched his face. "Can you feel where the texture is different?"

"No. It all feels the same to me."

"It will at first. You are new at this. But close your eyes and keep trying."

"This is hopeless," Yves declared a few minutes later, feeling decidedly foolish.

"You are too impatient."

Yves swore softly in French, but he kept his eyes closed and continued his tactile examination of the fabric. Then just as he was about to give it up . . .

"I think I have it," he cried. "A coarse, almost brittle feeling that makes my fingertips prickle—right here."

Rachel ran her hand over the area he indicated. "Yes! That is it! You can see now why I must search out every scrap of fabric into which the inferior wool has been woven. I would never market a serge under the Barton Mill name that made the wearer itch. Luckily our customer in this case requested that we deliver the material in thirty-yard bolts, so the search is at least possible."

Yves frowned. "But that could represent a serious loss if it turns out that a great many bolts are involved."

"No. We will have to produce new cloth, of course, which will necessitate long hours at the looms for my weavers, and contrary to popular practice, I will compensate them accordingly. But I will still make a good profit on the new cloth—and I will suffer no loss on the old."

"How can you say that?" Yves asked, staring at the huge stack of bolts sitting next to the loom.

Rachel shrugged. "I am prepared for such a contingency, and so should you be if you invest in a mill. I learned long ago that even using the best wools and hiring the finest weavers is no guarantee against the occasional mistake. Therefore, I have an outlet where I can market such mistakes under a name other than Barton Mills."

To Rachel's surprise, Yves greeted this information with a hearty laugh. "What is so funny?" she asked. "I am giving you some very good advice."

"I know. I know. I am not laughing at you, but at my own stupid sense of male superiority. Believe it or not, I asked to tour your mill, not so much because I plan to invest in one myself, but because I wanted to take the measure of the man—or men— who manage your mill for you."

"You did? Why ever for?"

"Because, my friend, despite your claim that you are a good businesswoman, I had my doubts. You told me a great deal about how you had improved the lives of your workers; you said little about the actual operation of the mill."

"So, of course, you assumed that unless some man was controlling my reckless spending, I must be driving it into bankruptcy."

"I wouldn't go that far."

"Don't deny it. You have already remarked that I seemed more inclined toward philanthropy than profit."

"Well, it is common knowledge that women are helpless, ineffectual creatures who need men to take care of them," Yves said, and though his grin made mockery of his words, Rachel still felt obliged to protest them.

"I thank you for your concern," she said stiffly. "But I assure you I am quite capable of taking care of myself."

"So I have come to realize." Yves's grin broadened. "I can see now there was no need to assure myself that you were taken care of before I sailed for America."

"America? You are not returning to France?"

"No. I love France but I can no longer live there." The words "It holds too many bitter memories," hung unspoken between them and Rachel felt the crack in her heart widen at the thought that soon a vast ocean would separate her from this man who had captured her heart.

She managed a wobbly smile. "What made you decide on America? A country founded on the principle that all men are created equal seems an odd choice for a titled nobleman."

"But I am not your typical titled nobleman. The truth is I have become accustomed to hard work and would find the idle life of an aristocrat unbearably boring. Also, my sister and her husband have settled in a place called Virginia, and she is all the family I have left."

"Then you should indeed learn all you can about operating a textile mill, for I understand the Americans are very successful at both raising sheep and growing cotton," Rachel declared with a heartiness that even to her own ears rang hollow.

Yves nodded. "My thought exactly."

"There you have it then. And what better way to begin your education than to help me search out the inferior wool in this serge? With two of us working at it, we should finish in time for the midday meal."

Though he seriously doubted he would ever invest his money in a textile mill, Yves lifted the top two bolts of fabric off the pile so they could begin their search. He had long ago decided that he was a farmer at heart and nothing he had seen in Rachel's mill had changed his mind. Still, pretending an interest in it would give him the excuse he needed to stay in Yorkshire until Fairborne arrived.

He chanced a glance at Rachel out of the corner of his eye. It was obvious from the firm set of her jaw that she was once again the pragmatic woman he had known in London. He told himself it was just as well. This was the Rachel with whom he was comfortable. The one with stars in her eyes made him too acutely aware that he was a man and she was a woman.

Two hours of intense scrutiny had proved to Rachel that every bolt of the serge recently woven on number four loom contained strands spun from the Karlsborough wool. She could only pray the problem was confined to the one loom and the one order placed by a tailor in York. That particular customer always ordered well ahead of his actual need and would suffer no hardship if she were a little slower than usual in producing the fabric. If no other problems arose, she would weather this latest storm as she had weathered all the others that had blown her way in the past three years.

But she was not without problems. She doubted even Jacob realized how low she had been on working capital since building the new cottages and raising the wages of her adult employees. Though she relied heavily on him when it came to production matters, she alone kept the books for the mill.

He was waiting for her when she and Yves returned to the office. "All ten bolts woven on number four contain inferior wool," she said immediately, and saw the concern registered on his face.

"My news is somewhat better," he declared. "From the amount of Karlsborough wool left in the carding baskets, I feel certain all that was spun found its way to the one loom and no fabric containing it has been delivered to customers. But to be safe, I will check again to make certain there is none of it already carded or spun. In the meantime, I've had it packaged up for donation to the Cottage Weavers' Society in Hammersville."

He hesitated, a frown darkening his brow. "This would not have happened if I had kept a closer watch on things."

"If you are looking to establish blame, at least be honest in doing so," Rachel said. "The mistake occurred because I let my heart rule my head and bought what I knew was inferior wool— then compounded the problem by haring off to London before I saw it off the premises."

She turned a baleful eye on Yves. "And if you say one word about women being ineffectual creatures who need men to look after them, I shall rescind my invitation and leave you to take your noonday meal at the inn—a fate worse than death if the rumors about the quality of the food served there are true."

"My stomach is empty. Ergo my lips are sealed," Yves said with a grin. "I have been thinking about Mrs. Partridge's mutton stew all morning."

"And what about you, Jacob?" Rachel asked. "Can I tempt you to join us?"

Jacob smiled. "I believe you can, Miss Barton. Mutton stew is a favorite of mine."

Rachel couldn't believe her ears. Since his wife's death, she had often invited him to take meals with her. Except for Friday night suppers, when they reviewed the week at the mill, he had always politely declined. She hoped his newfound friendship with

Yves was his reason for accepting today—not, as Mrs. Partridge claimed, a fancy for her pregnant maid.

Once they reached Barton House, she escorted the two men to the small parlor adjoining the dining room and poured them each a glass of Yorkshire ale. Then she excused herself, explaining she needed to apprise her housekeeper that she would have two guests at the table.

Yves could not stomach ale, especially dark ale; he was a brandy drinker. But as a courtesy to his hostess, he would either have to drink the vile stuff or dispose of it in such a way that it would appear he had done so. Luckily, it was a glorious autumn day and the window stood open. Now all he had to do was wait until Jacob looked the other way.

His problem was solved a few moments later when Mary Tucker appeared and began laying service for three at the long oak table. Jacob's gaze instantly riveted on the pretty maid as she moved gracefully around the table performing her task.

Yves quickly dumped the ale into the bushes outside the window and empty glass in hand, greeted her with a smile. "Good afternoon, Mary Tucker. I see from your sparkling eyes and rosy cheeks that you are feeling much better."

Mary dropped into a deep curtsy. "Aye, sir. That I am. My poor stomach didn't take well to a moving carriage—not even one as fine as yours." She sighed. "'Twas a long, hard trip to be sure But isn't Yorkshire a grand place now that we're here?"

"It is indeed. A great improvement over London to my way of thinking."

Mary's gaze shifted to Jacob Zimmerman and she bobbed another curtsy. "Good afternoon to you, too, sir," she said, and blushed prettily.

Jacob had talked nonstop about the finer points of the weavers' trade on the walk from the mill and had paused only long enough to quaff his ale since they'd stepped into the salon. Now suddenly he appeared incapable of speech. In truth, he looked rather like he'd sustained a heavy blow to the head, and his spectacles had definitely fogged over. The Yorkshire mill superintendent was obviously smitten with the pretty little maid from London.

Yves wondered if Rachel was aware of this interesting development and if she were, what she intended to do about it. Not that it was any of his concern. Still, much as he liked Jacob he felt a certain responsibility for a woman he had transported the length of England, even if she were a member of the servant class.

"Rachel's maid is a pretty little thing," he remarked idly once she had returned to the kitchen.

Jacob blinked as if awakening from a dream. "That she is."

"And a plucky one as well," Yves continued. "The trip from London had to have been a very difficult one for a woman in her condition, but she never once complained."

"Her condition?"

"Rachel warned me the widow was breeding and we might have to stop frequently if she continued to suffer bouts of nausea. And so we did."

Jacob blinked again. "She is with child?" he asked as if the possibility were beyond his comprehension.

"So it would appear." It had been Yves's experience that knowing a woman was breeding usually cooled the ardor of most men, and from the stunned expression on Jacob's face, he had to believe his stratagem had worked.

He glanced up to find Rachel entering the room, a smile on her face.

"Yves tells me your new maid is with child," Jacob said the moment she approached.

Rachel cast a questioning look in Yves's direction. "What he says is true. Though I cannot imagine of what interest the subject could be to two bachelors."

Jacob studied her intently. "Then that is why you brought her home to Yorkshire with you."

Rachel hesitated a moment too long to Yves's way of thinking before she answered, "As a matter of fact, it is. Heaven only knows how a young widow could support herself and her child in London."

A barely discernible flicker of her eyelids told him there was more to the story than she was telling. What it was, Yves didn't care to know. The little maid and her babe would be safe under Rachel's protection.

Jacob cleared his throat. "I take it then, Miss Barton, that you consider yourself Mary Tucker's guardian as well as her employer."

"I had not thought of it in that way," Rachel said. "But I suppose in a way I do."

"Then may I have your permission to call upon her?"

"Call upon her? You wish to 'call upon' my maid?" Rachel stared at Jacob as if he had lost his mind. "To what purpose?"

"Perhaps I should rephrase my request. May I have your permission to court her?" Jacob removed his spectacles and wiped them with his handkerchief. "I can see from the expressions on both your faces that you think I have gone mad. Maybe I have, since admittedly I first laid eyes on her less than four hours ago. But the moment she smiled at me in that shy way of hers, I knew she was the woman I had been waiting for. If I am successful in my suit, her child will be an added blessing."

Yves hid his amazement behind a purposely bland expression. He was well acquainted with the phenomenon of "love at first sight," but he would never have expected a prosaic fellow like Jacob Zimmerman to be bitten by the bug . . . and of all things, for a lady's maid.

"Why don't I go chat up Mrs. Partridge and leave you two to your discussion," he offered.

Jacob frowned. "Do not leave on my account. My interest in the Widow Tucker will be no secret once I begin courting her with Miss Barton's approval, of course."

A flush of embarrassment colored Rachel's cheeks. "I scarcely know what to say. I have been faulted for my democratic leanings by every other mill owner in Yorkshire, and with good reason. But even I have to wonder if it is appropriate for the superintendent of my mill to court one of my household servants."

"More appropriate than you might think," Jacob said, his brow darkening. "It is not common knowledge, but my father was a weaver by trade, my mother the daughter of a shepherd who spent his entire life guarding sheep, but never owned so much as a ewe lamb himself. I rose above my humble beginnings by teaching myself to read and write, and by listening to and carefully copying the manner in which my so-called betters spoke."

"That is a worthy accomplishment, Jacob, and one for which I sincerely respect you," Rachel said, and Yves could see she was as amazed by Jacob's admission as he was.

"However you got there, you are far above the station of a common domestic," she continued, "and you will be subjected to the cruelest kind of speculation if you marry a lady's maid, especially a pregnant one."

"If you are suggesting I shall be considered a social outcast

by the local squires, I believe I can survive the experience without too much damage to my self-esteem."

"Still, your first wife was the daughter of one of those squires."

"And in four years of marriage, she never let me forget for
one minute that she had married beneath her," Jacob said bitterly.
"I am proud of what I have made of myself, but I am not ashamed
of my parents. When I take another wife, she will be a woman
who will be a daughter to them and treat them with the respect
they deserve."

He searched Rachel's face with troubled eyes. "But there is
more to consider here than my feelings. Would this misalliance
I propose be an embarrassment to you, as my employer?"

"No, of course not. You should know by now that I care little what others think of me." Rachel hesitated, but only for a
moment. "Very well, if you are certain this is what you want, I
will speak to Mary on your behalf. She is a lovely, courageous
young woman who would make the right man a fine wife—and
I would be pleased to see her happily situated."

"Thank you, Miss Barton. I would appreciate that." Jacob
smiled. "Now if you will excuse me, I find I have lost my appetite. I believe I shall return to the mill and make certain we
have ferreted out every strand of that troublesome wool."

With a brief nod in Yves's direction, he strode toward the
doorway leading to the entry hall, but turned back just short of
passing through it. "You will speak to her today, Miss Barton?"

Rachel nodded. "I will."

Jacob disappeared into the hall, and a moment later Yves heard
the front door of Barton House close behind him.

"Well I never," Rachel declared in hushed tones.

"Nor have I." Yves shook his head in dismay. "Which only
proves that one can never be certain of anything. Until this moment, I'd have sworn that nothing life had to offer could surprise
me."

Yves had departed for the inn shortly after they finished the
midday meal, but with a promise to return that evening for supper. Rachel would have liked to believe it was her companionship that drew him back to Barton House, but she strongly
suspected part of the lure was Mrs. Partridge's excellent cooking.

Still, she saw him off with a smile; then went in search of

Mary to keep her promise to Jacob. She found the girl seated at the kitchen table, polishing a silver teapot and humming a happy tune slightly off-key. Mrs. Partridge was nowhere in sight.

Rachel pulled up a chair and sat down. "So, Mary, how has your first day at Barton House been so far?"

"'Tis been purely lovely, mistress. I feared at first that Mrs. Partridge didn't like me, but she come around soon enough once I told her about the babe, and she's been ever so kind since."

Color bloomed in Mary's cheeks. "I didn't tell her everything, of course, and I feel guilty, letting her believe I'm a proper widow."

"Don't. The unscrupulous man who fathered your babe is out of your life, and good riddance. The important thing is to be the kind of woman who will make your child proud you are his, or her, mother."

"And so I will be, mistress, thanks to you. I feel like I was newborn when the sun come up this morning, and 'tis a fine feeling."

Rachel racked her brain for a diplomatic way to bring up the subject of Jacob Zimmerman, and finally decided the best plan was to come directly to the point. No amount of dancing around it was likely to make his request seem any less bizarre.

She took a deep breath. "Mrs. Partridge tells me you met my mill superintendent this morning."

"Aye, I did," Mary said, and her cheeks promptly turned a bright pink.

"So, what did you think of him?"

"Ma'am?"

"Did you like Jacob—or at least think you could when you knew him better?"

Mary's eyes widened. "That's not for me to say, mistress, with him being what he is and me being what I am."

"No, I suppose it's not," Rachel agreed, and noting the wary look with which Mary regarded her, quickly added, "But I have a good reason for asking. Jacob may not have mentioned it, but—"

"He never said a word," Mary interjected. "Just stared at me, strange-like. And since you asks, it made me feel kind of . . ." She shivered. "You know."

Unfortunately, Rachel didn't know. She'd had little experience with men. She knew how Edgar had made her skin crawl when he'd looked at her with greedy eyes that last day in London, and she knew how her heart turned flip-flops whenever Yves looked at her. But she had no way of knowing if Jacob had made Mary feel one way or the other, or somewhere in between.

"Jacob told me he thought you a very pretty girl," she said somewhat lamely.

Mary tossed her head. "I know that. He's not the first man to look at me *that* way. But I took no notice. 'Twas that sort of thing that got me into the trouble I'm in."

"Jacob is nothing like that beastly footman; he is an honorable man. As a matter of fact, he asked my permission to call upon you."

Mary frowned. "Why ever for?"

"He hopes that once the two of you get to know each other— that is, if you enjoy each other's company . . ." Rachel registered the look of bewilderment on Mary's face and in desperation, blurted out, "Oh for heaven's sake, the man is interested in marrying you."

Mary dropped her polishing cloth and the teapot clattered after it. "Is he daft? Men like him don't marry lady's maids."

"No they don't, ordinarily. But Jacob is a very unusual man."

"He's attics to let, is what he is, and if I was you, mistress, I'd think twice about letting a bacon-brained fellow like him have a say in the running of my mill." She sighed. "But wouldn't I like to see my mam's face if I was to tell her I'd been asked for by a gentleman."

"Jacob is a gentleman by design, not birth, which is why he requires a unique kind of wife," Rachel explained. "But he is serious about wanting to make a home for you and your child. Do not be too hasty in your judgment of him. I doubt you'll find many other men willing to offer for a widow who is in a family way."

"But there's the rub, mistress. I'm not a proper widow. I'm an upstairs maid what lost her virtue to a mealymouthed footman. If this Jacob of yours is as good a man as you say, he deserves better than a fool and her bastard."

Rachel leaned across the table and covered Mary's hand with hers. "That is for him to decide. My advice to you is to allow him to call on you. If you find you like him well enough to consider marrying him, tell him the truth of your circumstances."

Mary's round blue eyes filled with tears. "Do I have to, mistress? Will you be angry at me if I don't?"

Rachel shook her head. "Of course not. You don't have to do anything you don't want to."

"Then I'd be much obliged if you'd tell Mr. Zimmerman I'd as lief not walk out with him."

"Very well, but knowing Jacob as I do, I am certain he will want to know why," Rachel said softly.

"It's not that I'm not proud he offered. But I don't want any man right now—not so soon after . . ."

She brushed away the teardrop sliding down her plump cheek. "I'm ever so happy just to be here at Barton House with you and Mrs. Partridge. Maybe I'll want to marry someday a long time off, but if I do, he'll be an ordinary fellow like a gardener or a groom. How could I feel comfortable growing old with a man so far above me I'd need to curtsy every time he came in sight?"

Yves made straight for the taproom when he returned to the inn and, as he'd expected, found Philippe there chatting up the innkeeper's daughter. But the dapper marquis immediately chucked the pretty girl under her plump chin and excused himself with a promise to see her later.

"You look to be a man deep in thought," he said in French as he followed Yves up the stairs and into his chamber. "Did you not enjoy your tour of Miss Barton's mill?"

"I enjoyed it very much," Yves replied, also in French.

"Well something is wrong. Did you and Miss Barton quarrel?"

"No, of course not." Yves was so grateful that Philippe appeared to hold no grudge over the ugly words they had exchanged the previous night, he forgave the fellow his nosiness. For all their differences, the two of them were as close as brothers and like brothers, could forgive and forget even the most bitter arguments.

As before, Philippe sprawled in the room's only chair. "So tell me then, what is this weighty matter troubling your mind?"

"Damn your eyes, I am not in the habit of baring my soul—not even to you."

Philippe merely stretched out his legs, crossed them at his ankles, and waited.

"All right. I met a remarkable fellow today—one of the few truly self-made men I have come across in my two-and-thirty years. I watched him, despite all odds, reach out for what he saw as his chance for happiness. It made me realize how empty my own life is."

He coughed to clear his throat. "It also made me rethink our rather heated discussion last night and wonder if there could be some truth in what you said."

"There is always truth in what I say, unless I am angling for the favor of a beautiful woman," Philippe declared. "But which of my truths has furrowed your brow at the moment?"

Yves sat down on the bed and faced Philippe squarely. "You said Rachel and I were made for each other."

"And so you are, if you would only admit it."

"I confess I admire her. What intelligent man would not, considering all she has accomplished in her short life. And I do enjoy her company. I like doing the most simple things with her—things like pondering a problem at her mill, arguing over a book we've both read, sharing a quiet supper. I find myself thinking of ways to make her happy because she makes me happier than I've been in a long, long time."

"Then I fail to see your problem." Philippe flicked a speck of lint off the shoulder of his jacket. "Unless, of course, you feel no desire for this woman you admire so much."

"That is the most confusing thing of all. Lately, every time I'm near her, I find myself wanting to take her in my arms. But the feeling is one of tenderness, as well as passion, and it has crept upon me so slowly, it has taken me unawares. Where are the thunderbolts I felt before? Where are the lightning flashes? If this is love, it is certainly nothing like what I felt for Amalie."

Philippe drummed his fingers impatiently on the arm of the chair. "Why should it be? I have been in love a hundred times and each time has been different from the rest. As I said before, I fail to see your problem. You desire her; she obviously desires you. Bed the woman and be done with it."

"How many times must I tell you Rachel is not the kind of woman with whom I can have a casual affair."

"Then marry her. Forget about America. Settle down in this valley and give her a dozen beautiful, black-haired children. You say you want to make her happy. That should do the trick."

"You make me sound like a stallion whose only function is to service a brood mare." Yves's jaw tightened. "But to be perfectly honest, what else would there be for me to do here in Yorkshire?"

"I cannot help you there, *mon ami*. It is beyond me what any man of our class would find to occupy his time once he climbed out of bed in this godforsaken place. But since you have already declared your intention to dabble in trade, it occurs to me that Mademoiselle Barton should be the perfect wife for you. I have been told that under English law, once a woman marries, all her monies and property belong to her husband. I assume that holds true if the husband is a foreigner. If so, you would have a woman you desire and your entreé to the world of trade."

"I would never exercise that right. The mill is Rachel's. She has paid dearly for it in more ways than you could ever imagine, and it would take me a lifetime to learn as much as she knows about running it."

Philippe frowned. "I fear your years of posing as a farmer's son have addled your brain. No self-respecting aristocrat would miss a chance to get his hands on a fortune."

"But I do not need a fortune. I already have one. The problem is that Rachel has built herself a little kingdom here in Yorkshire—one she rules with an iron hand and a compassionate heart—and I was never cut out to be any woman's consort. I would despise the role and eventually despise the woman for whom I played it."

"Then I fear, my friend, that there is no solution to your problem." Philippe yawned. "Ah well, you will soon forget your Yorkshire lady once you reach America. I have heard it abounds with untilled land and lusty women. You can farm to your heart's content there and sire sturdy little Americans as well. If I did not have such an abhorrence of the rustic life, I would join you in your wilderness adventure."

Yves had been lost in thought and only half listening to Philippe. But one phrase penetrated his fog and brought him instantly alert. "What was that you just said?" he demanded.

"I said if I did not have such an abhorrence of—"

"No, not that. Something about untilled land."

"I said you could farm to your heart's content in America."

"But why couldn't I do that same thing here in Yorkshire?" Yves posed the question as much to himself as to Philippe. "Rachel has a vast amount of untilled land, far more than she needs to graze her sheep. I remember remarking that it was a terrible waste."

He leapt to his feet and paced the small room, his hands

clasped behind his back. "Rachel is a very wealthy woman, but she is also one who is short of the ready if she must put off building her beloved school and cutting her workers' hours. In short, she has the land I want and I have the cash she needs."

Philippe regarded Yves with a beatific smile. "Now there is the perfect definition of a marriage made in heaven if ever I heard one."

The sarcasm was not lost on Yves, but he chose to ignore it. "I have to believe the land is arable. The grass certainly appears lush. I will suggest we take a ride across the meadowland so I can get a closer look. If the soil proves to be as rich as I think . . ."

He stopped short. "What am I thinking? I must finish dealing with the past before I can consider the future."

"And if you never find the evidence you need to see the black-hearted devil transported on a prison ship?"

"Then, regardless of my promise to Lord Castlereagh, I will settle the matter in my own fashion."

Philippe scowled ferociously. "And be forced to flee England to escape the hangman's noose. Brilliant thinking, my friend. Then the evil earl will have robbed you of your future twice over."

"What would you have me do? Forget about avenging Amalie's death?"

Philippe straightened in his chair. "Perhaps you should content yourself with the thought that by marrying the Yorkshire heiress you will accomplish two things—insure your own future happiness and deprive Fairborne of his. I doubt he will have enough time to find himself another heiress before his creditors close in on him."

He contemplated Yves through narrowed eyes. "It is enough, my friend. My sister gave her life to save yours. Has it never occurred to you that her sacrifice will have been in vain if you waste the precious years she gave you in a fruitless search for revenge?"

Chapter Fourteen

Yves had both surprised and delighted Rachel with his request to see the land where her sheep grazed. She had halfway expected him to announce he was returning to London once he'd toured the mill. Now she could count on another day of his company, and she could think of no way she would rather spend a sunny autumn morning than driving through the countryside in her pony cart with the man she loved.

They set out from Barton House shortly after ten o'clock with Yves at the reins and the blanket and picnic basket Mrs. Partridge had supplied stowed beneath the seat of the cart. Jacob was standing in the doorway of the mill office when they passed, a hangdog expression on his lean, craggy face.

"I take it our friend's courtship is not progressing as he'd hoped," Yves said, returning the mill superintendent's cursory nod with one of his own.

Rachel sighed. "I did my best to persuade Mary to let him call on her, but she would have none of it. She said she could not be comfortable with a man so far above her on the social ladder."

"The girl is wise beyond her years. I wish to God I had been as astute at her age." With that obtuse statement, Yves flicked the reins to urge the pony into a trot and left Rachel to ponder what his perplexing words signified.

She drew her pretty silk shawl tightly about her shoulders and found herself wishing she had worried more about warmth than vanity when choosing to wear it for their outing. For though the sun was a bright golden ball in the sky, a chill sharpened the breeze and the leaves of beech and maple showed the first hint of the vivid colors to come.

They rode in companionable silence beyond the brick building housing the mill, past the line of wool sheds, and onto the narrow lane that led to the northern half of the valley. By eleven o'clock they had left the mill and Barton House far behind and had come upon the first large flock of sheep grazing the vast meadow.

"These are Teeswaters," Rachel said, waving to the young shepherd who tended them. "A mile or two ahead we'll begin to see Shetlands, blue-faced Leicesters and Suffolks, and beyond them a flock of my prize Wensleydales."

"They appear to be fine, healthy animals," Yves remarked when after passing four more flocks they stopped to give the pony a rest. "But I know nothing about sheep. Monsieur Durand did not raise them, despite the fact that Madame was a weaver."

"These are but a few of my flocks," Rachel said. "I need a great deal of wool to keep my mill supplied and I try to raise a goodly portion of it myself. I have better control of the quality of wool that way." She felt a flush heat her cheeks when she remembered Yves had been present when her usual careful control had been noticeably missing.

"Still I find it amazing that you can distinguish one breed of sheep from another just by viewing them," he said. "They all look alike to me."

"I had a good teacher, who taught me that every breed has its own distinct quality and texture of wool."

Yves's black brows drew together. "I take it all the sheep in this half of the valley belong to you."

Rachel nodded. "They do, and the cattle you can see off in the distance as well. I am not so addicted to mutton that I do not enjoy a varied table. The chicken and pork Mrs. Partridge served last evening came from one of the small farms south of the village. I've no desire to take up hog or poultry raising."

"But all the land in the northern half of the valley is yours?"

"As far as the eye can see," Rachel said, wondering why he was belaboring the point. "My grandfather began acquiring it shortly after he arrived in Yorkshire. By the time he died, he owned a little over half the valley. I'm sure he would have purchased the other half also if he could have talked the owners into selling to him."

Yves raised an eyebrow. "Said 'owners' being?"

"Dozens of farmers with small, individually owned farms and a few country squires with tenant farmers, all as fanatically attached to their land as I am to mine."

"Ah!" Yves's curiosity temporarily satisfied, they proceeded at a slow trot for another hour. Topping a gradual rise, he brought the cart to a halt and stared at the vast, empty meadow, imagining how it would look planted in spring wheat or barley or maize—crops he could sell to the owners of the granaries in York and London.

Rachel studied his profile, a puzzled expression on her face. "You look as if your thoughts are thousands of miles away. America, I suppose."

Yves smiled. "Actually no farther than London. I was thinking about our first meeting that night in Fairborne's bookroom. I am convinced it was fate, *cherie*. We French are great believers in fate."

If it was fate, it was a pitiless one, she decided, noting how the sun glistened in his thick, black hair. For what could be more cruel than to tempt a plain-as-dirt countrywoman with the most beautiful male ever to walk the face of the earth.

She tossed her head. "Well I am not French and while I admit that meeting you has added an unusual element to my life, I find the idea that it was 'fate' much too farfetched for my taste."

"Is that so? Then we must do something about that." Yves tied off the reins and to her surprise, stepped from the cart, circled it, and reached up to hand her down.

"What are you up to?" she demanded as she felt his arms close around her the minute her toes touched the ground.

"Making a believer of you, Mademoiselle Skeptic," he said, brushing her lips in a brief but tender kiss that triggered the same quivery sensation in her stomach that she'd felt every time he'd kissed her.

She shivered in his arms and he regarded her with knowing eyes that brought her to the blush. "Now tell me you do not believe in fate, *cherie*."

Rachel gathered her befuddled wits and searched his handsome face. The sensuous lips that had claimed hers just moments before were grinning wickedly and an unmistakable air of male triumph had replaced the laughter in his eyes. He was apparently playing some sort of male-female game that she was too naive to comprehend.

"It would be rather pointless to deny that your kisses evoke feelings I have never before experienced," she said with quiet dignity. "But I fail to see what that has to do with fate."

Yves chuckled. "For shame, Rachel. Proper English spinsters are not supposed to admit they feel desire."

Rachel gasped. "I did not say I desired you."

"You didn't have to. You are too forthcoming to hide your feelings, and I have already admitted that I desire you. If that is not fate, it is most certainly a happy coincidence."

Rachel felt her cheeks flame at his teasing words, perhaps because she could not deny the truth in them. She had never seen him in such a playful mood as he was in today. Yet strangely enough, she sensed a hint of gravity in his laughter and a restiveness beneath his outward calm. She watched him narrow his eyes against the late morning sun and stare across the fields again, and wondered what mysterious thoughts were running through his clever mind.

In truth, Yves's mind was devoid of thought for the moment, so immersed was he in the feelings that washed over him. Not since he'd left the farm in Normandy had his heart been so cheered by a chorus of bird songs or his eyes so gladdened by the sight of grassy meadows and sparkling streams. Nor had he filled his lungs with air so gloriously free of soot and smoke as this air of Yorkshire.

He took a deep breath and acknowledged it had been a long time since he had felt so pleased to be alive and so attuned to everything around him. If a spirit as tired and jaded as his could be renewed, it would surely be in this place and with this woman who had become so much a part of his life.

He had dreamed about her last night—a frankly erotic dream that had left him to face another dawn with only a haunting memory to warm his lonely bed. Like wisps of smoke drifting on the wind, fragments of the dream still swirled about in his head. There had been a kiss, considerably more passionate than the one they had just shared, and he had touched her in intimate ways that he felt certain would have earned him a hefty slap had he been anywhere but in a dream.

It had, of course, been nothing more than a fantasy born of his own imagination. But how vividly he remembered the scent of her, the taste of her, the way her slender body had molded to his. Even now he felt plagued by the burning needs the dream Rachel had awakened in him.

It was a dangerous state of mind for a man who had been celibate much too long. It was an even more dangerous state for a man whose future depended on what he said and how he said it in the next few minutes.

He chided himself for succumbing to the temptation to kiss her. This was not the time to lose control of his emotions. Rachel was the most practical woman he had ever met. Therefore, it seemed only reasonable that he should approach the subject of their future together from a purely practical standpoint. For despite her passionate response to his kisses, she was still an innocent where pleasures of the flesh were concerned.

"What say you to taking a walk across the meadow," he asked after ascertaining she had worn sensible half boots.

"I should enjoy that very much, and we could have our picnic beneath that oak tree," she said, pointing to an ancient, gnarled oak atop a distant knoll.

Yves reached for the picnic basket and blanket. "Will the pony bolt if we leave him alone?"

Rachel scratched her faithful Galloway behind his ear and smiled at his satisfied whinny. "I doubt Toby would move an inch, but to be certain, we should unhitch him from the cart and turn him into the meadow. He is a greedy fellow. If he can nibble on some fresh, green grass, he will be content for hours."

Moments later, with the pony happily settled, the two of them set off on foot across the meadow, with Rachel carrying the blanket. Yves carried the basket in one hand and since the ground was soft and the grass slippery from a recent shower, he reached for Rachel's hand with the other. A shiver of awareness rippled through her when their fingers entwined and to her humiliation the wicked fellow cast her a smile that said he knew exactly how his touch affected her.

Twice he set the basket down, dropped to his haunches and pulled up clumps of grass. Both times he shook the soil from the roots in the same way Rachel did when weeding her flower garden. She watched, more perplexed than ever about what he was up to.

"Rich, black, and crawling with earthworms," he pronounced in a peculiarly satisfied tone of voice when he performed his odd little ritual for the third time at the base of the knoll. "This would be great soil for planting crops."

"So I've been told," Rachel said as they climbed the slope and spread the blanket at the base of the tree. "A number of the valley farmers have asked me to lease sections of land to them for that purpose, but I have always resisted doing so. It is land that has belonged to three generations of Bartons, and I'd not feel right trusting it to strangers."

Yves raised the lid on the basket and began lifting out the carefully packed dishes and arranging them in the center of the blanket. "I can understand that. But how would you feel about trusting it to a friend?"

Rachel shrugged. "I have but two friends in whom I place that much trust. I doubt Jacob knows one end of a plow from the other and you . . ." She swallowed hard. "You are planning to open a textile mill in America."

Yves glanced up from his task, a look in his eyes that she had never seen before. "I may have misled you on that score," he said softly. "While I thoroughly enjoyed my tour of your mill, I came away knowing I had no interest in owning one."

Rachel was not surprised. "I doubt many men of title would be happy involved in trade."

"My title has nothing to do with it. The older I grow, the more convinced I become that while I am an aristocrat by birth, I am a farmer at heart. It is a risky business, I know, with all the disasters that can befall a crop before it is ready to harvest. But there is something about planting a seed and watching it grow that satisfies my soul."

"Then you should be happy in America," Rachel said, though the pain of saying it took her breath away. "I understand it is a nation of farmers."

Yves regarded her through narrowed eyes. "I might have been had fate not brought me to Yorkshire. Perhaps this is the time to confess that I am no longer of a mind to sail to America."

"You're not?"

"No, *cherie,* and I further confess that I had an ulterior motive in asking to see your land."

Rachel's knees buckled beneath her at the implication she read into his quiet words and she sat down abruptly on the edge of the blanket. "Wh—what motive was that?"

"To put it simply, you have more land than you need, but lack the money to build your school and fund the other projects you have in mind; I have more money than I can ever spend, but I have no land. Surely there is a bargain to be struck in such a situation if only we look for it."

Rachel's heart started thumping so wildly, she feared it would burst from her breast. "Are you saying you are contemplating settling in Yorkshire?"

Yves smiled. "The thought has occurred to me, but the final decision rests with you at the moment."

"Because you want to buy some of my land so you can grow crops?"

"No. An outright sale was not what I had in mind. I was thinking more along the lines of a partnership."

"You want to go into business with me?" Rachel stared at Yves, mouth agape. "There is nothing I would like more than to have you stay in Yorkshire," she said when she finally found her voice. "But I must tell you a partnership between a single man and woman would be most irregular. I am not even certain it is legal."

"Oh it is legal, and I have to believe any number of such partnerships are formed every day in England. I know they are in France and I suspect the Church of England favors marriage every bit as much as the Church of Rome."

"M—marriage?" Rachel suffered a sudden attack of light-headedness and there was a definite buzzing in her ears. Still, she knew she had not mistaken what Yves had said. "Y—you are speaking of m—marriage?." she stammered.

"But of course, *cherie*. I am a man and I am French. I would find it most uncomfortable to form any other kind of long-term relationship with a virtuous woman whom I desired—and like your wise little maid, I recognize that I could never be happy if I were not comfortable."

He surveyed her with a wicked grin. "Furthermore, as my friend, the marquis, recently reminded me, I have two-and-thirty years on my plate and am long past the age when I should be setting up my nursery. To do so without a proper wife would be certain to create a bad impression with my Yorkshire neighbors."

His expression sobered. "So what say you, Rachel, shall we strike our bargain? I believe we shall deal well together, for we have much in common, and we already trust each other. How many couples can say that when they stand together at the altar?"

Rachel contemplated her hands, which were folded in her lap, and wondered how it was possible for her heart to be overjoyed and close to breaking at the same time. With quiet desperation, she reviewed the words with which Yves had made his offer.

We shall deal well together. We trust each other.

Never, in her entire life, had she wanted anything as much as she wanted to be Yves St. Armand's wife—to live with him, bear his children, grow old with him. But how sterile his offer of marriage sounded when it held no mention of the word "love."

She might want to deal well with the farmer who delivered her butter and eggs, and she would trust Jacob Zimmerman with her life; she had no desire to marry either man. But neither was she certain she could bear to live out her life as the wife of the man she loved, knowing she would never be loved in return.

Somehow, she must make him understand that.

She took a deep breath, expelled it slowly, and began with, "I can think of nothing that would make me happier than to become your wife, but—"

"It is settled then," Yves interjected.

"No, it is most certainly not settled. There is something I need to say—"

He raised a hand as if warding off a blow. "You are worried about my London mistress. I can understand that, considering the show I treated you to at Drury Lane. Believe me, it was just that—a show played out for a specific audience. Jacqueline Esquaré means nothing to me. I shall dispatch a note to my solicitor instructing him to purchase her an expensive bauble and arrange for another wealthy protector to keep her in the style she demands."

Rachel ground her teeth in frustration. "That is not what worries me—"

"And never fear that, like most aristocrats, I would betray my wedding vows," he continued, ignoring her feeble protest. "I was raised by a God-fearing French farmer who taught me to respect the sanctity of marriage."

He caught her hand in his and pressed a tender kiss to the palm . . . and every objection she had instantly took flight. It mattered not that he had never said he loved her or even that she had decided marriage was not for her. Her mind might harbor doubts; her heart recognized that life with Yves on any terms would be preferable to life without him.

"Very well, if you are certain it is what you want, I will marry you," she said softly.

"I am certain, *cherie*, and I vow on the soul of my mother that I will devote the rest of my life to seeing that you never regret your decision." His eyes darkened with emotion. "Have you any idea how good it feels to make such a vow? To plan for the future instead of dedicating every waking thought to avenging the past?"

Rachel curled her fingers into his. "I am glad you have given up the idea that the Earl of Fairborne is the traitor you seek. Granted he is a fool and a scoundrel, but I cannot believe he is so truly evil he could betray his country."

"Then we have been betrothed less than five minutes and already we have found reason to disagree," Yves said grimly. "For I will go to my grave believing he not only could, but did commit the most heinous of crimes. Unfortunately, there appears to be no way I can prove it to Whitehall's satisfaction, so I have decided to abandon him to the tender mercies of his creditors and get on with my life."

The sun had long passed its zenith and was heading toward the western horizon when Rachel and Yves packed up the remains of their picnic and made their way back to the pony cart. They had tacitly agreed to avoid the subject of the Earl of Fairborne, settling instead on her plans for her school, his plans for the land and the tenants he must find to farm it. Like two friends who had known each other forever, they had talked together and laughed together, and scarcely noticed that the afternoon shadows had begun to creep across the meadow.

An inexplicable excitement had heightened every word, as had a lingering gaze, a not entirely accidental touch of fingers, and Rachel had taken heart. If Yves liked her and desired her now, it was not unreasonable to believe he might someday love her.

Now with the basket again stowed beneath the seat and the pony once more hitched to the cart, he stepped forward as if to help her into her seat. Instead, he caught hold of her upper arms and drew her into his embrace.

"Now what are you up to?" she demanded, though the gleam in his eyes left little doubt what he had in mind.

"We have had enough of serious talk," he purred, very much like her old tomcat when he wanted to be petted. "Our bargaining is done for this day. It is time we played a little."

Rachel put up no resistance, but she managed a mock scowl. "If you are planning to tell me that kissing and playing are synonymous, you are wasting your time, sir," she chided. "For even an aging Yorkshire spinster knows that to be untrue."

Yves grinned wickedly. "*Au contraire, mademoiselle.* Kissing is a most delightful kind of play particularly designed for two friends who are about to become lovers."

Lovers. The very word stirred something reckless and wanton deep inside her. His lips brushed hers with a feather-light touch, and with breath suspended she waited for him to deepen the kiss. When he did not, she parted her lips in a blatant invitation.

"Ah, Rachel, what you do to me," he growled deep in his throat and gave himself over to ravishing her mouth with a passion that left her clinging to his broad shoulders for support when he finally raised his head.

Eyes closed, she rested her head on his shoulder and gave herself up to the wonder of being in the arms of the man she loved. Then she heard it. Faintly, as if from a far distance—a familiar melodic chiming that could only be the string of bells hanging from the neck of the lead Wensleydale ram. She knew from experience the shepherd could not be far behind.

How annoying! When she was just beginning to enjoy being a wickedly wanton woman. She peeked over Yves's shoulder, but the flock was nowhere in sight.

But there was the sound again—and it was definitely closer. It seemed to be coming from behind the hillock she and Yves had just vacated. She had known the old hermit who tended her Wensleydales since she was twelve years old, when her father had sent her into the fields each summer morning to learn about sheep from the gruff old herdsman. She would be mortified if he came upon her in such a compromising situation.

Quickly, she freed herself from Yves's arms. "It is time we were on our way," she declared more sharply than she intended.

"But why?" His arms dropped to his sides and he stared at her with emotion-glazed eyes.

"There is the smell of rain in the air," she improvised. "I've no desire to arrive home soaked to the skin and have to choke down one of Mrs. Partridge's tisanes."

Yves shook his head as if rousing himself from a dream. "Odd, I smell no rain. But I shall take your word for it as you know this climate better than I." Without further ado, he helped her into the cart, then took his seat beside her and picked up the reins.

They drove back to Barton House at a brisk trot, stopping only twice to let the pony rest and drink from the small stream that bordered the lane. Rachel prayed for even a drop of rain to make her prophesy ring true. But the closer they got to Barton House, the fewer the clouds in the sky. By the time they drove through the gate and onto the long tree-lined driveway, the sun was so bright even her thin, silk shawl felt uncomfortably warm.

Yves walked her to her door, but he seemed oddly distracted, and Rachel feared she had offended him by cutting short their intimate moment together.

"Is something wrong?" she ventured when he failed to execute his usual courtly bow before taking his leave of her.

"Wrong? No." He stared at her, an odd expression on his face. "Confusing? Yes."

There was nothing for it but to tell him why she had been so anxious to end their embrace, though he would undoubtedly think her a silly priss to worry about scandalizing an elderly hermit. The French appeared to have no qualms about openly displaying affection.

"I enjoy it when you kiss me," she blurted out, then stopped short, tongue-tied with embarrassment.

"I enjoy kissing you," he responded gravely. "Each kiss seems more enjoyable than the last and the one we shared this afternoon the most remarkable of all."

Rachel blushed, remembering it was a kiss she had initiated. He frowned. "I will not lie to you, *cherie*. I am no saint. I have kissed many women—more than I care to admit."

"I am sure you have," she said stiffly. "You could not gain such expertise without considerable practice."

"Some kisses have been better than others, of course, but I have enjoyed them all."

Oh dear. She knew what he was trying to say. She would save him the trouble. She raised her chin defiantly. "I had done very little kissing before I met you, but I am certain I shall get better at it as I go along."

"Better? *Sacré bleu*, woman. You curl my toes now!"

"I do? What a lovely thing to say." She searched his face to see if he was teasing her—but he appeared to be deadly serious.

His frown deepened. "It is not as if I have not had my toes curled before. As my friend, Philippe, is fond of pointing out, I am a man with a powerful carnal appetite. I have even, on occasion, imagined I heard thunderbolts and saw lightning flashes when a kiss was particularly pleasurable."

Rachel didn't doubt his word. She had seen a few lightning flashes of her own when Yves's lips had touched hers.

He took an impatient swipe at a lock of hair that had fallen onto his forehead. "But I swear that never until today have I heard bells."

Rachel blinked. "You heard bells?"

"I hesitated to mention it for fear you would think me a raving madman. But as God is my witness, when we kissed today I heard bells chiming—sweet, silvery bells not unlike those our village priest rang at Mass each morning. It was as if the angels themselves were blessing our union."

Rachel's spirits sank like a stone tossed into a pond. For one brief, impossible moment, she was tempted to let Yves go on believing his lovely fantasy. But how could she live with her conscience if she did? More important at the moment, how could she tell him the truth without sorely embarrassing him, to say nothing of wounding his masculine pride?

She shifted uneasily from one foot to the other. "There is something I must tell you, Yves," she said, fixing her gaze on his cravat. "I, too, heard those bells—"

"You did?" The look that crossed his face was a combination of relief and amazement. "Then I did not imagine them! Ah *cherie*, if I did not already believe we were fated to wed, I would certainly believe it now."

"But, Yves, you don't understand—"

"Hush, Rachel. Not to worry. What could possibly upset our plans for the future when the angels are on our side?"

Drawing her into his arms, he murmured in her ear, "I'll have one more kiss to celebrate our betrothal before I bid you good-day, my Yorkshire lady." But before he could claim his prize, the door burst open to reveal Mary Tucker, her golden curls awry and her face puffy and tearstained.

"Oh mistress, I am so glad you're back. I've had such a fright."

"What in the world?" Rachel quickly slipped from Yves's arms and faced her abigail. "What happened? Who frightened you?"

"Mrs. Partridge sent me to the village on an errand," Mary said, choking back a sob. "It was then I saw the evil fellow, peering from the window of his fine coach. I turned my head so he wouldn't recognize me, but he will for certain once he sees me up close."

Tears flooded her round blue eyes. "Then everybody in Yorkshire will know my shame."

"Stop your crying and tell me who it was you saw in the village," Rachel demanded, more to give herself time to gather her frazzled wits than because she had any doubt as to the identity of the "evil fellow."

"It were him, the Earl of Fairborne," Mary wailed. "He's here in Yorkshire, and I'm sure as I am of my own name, he means to make trouble for both you and me."

Chapter Fifteen

"Are you certain the man you saw was the Earl of Fairborne?" The harsh tone of Yves's voice made Rachel want to cover her ears. Just moments ago she had been certain he had put the past behind him and was eager to embark on the future they had spent the afternoon planning. Now, at the mere mention of the earl, he changed from a man happily planning his future into a grim-faced fellow she scarcely recognized.

"I am certain, sir," Mary said. "Even if I hadn't seen his face, I'd not mistake that carriage of his." She grimaced. "Not with that dreadful creature on the door."

Yves raised a questioning brow and Rachel explained, "The earl's travel coach bears his coat of arms, as do the carriages of most aristocrats. His is particularly distinctive because it features a rather unusual dragon."

"A dragon?" Yves reached into his pocket, pulled forth a small silver object and held out his hand with it in his palm. "Similar to this one perchance?"

Mary gasped. "La, sir, 'tis the very same beast all right. Only the one on the earl's carriage is larger by tenfold."

Rachel stared in disbelief at the emerald-eyed miniature of the dragon in Edgar's coat of arms, instantly recognizing it for what it was. She managed to hide her shock sufficiently to direct Mary to bring a tea tray to the small parlor next to the dining room and direct Yves there.

"How did you come by that button?" she asked the minute they had seated themselves side by side on the parlor sofa.

He pondered her question gravely. "Are you certain you want to know?"

"Of course I want to know. I told you once before I don't like mysteries."

"Very well. I found it in Dover in a narrow alleyway behind an inn of dubious repute."

It was Rachel's turn to raise a brow. "How in heaven's name did it end up in a place like that? For that matter, what were you doing there?"

"At Lord Castlereagh's request, Philippe and I rode to Dover to investigate the murders of three people whose bodies had been found in that same alley a day earlier. That was why I was not at the Pulteney when you came looking for me."

Rachel gaped at him, momentarily frozen with a nameless fear. "Who were these people and why were you asked to investigate such a crime?" she asked when she found her voice.

"Lord Castlereagh felt I would have a particular interest in the murders since the victims were a Dover whore, a Frenchman recently arrived from the Continent, and the Bow Street runner who had been assigned to shadow the Earl of Fairborne."

"Dear God! It cannot be!" But even as she voiced her denial, Rachel sensed that what Yves said was true. She gripped the arm of her chair with rigid fingers as the full impact of his words seeped into her brain. But surely there was some mistake—some logical explanation that escaped her at the moment.

Yves searched her face. "You are pale as a ghost and have been since you first laid eyes on the bizarre button. Where have you seen one like it before?"

Her lips seemed incapable of forming the words to answer his questions. She could only continue to stare at him, speechless with horror.

Yves dropped the button back into his waistcoat pocket. "Damn it, Rachel, speak up. Tell me what you know."

She cleared her throat. "On my last day in London, when Edgar returned from his estate in Surrey—"

"Fairborne has no estate in Surrey or anywhere else. That was one of the first things Bow Street verified."

Rachel closed her eyes against his piercing gaze, and against the awful truth he was forcing her to face. "The earl is usually so fastidious, but he looked a bit disheveled that day," she said dully. "There was a black stain on the sleeve of his jacket and one of the buttons was missing from his elegant watered-silk waistcoat. I remember thinking what a shame since the little emerald-eyed dragons were so unusual."

Yves cursed softly in French. "Something told me it belonged to Fairborne the minute I found it. Just touching it conjured up something unspeakably dark and evil. But I couldn't imagine why it seemed familiar. Now I know. I must have caught a glimpse of the insignia on his town coach that day I met you outside Hatchard's Bookstore."

Warily, Rachel studied Yves's stern profile. "What are you going to do now that you have proof that the earl is . . . is what you claimed him to be?"

He turned his head. "What proof? A distinctive button may be enough for me, but I doubt that either Whitehall or the Privy Council will consider it sufficient to have a belted earl transported to prison for the rest of his life."

Visions of the three lifeless bodies left in that Dover alley like so much garbage swam before Rachel's eyes and she swallowed the bile rising in her throat. "But if I tell them—"

"Tell them what? That while a guest in the Earl of Fairborne's London townhouse, you noticed a button missing from his waistcoat that resembles one I found in Dover? He will, of course, deny that he has ever owned such a waistcoat—and since he has undoubtedly disposed of it long ago, how can you prove otherwise?"

He surveyed her abjectly. "I mean no disrespect, Rachel, but how much weight do you think such testimony would carry if offered by a commoner, and a woman, against a peer of the realm who is a close friend of the Regent."

"Very little, now that I think about it," Rachel said, slumping against the back of the loveseat. "But he has to be brought to justice. As difficult as I find it to believe, I must accept that the man I once considered a friend is evil incarnate. He has apparently already killed when he felt threatened. What is to stop him from killing again?"

"What indeed, since I've yet to find any convincing proof of his infamy."

She stared at him with wide, terror-filled eyes. "He will kill *you* if he finds out you mean to expose him."

"He will undoubtedly try . . . again," Yves said grimly. "But this time I will be ready for him."

"Do you think he followed you to Yorkshire for that purpose?"

"No. He would have no way of knowing I am here. I think he followed you to have one more try at getting his hands on your fortune."

Rachel's knuckles whitened as she tightened her grip on the arm of the sofa. "Why do I have the feeling you were not surprised when Mary said the earl was in Yorkshire?"

Yves gave careful consideration to his answer. He knew the truth could incriminate him in her eyes, but he had lived too long with lies and evasions. If he hoped to build a solid future with Rachel, he would have to begin by laying a foundation of honesty between them.

"I was not surprised," he said softly. "In truth, I had every expectation that he would attempt to mend his fences with you. He is in desperate financial straits and you are the means by which he'd hoped to recoup the fortune he lost at the gaming tables." He refrained from mentioning that Fairborne's obsession with Jacqueline Esquaré and other "birds of paradise" had cost him nearly as much as his addiction to green baize. There was such a thing as too much honesty.

Rachel raised her chin to a haughty level, and he held his breath, waiting for her reaction to his confession. "Your candor comes a bit late in the day, Yves," she said quietly. "I hope you will be more honest with me in the future."

Any other woman he'd known, Amalie included, would have demanded countless reassurances that he hadn't proposed to her merely to thwart his enemy. Rachel had dispensed with the touchy subject in two terse sentences that had let him know she was displeased with him, but at the same time trusted him sufficiently to believe his offer sincere. He was tempted to kneel at her feet and tell her how lucky he felt to have found her.

"You are right, of course," she continued. "A man so deeply in debt would not give up with one setback." She sighed. "I wonder I didn't discern what he had in mind when he asked the vicar to introduce us this past July. He has spent a month or more in this valley every summer visiting a relative for as long as I can remember and never before taken a moment's notice of me."

Her eyes widened and Yves could see the same thought that had just struck him had occurred to her as well. Unfortunately, Mrs. Partridge chose that moment to deliver the tea tray, and he waited until she'd withdrawn before he said, "Tell me about this relative Fairborne visits every summer."

"Lady Helen is his great aunt and a widow of many years. Her father was a baron and her husband Squire Ostrander, whose family has owned a small estate in the valley for generations.

She is very elderly and rumor has it she has become rather dotty in the past few years."

"Does Fairborne stand to inherit the estate?"

"No. As I understand it, the squire's heir is a nephew who is with the East India Trading Company in Bengal, but the will stipulated that Lady Helen should have the use of the house for as long as she lived."

Rachel paused to search Yves's face anxiously. "You're thinking if this proof you seek exists, it may be hidden somewhere in his aunt's house?"

"It is possible if Fairborne has spent a part of each year there. It would certainly be a safer place than his London townhouse to hide incriminating papers, and God knows I have no other leads to follow."

Impatiently, he drummed his fingers on the arm of his chair. "Do you know this house? Can you point it out to me?"

"Yes, as could anyone else who lives in the valley. But it would be much too risky to search it while the earl is in residence. If you are right about his coming here solely to plead his suit with me, he'll not stay long. I'll send him on his way as soon as he shows his face at Barton House. I beg of you, wait until he leaves Yorkshire to make your search."

Yves leaned forward, his elbows on his knees, his head in his hands. "An hour ago I might have agreed to your request. Against my better judgment, I had already let myself be talked into believing I had done all I could to bring Fairborne to justice and should let his angry creditors deal with him."

He raised his head and his anguished expression brought tears to Rachel's eyes. "I knew better, but I wanted so much to put the ugly past behind me and begin to build a future. Ironically, it was what you said a moment ago that made me realize that as long as Fairborne walks free, the past will rise to haunt me again and again."

Yves's mouth curved ruefully. "You asked what would stop him from killing again. The answer is the same as with any other dangerous predator. Confine him in chains or kill him."

The shocking words sent chills down Rachel's back, as did his tight, unreadable expression.

"There is more than revenge involved here," he continued in the same dispassionate tone of voice. "I cannot in good conscience let Fairborne return to London to seek out another unsuspecting heiress once he becomes convinced you are out of his reach. Ask yourself this, *cherie*. What is to stop him from disposing of a wife he doesn't want as soon as he controls her fortune?"

Rachel shivered. "As he would have disposed of me. Very well, I grant that you must find a way to bring him to justice while he is still in Yorkshire. But I pray you may do so by returning him to London in chains. All our plans for the future will be for naught if you . . ." She couldn't bring herself to say the word. "If you are forced to flee England with the Bow Street runners at your heels," she finished lamely.

She folded her hands in her lap. "I'll tell you my thoughts on how we should go about searching the manor house. Then you tell me yours. Between the two of us we are certain to find the best way."

"We?" Yves shook his head vehemently. "You are not to become involved in this. I forbid you to have anything to do with Fairborne other than send him a note saying you will never again receive him at Barton House."

"You do not yet have the right to forbid me to do anything," she answered with equal vehemence. "I choose to help you find the proof you need to put the Earl of Fairborne aboard a prison ship. I, too, want to forget the past and build the future we have talked about."

A sudden clap of thunder turned her attention to the window. The rain she had prayed for earlier had arrived with a vengeance. Drops of water pelted the glass and the world outside the cozy parlor looked dark and ominous. If she were as superstitious as Yves, she might think it an omen of trouble ahead.

She chose not to, and after a moment of thought she presented what she considered a foolproof plan for what they had in mind. "I will receive the earl when he calls and keep him entertained long enough for you and the marquis to search Lady Helen's house," she said and waited for Yves's response.

"I cannot let you do that," he protested. "I would never forgive myself if Fairborne harmed you."

"He won't harm me," she declared with a certainty she had already convinced herself she felt. "He will do everything but wag his tail and bark to gain my favor, and I will let him do so for an hour or two. But I shall make certain I am never alone with him. Mary and Mrs. Partridge will be in the house and I will alert the stable boy to fetch Jacob the minute the earl's carriage enters the driveway.

"Then once you are finished with your search, return to Barton House. Between you and the marquis, you should have no trouble overpowering him and delivering him to Whitehall if, God willing, you have the proof you need to see him transported. If you do not—but I refuse to think of that alternative."

Yves cradled her hands in his. "Ah, *cherie,* you make it sound so simple."

"It is simple," Rachel said. "So simple it cannot possibly fail. Since this is Friday and Jacob will join us for supper, we can apprise him of our plan, and Mrs. Partridge and Mary as well. Then tomorrow I will show you how to find Lady Helen's estate. What could be easier than that?"

Unfortunately, as it turned out, there was one flaw in Rachel's foolproof plan. She had failed to take into consideration how desperate the Earl of Fairborne was to get back in her good graces. She had expected him to take a few days to settle in at his aunt's estate before he called on her. Instead, promptly at one o'clock the following afternoon, his travel coach lumbered up her driveway.

She quickly scribbled a note to Jacob telling him of the unforeseen development and informing him that he would have to lead Yves to the estate immediately, while she kept the earl entertained. This she gave to Mary to pass to the stable boy to deliver to Jacob—a somewhat risky roundaboutation to be sure, but she had no choice. Then squaring her shoulders, she waved Mrs. Partridge aside, stepped to the door where the earl stood waiting, and pretended shock at finding him on her doorstep.

"All things considered, I would not have thought you'd have the audacity to call upon me, my lord," she said in a voice edged with ice.

"I was duty-bound to visit my dear aunt. She counts heavily on me now that she has become a recluse. And since I was so close to Barton House, I felt I must make an effort to mend my fences with you, dear lady."

Fairborne pressed a hand to his brow in a dramatic show of distress. "You will never know what courage it took for me to come here. Coward that I am, I used the books you left behind as my excuse to call upon you." He waved a hand in the direction of the coach and his coachman came forth with the stack of books Rachel had purchased at Hatchard's.

"*They* are most welcome," she said, directing the coachman to set them just inside the door. "I was sorry that circumstances forced me to leave them behind. Thank you and good-bye." She made as if to close the door, though she could plainly see Fairborne's boot was lodged against the jamb.

"At least receive me long enough to let me explain my behavior when I was your host," he begged.

Rachel shook her head. "I think not, sir. I really do not care to hear what you have to say, and after the treatment I suffered at your hands in London, I fear I do not trust you." A nice touch, she decided. It would not do to appear too eager to lure him into her parlor.

"Please, dear lady. I will beg you on bended knee if that is what you wish."

"I wish no such thing, sir, of you or any man. Do not even consider embarrassing yourself, and me, in such a way."

In truth, if she could do as she wished, she would slam the door in his face and never set eyes on him again. Now that she knew him for what he was, the very sight of him made her skin crawl. But for Yves's sake, she must play out this silly game.

She surveyed Fairborne through narrowed eyes. "Oh all right, if you insist. You may come in for a few minutes. But you are wasting your time, my lord, for nothing you can say will make me change my mind about you."

With a secret smile for the complacent look on the earl's face, she led the way to the parlor and instructed Mrs. Partridge to bring a tea tray and some of the poppy seed cake she had baked that morning.

Moments later, as she poured the tea, she saw Jacob fly past her window astride the lively mare from her stable, and breathed a sigh of relief. He was probably the world's worst horseman, and it would be a miracle if he managed to stay on the mare's back until he reached the inn, much less the Ostrander estate. But knowing her conscientious mill superintendent, she felt certain he would do so or die trying.

With a start, she realized the earl had been talking continually since he'd planted himself in the chair opposite her, and she hadn't heard a word.

"And that, dear lady, is why I did what I did."

"Ummm," she said, drawing her brows together as if giving serious thought to what he'd said.

"Love!" He raised his hands in a gesture of frustration. "It makes fools of the best of men."

"Love drove you to threaten me and post a guard outside my bedchamber? I find that difficult to believe, my lord. Your actions appeared more like those of a man driven to desperation by the thought of a fortune slipping through his fingers."

He managed to look both startled and offended by her accusation. "I am the Earl of Fairborne, not some fly-by-night Corinthian," he declared with haughty disdain. "You have seen my home, my carriages, my cattle. Think you a man of my means must marry for money? True, I acted out of desperation. But it was the desperation of a man in love, not a fortune-seeker."

He shook his head sadly. "I was afraid you would misconstrue my impulsive actions. What pangs of remorse I've suffered, knowing the woman I admire above all others must despise the very ground I walk on."

Fairborne took a sip of tea, put his cup down and gazed at her with a tortured expression. It occurred to her she probably would have believed every word he'd said if she did not know the truth about him. He could have taught Edmund Kean a thing or two about acting.

"Try a slice of Mrs. Partridge's poppy seed cake," she suggested. "I recall it was one of your favorite sweets."

"You remembered," he cried. "I knew that what we'd had together was too precious to be destroyed by one foolish act." He made short work of the cake she offered, washed it down with his tea and promptly consumed another slice. His "pangs of remorse" had apparently not affected his appetite.

But how much tea and cake could she expect him to consume. She had promised Yves she would keep him occupied for two hours. Scarcely fifteen minutes had passed and she could think of nothing more to say to him. Frantically she racked her brain for some topic of conversation she could safely discuss with him. The life of the man she loved could depend on her ability to keep Fairborne away from his great aunt's manor house for the next couple of hours.

Mrs. Partridge, bless her, saved the day in her usual inimitable fashion. "Thy midday meal is ready to serve, Miss Rachel," she said from the doorway of the parlor. "Shall I put it back? Or will the gentleman be joining thee."

How clever of the old dear to remember that all men, good or evil, enjoyed filling their bellies. Rachel felt as if an anvil had been lifted off her shoulders. Her immediate problem was solved. The earl could be counted on to spend a good hour or two stuffing himself with Mrs. Partridge's delicious food.

Still for the sake of appearances, she scowled as if displeased by her housekeeper's suggestion and checked her chatelaine watch. "I shall be ready to partake of my meal at precisely forty-five minutes past the hour of one," she snapped. "However, I am certain the earl has other plans."

Fairborne brushed the crumbs off his waistcoat. "On the contrary, my dear, I am deeply honored by your offer of hospitality and look forward to once again partaking of the excellent cuisine of Barton House."

Rachel had to laugh at how he twisted her words to suit his purpose. But the look of cunning on his handsome face reminded her there was nothing comical about her narrow escape. Had it not been for Yves's intervention, she might have made the fatal mistake of wedding the villain.

Gritting her teeth, she led him into the dining room at the appointed time and took up the task of plying him with food and wine for the next two hours. As was her habit, she bowed her head before lifting her fork. But instead of blessing the food they were about to eat, she offered a silent prayer for the success of the "simple plan" that was the key to hers and Yves's future together.

Yves was at the window of his bedchamber when Jacob came clattering into the stable yard of the village inn on a sorrel mare. Heart pounding, he rushed down the stairs to meet Rachel's mill superintendent, certain something was amiss.

Jacob wasted no time with preliminaries. "There's been a change of plans," he said somewhat breathlessly. "The earl is at Barton House and I'm to lead you to his aunt's estate posthaste."

"The devil you say! And leave Rachel with no man to protect her from Fairborne? I think not!"

Behind him, Philippe emerged from the taproom in time to hear what was said. "Go, for God's sake, Yves. It may be your last chance to see justice done without both of us having to flee

England to escape the hangman's noose. I'll protect your lady, with my life if need be."

Yves waited no longer to head for the stable and his trusty mount. Whatever else he might be, Philippe de Maret was a man of his word. Rachel would be safe with the marquis as her guardian.

However, it soon became apparent that the "plan" she had devised was not as simple as it had sounded. To begin with, the Ostrander estate was farther out in the valley than Yves had expected, and he could not ride hell-bent for leather as he and Philippe were wont to do when the need arose. Jacob did his best, but it was touch and go all the way as to whether or not he could manage to stay in the saddle. By the time they arrived at their destination, they'd used up close to thirty minutes of the precious two hours allotted them.

The estate, when they finally reached it, consisted of a large, overgrown park in which Yves spied a flock of sheep grazing side by side with a small herd of red deer. What had apparently once been a gravel drive was now just a weed-choked lane bordered by two lines of massive trees, whose twisted branches groped toward the sky like ancient supplicants praying to some long-forgotten Celtic god.

The house at the end of the lane looked even older than the trees. A two-story timber and plaster structure, it boasted a projecting porch, shallow bay windows, and a cluster of nondescript brick chimneys that had obviously seen better days.

"With the shrubbery surrounding the house so dense, I doubt if anyone will notice our approach," Yves observed. "Let's see if we can find an open window. I'd rather not have to break one."

Jacob sent him an uncertain look. "I should hope not. Breaking and entering is a serious crime in Yorkshire."

Yves scowled. "What would you have me do? Knock on the door and ask the old woman's permission to search for evidence to prove her nephew a traitor?"

A dark flush stained Jacob's sallow cheeks. "Forgive me if I find all this a bit confusing," he said stiffly. "I am not accustomed to acting outside the law, however valid the reason."

Yves bit back the scathing retort he was tempted to make. This was a chancy undertaking at best. He had counted on the daredevil marquis guarding his back. He feared Rachel's stoic mill superintendent would turn out to be more hindrance than help.

But luck was with him in one respect. The day was warm and most of the windows on the ground floor were wide open, including the French windows of what looked to be the library. Though, as Yves could readily see when he poked his head in, the high-ceilinged, dark-paneled room scarcely warranted the name. For unlike the bookroom in Fairborne's London townhouse, the floor-to-ceiling shelves in this room were empty except for a few dusty volumes scattered here and there.

Jacob stepped into the room and gazed about him with wary eyes. "We know the earl is at Barton House. But where is the old woman? And surely the servants will be about their tasks at this time of day."

"The old woman is probably in her bedchamber," Yves said. "I understand she is something of a recluse, and there could not be many servants about, unless they are exceptionally lazy. Everything in this room is covered with dust."

The words were barely out of his mouth when he heard the sound of approaching footsteps. Quickly, he pushed Jacob out the open window and told him to stand guard outside. Then he slipped behind the drape.

A moment later the door creaked open and from his vantage point, he saw a bald-headed ancient in tattered blue butler's livery and scruffy house slippers step into the room. An elderly maid in a dingy white mobcap followed close behind, feather duster in hand.

"Thee had best get to dusting afore the earl comes back," the old man said. "He near had a fit when he saw this bookroom last night. Accused me of not having it cleaned since he left for London."

"Why should thee, when he's the only one ever uses it. And what's he doing here in September anyways?" the maid grumbled, swishing her duster over the desk. "He's nowt come any month but July long as I remember."

"Hoping to get his hands on the Barton woman's fortune, I suspect," the old man said, busy rearranging the few items on the desk into some semblance of order. "His coachman claims the ornery bugger is at low tide and I believes him. Why else would he show up without that stiff-necked valet of his?"

"Humph! He's sniffin' round the wrong woman if thee asks

me. No daughter of old Ben Barton is fool enough to buy herself a kite that can't catch the wind."

Yves stifled a chuckle that quickly turned into a sneeze.

"What was that?" the maid asked.

"The house most likely," the butler answered. "The old place has more creaks in its joints than I do."

Yves pressed his finger beneath his nose. Surrounded as he was by dust-filled fabric, one sneeze begged another and it was all he could do to keep from giving his hiding place away before the maid finished her job of slap-dash dusting. However, finally she and the old butler left, closing the door behind them—but not before another fifteen minutes of his precious two hours was used up.

He wasted no time, but got quickly to work searching the drawers of the massive desk. They yielded nothing but a few more of the earl's unpaid bills. Nor did he find anything of import in the many drawers and cubbyholes of the ancient escritoire, which aside from two straight-backed chairs was the only other piece of furniture in the room. Next he riffled the pages of the dozen or so books, but to no avail.

In desperation, he surveyed the room in the hope of spying a likely hiding place for what he sought. This was even more discouraging than the search he'd just conducted.

It was a multi-angled affair with any number of odd nooks and crannies which could very well contain numerous ingeniously devised hiding places. There had been no such thing as a bank in either England or France when houses of this vintage were constructed. Hence, the builders had designed secret cupboards where the owner could safely hide his money and jewels.

It was in just such a "priest hole" in the family chateau that Yves's grandfather had hidden his fortune and entrusted his grandson's faithful nurse with the secret that unlocked it. Yves knew all too well such secrets were virtually impossible to uncover. He could search for days and never come upon the earl's hidey-hole, if indeed he had one. His time was running out and so far his guardian angels had showed no sign of performing another miracle on his behalf.

He moved to the fireplace, hoping to find a loose brick behind which a piece of paper could be hidden. He had pressed every brick just below the mantel and was starting on the second row when once again he heard the creak of the door hinges.

This time he was too far from the window to dive behind the drape.

Gripped by an unnerving sense of *dejà vu*, he straightened up and watched a woman come through the open doorway. But there the resemblance to that fateful night when he'd first met Rachel ended.

This woman's hair was the dingy white of trampled snow and vacant blue eyes peered from a face as wrinkled as the dried apples with which Madame Durand had made her winter flans. A cap of yellowed lace perched precariously atop her head and her frail body was encased in a purple satin panniered gown that had been in vogue when Louis XVI still sat on the throne of France.

Yves knew without asking she was Fairborne's great aunt and the lady of the house in which he was an intruder. He held his breath, afraid to move lest he frighten her into screaming for help.

To his surprise, she surveyed him as calmly as if finding a stranger rifling her bookroom was an everyday occurrence. "If you're looking for the cache of brandy my nevvie brought from London, you're looking in the wrong place, young fellow," she said in a voice as thin and dry as a leaf in winter.

Since he could think of no reply to that amazing statement, Yves exhaled slowly and watched her shuffle across the room to stand beside him.

"Thinks he's so clever, the cheese-paring clunch," the old woman muttered. "Fills my decanter with swill would choke an East India sailor and hides the good stuff for himself in a place he thinks no one else knows." She chuckled. "But I came to this house from Devonshire as a bride nearly sixty years ago and I know every hidey-hole in it."

She lowered one eyelid in a broad wink. "Just watch me, laddie, and I'll show you something that'll make your eyes pop out of your head."

Yves gave her a friendly smile and moved a step closer. The poor old thing was obviously mad as one of the inmates of London's infamous St. Mary of Bethlehem Hospital, but she seemed harmless enough.

He watched her grasp one of the ornate knobs decorating the fireplace mantel and give it a sharp twist. Instantly a panel in the wall beside the fireplace slid open, revealing a cupboard with four deep shelves. On the top shelf stood a cut glass brandy decanter, slightly over half full, and beside it a matching glass.

Yves blinked and looked again. On the second shelf, arranged in three neat piles, was a stash of papers, some of which appeared to be official-looking documents. His heart banged against his ribs like a wild bird trapped in a cage, as with grateful reverence he made the sign of the cross.

It appeared his guardian angels had not forsaken him after all. For unless he was mistaken, he was looking at the priest hole in which the Earl of Fairborne hid his secrets from the rest of the world.

Chapter Sixteen

The old woman reached for the decanter, but he stayed her hand. "Let me, my lady. A beautiful woman should never have to pour her own drink."

She giggled girlishly. "Now that's what I call a gentlemanly offer. But mind you pour but a wee one. 'Twouldn't do for my skinflint nevvie to know I've been tippling his fine French brandy. He turns mean as a corsair if he's crossed—especially if he's had a nip or two."

Yves poured a small drink, which she downed in one gulp. Then pulling a linen handkerchief from her sleeve, she wiped the glass dry. "There now, he'll ne'er be the wiser. Sorry I can't offer you a drink, but you can see how things are around here."

"I can indeed, my lady."

She reached for the knob, but again Yves stayed her hand. "I'll take care of closing it for you. Save your delicate hands for more ladylike tasks."

"Well now ain't you the sweet one. And handsome too. I always was partial to dark men." She sighed. "If you were twenty years older and I was twenty years younger . . ." She gave him a coy smile that revealed two missing teeth. "But I give you leave to kiss my hand if you'd like."

Yves felt an odd affinity for the dotty little woman, whom he suspected was ill-treated by her greedy great nephew. Raising her bird-claw hand to his lips, he lingered a moment longer than was proper over her parchment fingers.

"Wicked devil," she chided, giving him another conspiratorial wink. "If 'tis one of my nevvie's bits of paper you've come for, take it with my blessing. There's nothing would please me more than to tie the skinflint's tail in a knot."

"I may just do that," Yves said, winking back. He waited until she had shuffled out of the room, then closed the door behind her and set to work examining the contents of the priest hole. The stack on the left appeared to be all official documents, one of which was the deed to the earl's London townhouse issued some fifty years earlier to his grandfather.

The middle stack was comprised of letters and notes, many of which were written in the rather childish hand of Jacqueline Esquaré. The earl was evidently seriously smitten with the French trollop.

The third stack contained only two items, but the very sight of them was enough to make Yves shout for joy. For both were passes through the French lines issued to Fairborne. One was signed by Joseph Fouchet, the Minister of Police; the other carried the distinctive signature of Napoleon Bonaparte, the former Emperor of France.

Without further ado, Yves folded them neatly, slipped them into his pocket and twisted the knob to close the priest hole. Less than five minutes later he had apprised Jacob of his miraculous find and was on his way to Barton House, and Rachel, secure in the knowledge that he was at last in command of his future.

The Earl of Fairborne was foxed. Rachel had made the mistake of offering him a glass of Mrs. Partridge's famous elderberry wine and his consumption of food had dwindled in direct proportion to his growing interest in her housekeeper's skills as a vintner. But unlike Jacob, who had fallen asleep with his head in his plate when he'd imbibed too freely of the potent wine, the more the earl drank, the more ebullient his mood.

From a man who had begged for the right to apologize for his reprehensible behavior, he had quickly evolved into a cocky fellow, certain that with a mere snap of his fingers, he could charm his way back into her good graces. By the time the bottle was empty, Rachel could see he had convinced himself that she and her fortune were his for the taking.

How she longed to tell him the truth—that he was the last man on earth she would consider marrying. How she ached to call him the traitor and cold-blooded killer she now knew him to be. But prudently she kept silent and watched the hands of the mantel clock slowly creep toward thirty minutes past the hour of three when Yves would arrive at Barton House to deal with the earl one way or another.

Two o'clock . . . two and thirty minutes . . . three o'clock.

Rachel felt as if her heart had slowed to the deadly cadence of the passing minutes—and all the while Fairborne talked on and on and on. About what, she hadn't the slightest idea. She had stopped listening long ago.

The clock on the mantel chimed again. The interminable two hours were over at last . . . but her savior was not in sight. Fifteen minutes later he was still nowhere to be seen. Something unforeseen must have happened; Yves should have arrived by now. She fought to control her rising panic—not an easy thing to do with both Mary and Mrs. Partridge hovering in the doorway, their faces gray with worry. Something had definitely gone amiss with her "simple plan."

"We must decide how to proceed, dear lady," Fairborne said, his voice slurring. "We should make arrangements with the local vicar to begin reading our banns this coming Sunday." He reached across the table and grasped her hand, a triumphant smile on his wine-flushed face, and it suddenly occurred to her the drunken fool had taken her silence as acquiescence to his latest offer.

She snatched her hand from beneath his, sickened by the thought of his bloodstained fingers touching hers. She could wait no longer for help to arrive; she would have to deal with the despicable earl herself.

"What is this foolishness about banns being read?" she demanded. "However did you come by such a far-fetched idea?"

"Ah, my beloved, we are of the same mind." Fairborne hiccoughed. "How fortuitous, for I, too, am inclined toward elopement."

"Elopement?" Rachel rose from her chair and tossed her serviette to the table. "You must have attics to let, sir, if you harbor the notion that I would ever consider marrying you."

The earl pushed back his chair and stood up—surprisingly steady on his feet considering all he had drunk. "But that is exactly what we have been talking about for the past two hours."

"What you may have been talking about. I do not recall saying a word."

Fairborne hiccoughed again. "But naturally I construed your silence to mean—"

"If you were not so taken with yourself, my lord, you would have construed my silence for what it was—monumental disinterest."

"You jest, of course." Swift as a cat, Fairborne circled the end of the table and grasped Rachel's upper arms in his strong fingers. "Getting back some of your own, are you, my dear? Very well, I will allow that. But now that I think on it, elopement is the only way. I am much too eager to make you mine to wait another three se'nights to do so."

Rachel gritted her teeth. Things were rapidly going from bad to worse. Nothing she said seemed to penetrate Fairborne's alcohol-soaked brain. In desperation, she blurted out, "Stop this nonsense about my marrying you, Lord Fairborne. If you must know, I am betrothed to another."

Too late, she realized it was the worst possible thing she could have said. Rage contorted the earl's flushed features and his fingers dug into her arms with bruising force. "Who is he? When did this betrothal take place?" He snarled.

"The betrothal is very recent and he is no one you know."

"His name, madam?" Fairborne's grip tightened and he shook her as if she were a rag doll. "I would know what to have inscribed on this interloper's gravestone."

"He—he is a local farmer, " Rachel gasped, paralyzed with fear—for herself, for Yves. Fairborne's rage seemed to have had a sobering effect on him, but drunk or sober he was as dangerous as a rabid dog, and as impossible to deal with on a rational level.

"You chose a country bumpkin with dirt beneath his nails over a peer of the realm? I would not have believed even *you* could be that stupid." His eyes narrowed to angry slits. "But your lack of good judgment need not concern you, my dear. For I have decided to save you from your own folly. Luckily the border of Scotland is not that far from here and once we are man and wife, I will do your thinking for you."

Rachel knew she would only be wasting her strength if she tried to free herself from his hold. Physically, she was no match for a man his size. Her only hope was to outwit the evil fellow. Unless . . . out of the corner of her eye, she spied a small knife beside the platter of roasted chicken. She had armed herself against one bully with a knife; she would arm herself against another. Then she would at least have a chance of defending herself.

"Your greed for my fortune has addled your brain, my lord," she said with icy disdain. "Even in Gretna Green I would have to agree to the marriage and that I will never do."

"Oh I think you will, my dear. I am very skilled in the art of persuasion, as you will soon learn if you persist in defying me." With that he loosed his hold on her arms, stepped back, and opened his jacket to reveal a deadly multichambered pepperbox pistol, identical to the one her father had owned, tucked in the top of his breeches.

Rachel stared at the pistol, then raised her eyes to meet his. "If you are threatening to kill me, it is an idle threat, my lord. Surely not even *you* could be stupid enough to think you would see a penny of my fortune if you did that." She marveled that her voice could sound so calm when her hands were shaking uncontrollably and her pulse pounded in her ears like raindrops on a tin roof.

"I would not think of harming a hair of your head, my precious," Fairborne purred. "But surely you're aware we've had an audience for the past half hour—and it would not bother me in the least to put a bullet into the heart of one of your faithful servants." With that, he grasped the pistol, wheeled around, and strode toward the door.

For one brief moment, shock froze Rachel in place. But even as she heard Mary's shriek of terror she snatched the knife off the table and slipped it into the pocket of her dress. Then dashing after the earl, she cried, "Stop! Do not harm them. I will go with you."

"I rather thought you would. But just to make certain you are as cooperative in Gretna Green as you are here, I will take one of them with us." Fairborne frowned thoughtfully. "But which one should it be—the old woman or the young one?"

Mrs. Partridge stepped forward, her face as white as her pristine apron. "I'll go with thee. Mrs. Tucker is in a delicate way and the ride could harm her babe."

Fairborne stared at Mary, a look of dawning recognition on his face. "By George, if it isn't the trollop who seduced my footman so her mistress could escape me. That settles it." Rage contorted his features into a menacing caricature of his usual handsome self. "You will act as witness at your mistress's wedding."

"Do not do this, my lord," Rachel pleaded. "I have said I would go with you."

"True. But you also reminded me that our nuptials could not take place without your cooperation. I am merely making certain

I have it." A subtle change in his voice rendered it undeniably lethal. "Furthermore, I have a score to settle with this slut—one I have already settled with her foolish lover."

"And I have a score to settle with you, monsieur."

Rachel instantly recognized the voice as that of Yves's friend, Philippe de Maret. Weak with relief, she spun around to find the handsome Frenchman standing in the doorway that led to the kitchen, pistol in hand. Too late, she realized she was between him and the earl, and he could not see the earl's pistol, nor know it was cocked and ready to fire.

"Look out! He has a gun," she shouted. But even as the words left her mouth, Fairborne flung her aside and fired. Mary screamed, Mrs. Partridge fainted, and Philippe de Maret slumped to the floor as blood spurted from the wound above his left eyebrow.

"Dear God! What have you done?" Rachel gasped.

"Nothing of consequence. Merely rid the world of yet another foolish Frenchman who made the mistake of threatening me," the earl said in a flat, emotionless voice.

Sick with horror, she started toward the fallen marquis, but powerful fingers gripped her arm and swung her around to face the opposite direction. "To the carriage, my dear, if you please. We have a long ride ahead of us."

He waved his pistol in Mary's direction. "You too. Walk ahead of us, and in case you are not familiar with a pepperbox pistol, I need only cock it again to fire another shot."

"Let me go, you fiend," Rachel cried, trying desperately to wrench free of his hold. "I must help the poor man."

"A waste of time. The Marquis de Brune is quite capable of dying alone."

"In which case you will hang for his murder."

"Nonsense. I am an English nobleman. I need only assert I acted in self-defense against a rabid French insurgent, and I shall be acquitted of any blame," Fairborne said, yanking her along beside him as he strode toward the carriage. "The mystery is how he came to be in your house."

Instinct warned Rachel to pretend ignorance about the marquis rather than risk betraying Yves's part in the plot against the earl. With monumental effort she managed what she hoped looked like an indifferent shrug. "Whoever he is, he would have had no trouble gaining entry. The doors to Barton House are never locked."

"But alone? I know this fellow, and find it hard to believe he took it upon himself to follow me to Yorkshire without the aid of his close friend, the Comte de Rochemont."

He tightened his grip on Rachel's arm. "It occurs to me you may have more knowledge of this than you are admitting, madam."

"I have no idea what you are talking about," Rachel said. "I remember there was a Frenchmen you disliked in London, but foreigners are thin on the ground here in Yorkshire."

She held her breath, wondering if she had done it up too brown. But to her relief, the earl appeared to accept her explanation without question. Entering the carriage directly behind Mary and her, he settled on the seat opposite them, tapped on the trapdoor and ordered the coachman to drive north to Scotland without delay.

Mary stared at her with wide, terrified eyes and Rachel suspected she was thinking of the earl's threat to "settle a score" with her. Rachel could do no more than give her hand a comforting squeeze. The girl was no fool. She had to know that as long as the earl held a loaded pistol, he had the upper hand and there was nothing they could do about it.

Until a few minutes ago, Rachel would never have believed she could feel such hatred for another human being that she would harbor murder in her heart. But the Earl of Fairborne's cold-blooded slaying of the marquis had destroyed any lingering spark of compassion she might have had for a man she'd once called "friend."

At long last, she understood Yves's obsession with the villain. Beneath the mask of charm and affability Fairborne wore so well, there lurked a dangerous predator, who would kill again and again until someone found a way to stop him.

She knew Yves would follow them, all the way to Scotland if need be, both to avenge the death of his friend and to rescue her from the monster's clutches. This time there would be nothing to prevent the two men from meeting face-to-face in a classic battle of good versus evil. It was enough to make her believe in the "fate" Yves had touted so eloquently.

She breathed a fervent prayer that good would triumph. But she had never been one to leave the important matters in her life to chance. Surreptitiously, she fingered the sharp little knife concealed in her pocket. It would take a good while to reach the Scottish border . . . and not even the devil himself could remain vigilant every second.

The ride from the Ostrander estate to Barton House was long, slow and frustrating, due mostly to Jacob's incompetent horsemanship. Then just when Yves had hopes the poor fellow had mastered the knack of staying in the saddle, his horse shied at a farm cat crossing the road. Jacob flew in one direction, his spectacles in the other, leaving Yves to chase down the riderless horse while Jacob crawled about on his hands and knees searching through the tall grass bordering the road. Ten minutes later, the bruised mill superintendent remounted the testy little mare—but without his spectacles. They were smashed beyond repair.

If patience was a virtue, Yves felt he had surely earned his place in heaven playing nursemaid to the clumsy fellow. But finally, more than an hour past his promised arrival time, he spied the four tall chimneys of Barton House and breathed a sigh of relief that Philippe had been there to protect Rachel during his long absence.

Still, late as they were, they dared not ride up the broad, tree-lined driveway to the front door, lest they warn the earl of their coming. With Jacob leading the way, they spent another ten minutes circling around the wool sheds, through the mill yard and past the beech grove. Then stabling their horses, they approached on foot through the kitchen garden.

The afternoon sun was beginning its descent toward the western horizon, but it still shone bright and warm, and Yves found himself temporarily blinded when he stepped into the cool, deeply shadowed kitchen. Behind him Jacob murmured, "I can't see a thing without my spectacles . . . but something is wrong."

Yves glanced about him at the immaculate kitchen. "What do you mean 'wrong'?"

"This time of day there should be the smell of bread fresh from the oven, stew bubbling on the range." Jacob scowled. "Where is Mrs. Partridge? She should be busy preparing supper."

"It is extraordinarily quiet," Yves agreed, and promptly stumbled over a tin bucket sitting in the middle of the floor. The racket shattered the eerie silence of the large, oak-beamed kitchen and he spat out an explicit curse in gutter French as he bent to pick up the offending item.

"What the devil is this?" he exclaimed when he saw the contents.

Jacob peered over his shoulder, eyes narrowed in a tight squint. "It looks like a piece of cloth. Good God it is . . . a piece of blood-soaked cloth. Someone has been badly hurt."

With quiet care, Yves set the bucket down beside the round oak table, pulled his trusty knife from its sheath, and slowly opened the door leading to the hall. No one was in sight, but he could hear the muted sound of a male voice coming from the small parlor, and something that sounded suspiciously like a woman weeping.

Heart pounding, he waved Jacob back and moved silently across the stone floor to the parlor door. "If Fairborne has dared lay a hand on Rachel, I'll kill him first and then see him transported," he muttered under his breath.

His first glimpse of the room told him Rachel was nowhere to be seen and the woman sobbing quietly into her handkerchief was Mrs. Partridge.

His second glimpse set him back on his heels. Someone in a pair of familiar, silver-tasseled boots lay propped up on two feather pillows on the sofa, his head swathed in a white, blood-spotted bandage. Beside him stood a giant of a man with a shock of flaming red hair and a round, youthful face peppered with cinnamon-colored freckles.

"Stop hovering over me like the angel of death, you great, clumsy oaf and go look for Yves St. Armand," the injured man chided in a petulant voice that could only belong to the Marquis de Brune.

"Devil take it, what is going on here?" Yves demanded, stepping through the open doorway. "Where is Rachel?"

"Yves! Thank God you're back." Philippe struggled to a sitting position and peered at him with one eye. The other was hidden beneath a bandage that was only a shade whiter than his pasty complexion.

Yves gaped at his wounded friend. "How did all this happen to you in the three hours since I saw you last? And where is Rachel?"

"I'm ashamed to say Fairborne caught me unawares," Philippe said bleakly, sinking back onto his pillows. "Luckily he merely creased my skull instead of putting a bullet through it as he intended." He gestured weakly toward the red-haired giant. "This fellow is the new Bow Street runner assigned to follow the earl."

"Daniel Monahan at your service, sir," the runner said. "But I arrived too late to be of help."

Yves's stomach clenched. "You've told me everything except the one thing I want most to know. Where the devil is Rachel?"

"She's gone," Mrs. Partridge wailed. "The earl took her in his carriage and Mary with her. Miss Rachel had no choice but to do as he said, with him holding a gun to poor Mary's head."

Yves heard Jacob's groan of distress and silently echoed it. How could such a thing happen? Philippe was no green boy to be outsmarted by someone like Fairborne. He wanted to yell down the house, smash something, punch someone—get his hands around Philippe's neck and throttle him for failing to protect the woman he loved.

The woman he loved. The shock of realizing the true extent of his feelings for Rachel was almost as great as the one he'd suffered at hearing she was once again in Fairborne's clutches. It sobered him instantly. He had loved but two women in his entire life. The Earl of Fairborne had robbed him of one; he was not about to let the black-hearted devil harm the other. A sick feeling in the pit of his stomach told him if he'd had that insight a day earlier, he would never have agreed to put Rachel's "simple plan" into motion.

But this was not the time to indulge in self-recrimination. "Think carefully, Mrs. Partridge," he said quietly. "Do you have any idea where he took them?"

"Aye, sir. 'Tis for Scotland he's headed. To that place called Gretna Green just across the border. I heard him threaten to kill Mary unless Miss Rachel agreed to marry him." Mrs. Partridge sobbed anew. "And 'twas plain he meant what he said."

Jacob stepped forward. "How long have they been gone?"

The housekeeper blew her nose. "More than an hour, and the earl had his heavy travel coach and four horses that looked to be grand, strong animals."

Yves took a deep breath. "I doubt they can outrun my gelding."

"I'll ride with you, sir, if I can find a fresh mount," the runner declared. "Mine is pretty well spent."

Jacob frowned. "Miss Barton has but two horses besides her

favorite mare, which I shall be riding as soon as I pick up my extra pair of spectacles at the mill office."

"Not with me, you won't," Yves said. "I'll be traveling far too fast for you to keep up." He glanced toward the runner. "I'll not hold back for you either, Monahan."

The runner snorted. "'Tis more likely you'll be the one having trouble keeping up. Now where are these two horses?"

"In the stable out back," Jacob said. "But I doubt you can handle either one. They're both ill-tempered brutes Miss Barton bought because she heard their owner was mistreating them."

"I may be England-born, but I'm an Irishman by blood, and the son of Jock Monahan, who manages the Marquess of Haversham's stud farm. There's not a horse born I can't ride." The runner's expression was grim. "Besides, I've good reason to want justice done, and I'm thinking there's evidence enough to warrant taking the blighter back to London to pay for his sins."

Yves tapped his breast pocket. "With what I have in here, I guarantee it," he said, remembering the runner found murdered in Dover had been named Monahan too.

He exchanged a telling look with Philippe. "It appears the Earl of Fairborne is about to begin paying for *all* of his sins."

Chapter Seventeen

They had been on the road for what seemed an interminable time. Dusk had given way to night and for a while Rachel could see nothing in the inky blackness outside the carriage windows except an occasional pinpoint of light from a distant cottage. But at last a three-quarter moon had risen, bathing the landscape in an eerie silver light.

The interior of the coach was even brighter, since the earl had lighted both lamps shortly after they'd left Barton House. "The better to see you with, my dear," he'd said, as if warning her he was aware she was plotting against him. He'd settled back against the squabs, pistol in hand, and advised her to "relax and enjoy the ride" exactly as he'd once done when he'd driven her through Hyde Park on a sunny afternoon.

"I imagine you consider my handling of this situation a bit highhanded," he said conversationally. "But you will come to realize that what I have done is for your own good. For what has a Yorkshire farmer to offer you but a parcel of grubby brats no better than yourself. Despite your obvious shortcomings, I am willing to make you my countess—an honor for which any woman of your background should be sincerely grateful."

Rachel heard Mary's gasp of dismay at his insulting words, but she maintained a stubborn silence, letting a glare of animosity speak for her.

"A word of advice," he continued. "Do not waste your time complaining to the local magistrate that you were forced to marry against your will. I have known the fellow since I first visited my aunt as a green lad, and we are in accord about women who overstep the bounds society has wisely set for them. As a matter of fact, your name came up as a prime example of such a woman the last time I dined at his home."

Rachel's spirits sank. It was plain to see that if she defended her virtue, and Mary's life, by sinking her knife into the evil monster who sat opposite her, she could expect no sympathy in the local courts. Yves had known whereof he spoke when he'd said a commoner and a woman could not prevail against a nobleman.

But sink it she would if Yves did not catch up with them before they reached the border of Scotland. For she would never surrender to Fairborne like a lamb going docilely to slaughter. Then unless Yves had found written proof that the earl was the traitor Whitehall sought, she would be the one who would be forced to flee to America.

"What the devil!" Fairborne's angry voice interrupted her musings. Puzzled, she wondered what had set him off now, until she realized the carriage was slowing down.

"Ho! Coachman!" Fairborne rapped on the roof trap with the barrel of his pistol. "What is going on out there?"

The coachman lifted the trap. " 'Tis highwaymen, milord. Two of 'em as far as I can tell from their shouting."

"Then why are you slowing down, you fool? Outrun them."

"And get me head blown off? Not me, milord. I've a wife and two babes waiting for me back in London." The trap slammed shut and the carriage slowly rounded a curve and ground to a stop at the side of the road.

Rachel gripped the handle of her knife. This might be the chance for which she'd been praying, though it could not be Yves and his friend, since she'd seen the poor marquis brutally slain. But she would sooner take her chances with "knights of the road" than face what Fairborne had in mind for Mary and her.

"You in the coach, come out."

Her heart skipped a beat. It was Yves. She would recognize his voice anywhere. She nearly laughed out loud from pure relief. But a glance at the earl's face told her he would not surrender easily.

"Be careful," she called out, "he has a gun," and prayed her warning would be of more help to Yves than it had been for his friend.

The earl pinned her with a venomous look. "You know these men?"

"No, but whoever they are, they have to be preferable to you."

"You have a vicious tongue, madam—one I will enjoy curbing once we are married."

He cocked his pistol, then snuffed the interior carriage lamps. "Very well, let us do as this thatchgallows demands, for it may well be the last demand he ever makes of any traveler."

Rachel shivered, suddenly far more afraid for Yves than for herself. But the moonlight streaming through the window plainly outlined the gun Fairborne held pointed at her, and she knew it would be a futile gesture to try to use her knife at that moment.

"Forgive my lack of manners, my dear. But due to unforeseen circumstances, I fear you will have to exit before me and make your way down the carriage steps without assistance."

He waved the pistol in Mary's face. "You stay here and keep quiet unless you want to see your mistress meet the same fate as that fool Frenchman back at Barton House." The earl's voice seemed strangely disembodied in the half-light of the carriage—smooth and oily and so darkly dangerous, it was all Rachel could do to keep from giving voice to her fear.

He undid the latch and kicked the door open. "Proceed, madam, and do remember to watch your step."

Rachel felt Mary stir beside her. "Do as he says," she whispered and sensed the little maid promptly huddled into the far corner of the seat.

"I am coming out first," Rachel called in a voice gone strangely hoarse, before she made her careful way down the carriage steps with the earl behind her.

Between the moonlight and the running lights of the carriage, the area was almost as bright as day. She could see Yves and another man she didn't recognize. Both were still mounted on their horses and spaced some ten feet apart. Light glinted off the barrels of their pistols and the horses beneath them snorted and pawed the ground, keyed up from their long run.

Behind her, the earl spat out a curse. "You!" he exclaimed, when he recognized Yves. "I should have known!"

Yves made no response to Fairborne's angry invective. "Are you all right?" he asked Rachel.

"I am fine," she answered, though he could plainly see the barrel of Fairborne's pistol pressed against her back. He felt consumed with rage. How like the coward to hide behind a woman—and how like Rachel to stand pale and rigid with fear, yet bravely defiant in the worst of circumstances. He wondered if any man alive could match his Yorkshire lady for courage.

Fairborne studied him through narrowed eyes. "So, we meet

again, St. Armand." The name was a curse on his lips. "Since when have you taken to the high toby?"

"Since my sworn enemy has resorted to kidnapping women now that he can no longer sell England's secrets to Napoleon Bonaparte." Yves responded in the coarse gutter French of the Parisian riffraff with whom the earl had transacted much of his nefarious business.

The angry twist of Fairborne's mouth told Yves he recognized the insult dealt him. "I cannot picture a man with your rakish reputation as a knight errant," he said in his cultured English. "But this moment has been a long time coming. How ironic that it should be brought about by a common antidote from Yorkshire—and how embarrassing for you that your 'chivalry' is in vain. For we appear to be at an impasse. My coachman carries a pistol, as do I, which makes us two against two."

"The devil it does," the coachman said, tossing his pistol to the ground and climbing down after it. He extended his hands to Yves to show he was unarmed. "I can see you're no highwayman, sir, and I wants no part of this havey cavey business the earl is up to. I just followed his orders up to now 'cause he paid me to drive his carriage. But I've collected no wage for a quarter or more, so he's on his own far as I'm concerned."

Yves nodded. "Very well. Then see to the horses and make certain that whatever happens, they don't bolt."

He turned his head and again surveyed the black-hearted devil with whom he'd been obsessed for three long years. "Since you now stand alone and there are still two of us, one of whom is a Bow Street runner, we appear to have the advantage."

"Only if you choose to sacrifice the woman you planned to rescue," Fairborne sneered.

"Turn her loose and I will dissuade the runner from killing you outright, which I can see he is eager to do, since he is the brother of the man you murdered in Dover."

Fairborne looked momentarily taken aback. He cast an uneasy glance at Daniel Monahan, whose tense figure was outlined against one of the carriage lamps. "What has this dowdy commoner to do with the trouble between you and me, St. Armand?"

"Not a thing," Yves snapped. "I barely know the woman. But as a man who enjoys all women, I have a natural inclination to save any female from the clutches of a minion of the devil."

Yves saw the momentary shock registered on Rachel's face

and prayed that she would understand that if Fairborne had an inkling of how much she meant to him, he would use it as a weapon against him. Her brief smile told him that her quick mind had grasped the truth behind his careless words.

"Come now, St. Armand, do not think to hoodwink me, of all people. We are both men of the world and cut of the same cloth. If you feel you must avenge the death of your French lover, do so on the field of honor as a nobleman should. Name the time and place and I will be there. But for now, leave me to wed my Yorkshire heiress."

Yves shrugged. "Even if I were inclined to do so, I could not, my lord. For I promised Whitehall I would provide them with the proof they need to send you to prison for the rest of your life."

"Whitehall?" The earl cast a furtive glance at the imposing form of the Bow Street runner and Yves could see the full gravity of his situation was just dawning on him. It had obviously never occurred to him that the runners who had followed him these past months had been hired, not by his enemy, but by Whitehall.

"The game is up, my lord," Yves said. "Thanks to your charming great aunt and her proclivity for French brandy, that proof is now safely in my pocket."

His eyes sought Rachel's in one glorious moment of triumph that only the two of them shared. Then once more he gazed beyond her to Fairborne. "Ergo, as I see it, you have a choice between a bullet in the heart and a trip aboard His Majesty's transport ship to Van Diemen's Land."

In the space of a second, Fairborne seemed to shrink before his very eyes. Fear and rage transformed his once handsome features into an ugly mask and the hand that still held the gun to Rachel's back now trembled as if with ague.

Yves cursed himself for a fool. How could he have failed to remember that a cornered rat was always more dangerous than one that freely roamed the barn? Now Fairborne would be more inclined than ever to use Rachel as a shield.

Slowly, Yves dismounted and faced his enemy eye to eye. "You cannot escape, my lord. Accept that your luck has run out. The most you can do is prolong the agony." He paused to let the words sink into Fairborne's stunned brain, before he added, "Let the woman go; she has no part in this."

For a long moment Fairborne stared at him with hate-filled eyes. Then in a move so sudden it caught Yves unawares, he circled Rachel's waist with his left arm and raised his right hand to press the barrel of the pistol against her temple. "I believe I shall take my chances with the bullet—or rather with your sense of chivalry that will not allow you to risk the life of an innocent woman."

"Luckily I have not a drop of chivalrous blood in my veins," Monahan growled, and out of the corner of his eye, Yves saw the runner raise his pistol and point it at Fairborne's head.

"Hold!" he barked, but Monahan's hand didn't waver.

"I will wait for the traitor to surrender, but only so long," Monahan declared in a chilling tone of voice. With those ominous words an eerie silence descended on the tense drama being enacted beneath the pale autumn moon and for a long moment all four players seemed frozen in place.

Then from out of nowhere came the sound of hooves thundering on the hard-packed dirt of the road. Yves glanced up and instantly recognized the horseman as Jacob Zimmerman. Both he and the mare beneath him looked dangerously out of control, and they were heading straight for the spot where Rachel and Fairborne stood.

Throwing caution to the winds, Yves sprinted forward, grabbed Rachel's arm and dragged her behind a tree that stood between her and the oncoming horse. Only once did he look back into the muzzle of Fairborne's gun. Then heart pounding, he pressed her against the tree trunk and protected her body with his own.

He raised his head and chanced a look as the rider approached. Coattails flapping and hair on end, the mill superintendent clung to the horse's mane, a look of fierce determination on his chalk white face. "Do not despair, Mrs. Tucker," he shouted at the top of his voice. "I have come to save you from the monster's clutches."

Shocked into action by the horse and rider bearing down on him, Fairborne backed up, took frantic aim and fired a quick shot. At the same moment another shot rang out and even as Jacob's battle cry ended with a yelp of pain, Fairborne crumpled to the ground next to the front wheel of the carriage.

"Whoa!" Yves shouted to the little mare and grabbed at the reins as it galloped past him, since it was obvious Jacob was too befuddled to do so. Rachel's obedient mare came to an abrupt stop, catapulting Zimmerman into an aerial somersault that landed him on his back on a grassy hillock beside the road.

Miraculously, his spectacles appeared to have survived the acrobatic maneuver. But a trickle of blood seeped down his left sleeve from where Fairborne's bullet had grazed his arm.

Slowly, Yves straightened up and gathered Rachel into his arms. Her face was streaked with dirt, her hair an unruly tangle of leaves and twigs. She had never looked more desirable. He picked a twig from her hair, tossed it aside and kissed her with the tender passion of a man who knew how close he had come to losing heaven.

Rachel slipped her arms around his waist and laid her head on his shoulder. Yves might not love her; the word had never passed his lips except in reference to Amalie de Maret. But he cared enough about her to risk his life to rescue her from the evil earl. And he desired her. Even now, pressed against him as she was, she could feel the evidence of that desire. It was enough. It was, in fact, far more than she had ever expected when first she'd realized how she felt about him.

"What happened?" she asked. "I couldn't see a thing with my nose pressed into that tree trunk."

Yves picked another twig from her hair and buried his nose in the spot where it had been. "I am not entirely certain, but I believe we were the victors in whatever war it was we just fought. But here comes Daniel Monahan and he does not look happy, so maybe I am mistaken in that assumption."

Rachel watched the grim-faced Bow Street runner approach—his own pistol in one hand, Fairborne's in the other. Pulse quickening, she slipped out of Yves's arms to stand beside him.

Monahan acknowledged her with a courteous nod of his head, but addressed his remarks to Yves. "It is a good thing that fool mill superintendent is already wounded," he roared, "or I would be tempted to spill a little of his blood myself. My horse reared when the idiot came galloping past and I shot Fairborne in the knee instead of the heart, as I intended."

Yves smiled. "On the other hand, Jacob is something of a hero," he said loud enough for all to hear. "We were at a hopeless impasse with Fairborne. Who knows on whom the villain might have turned his gun had the brave mill superintendent not arrived to defend Mrs. Tucker." He winked at Rachel as Mary made a gingerly descent from the carriage and rushed to the side of the fallen hero to tend to his wound.

"Very well, I grant you that," the runner grumbled. "But there is still the question of what to do with the blackguard." He glanced at the pistol Yves had returned to the waist of his breeches. "You are the one who found the proof that he was a traitor. You have earned the right to shoot him."

Rachel looked at the earl, still moaning over his knee, then at Yves, who appeared to be seriously considering the runner's suggestion—and felt her breath catch in her throat.

"Alas," Yves said sadly, "I cannot shoot a man, even an evil one, who is not in a position to defend himself. It is not my way."

Monahan scowled. "More fool you. As my poor brother could attest if he were alive to do so, Fairborne would shoot you without a second's hesitation."

Yves shrugged. "I know that. But that is the difference between us. Furthermore, as Lord Castlereagh said, death would be preferable to spending the rest of one's life in one of England's prison colonies."

The runner's scowl grew even darker. "Still, there is always the odd chance the devil could escape. Better to put paid to his miserable existence here and now."

Rachel had to admit she could see the runner's point. Still she hoped Yves would prevail. She sidled closer to him and felt his arm slip around her waist.

"But the most important reason why I cannot do this thing you propose," Yves admitted, "is that I do not think my gentle, kindhearted Yorkshire lady would approve."

"Then I'll not argue with you, sir. I'll do as you wish."

Yves smiled. "What I wish is for you to deliver Fairborne to the village constable and ask that he provide you with a couple of stalwart men to help you transport the traitor to Lord Castlereagh along with this." Yves removed the incriminating letters from his pocket and handed them to Monahan.

"But you are the one who hunted him down," Rachel said. "You are the one who has lived only for the day when you would bring him to justice. It should be your moment of triumph at Whitehall."

"Ah, but I have something else to live for nowadays, thanks

to you, and I cannot go to London right now because I have a more important appointment elsewhere."

The runner shrugged. "In that case, I suppose I cannot refuse your request. But I warn you, if Fairborne gives me a single moment of trouble, I will put a bullet in his black heart."

"You have my permission to do as you see fit, and my blessing as well."

Rachel smiled at the huge red-haired man. "You have my blessing too, sir, but perhaps this will be of more practical use." She reached into her pocket and withdrew the knife she'd found no occasion to use.

"A knife?" Monahan stared at the weapon she'd handed him and roared with laughter. "I think, sir, that our problem with the Earl of Fairborne might have been better solved had we left him to the tender mercies of your gentle, kindhearted lady."

Yves shook his head. "I might have known Rachel would find a way to defend herself. I have always said she was a unique woman."

Monahan wiped his eyes. "So she is, sir. So she is, and I wish you luck with her. I have a feeling you are going to need it."

Dawn was breaking by the time Rachel had bound the earl's knee with his own cravat and seen him loaded into his carriage for the trip back to the village and thence to London to pay for his crimes. Evil as he was, she could not help but pity him, for Yves was right—death would be preferable to the bleak future the Earl of Fairborne now faced.

"Now where is this appointment you claimed you had and with whom is it?" she asked as she and Yves watched the carriage drive off, leaving only the two of them, her mare, and his gelding behind.

"*Our* appointment is with fate, for once again that mysterious force has worked in our favor. More so than ever, for this time it has shown me the way to achieve my fondest dream when it seemed all but impossible." He smiled. "And as I've said before, who are we to argue with fate?"

"And is this a new dream, or one of those you shared with me about your plans for the future?" Rachel asked, reveling in the look of quiet excitement in his eyes and the knowledge that she was the one with whom he wanted to share his dream.

He shook his head. "This dream is not about my farm. I paid

a visit to your village vicar yesterday morn." He hesitated as if choosing his words carefully. "I know I should not speak ill of a man of the cloth, but the fellow is a pompous ass, more concerned with rules and regulations than doing the work of God."

"What happened? Did he refuse to read the banns of a papist?"

"He did. Indeed, I think he felt my very presence in his church contaminated the holy ground."

"And do you think your priests would feel any differently about marrying a Roman Catholic to an Anglican?" Rachel asked.

Yves's black brows rose slightly. "Probably not, but what care we when the angels are with us."

In the cold, clear light of dawn, with his shirt open at the throat and a black stubble on his usually clean-shaven face, he looked more like a pirate of the Spanish Main than a French aristocrat. She smiled to herself. A pirate who believed in angels.

"Our first sunrise together," Yves said, and the look on his face was one of pure contentment. "But we have a lifetime of sunrises before us."

He drew Rachel into his arms and together they watched the glorious spectacle unfold before them. "At long last I have put the past behind me forever," he said softly. "And where did fate decree this auspicious event should take place?"

"On the road to Gretna Green, thanks to that scoundrel, Fairborne."

"Exactly. A place, I've been told, where no one asks if one is papist or Anglican or even a son of Mohammed."

Rachel smiled, certain now where this mysterious appointment of theirs was to take place. "As I understand it, one has only to jump an anvil to be properly married in Scotland."

"And I thought the French were practical. Think about it, *cherie*. If that is not a sign from the angels that I should marry the woman I love, then what, pray tell, is it?"

The woman I love. He had finally said the words she had thought she would never hear. The brilliant colors of the sunrise blurred before the tears of happiness filling her eyes. But now that he'd finally said them, she realized they were, after all, only words. In a hundred different ways he had already shown her how deeply he cared for her.

He cocked his head, as if listening for something. "What is it?" she asked. "What do you hear?"

"Not a thing but a bird waking to the morning. But I feel certain that at any moment I shall hear those angelic bells again."

Rachel raised her head from his shoulder and smiled into his beautiful silver eyes. "Ah yes," she sighed. "About those bells—"

PENGUIN PUTNAM INC.
Online

Your Internet gateway to a virtual environment with hundreds of entertaining and enlightening books from Penguin Putnam Inc.

While you're there, get the latest buzz on the best authors and books around—

Tom Clancy, Patricia Cornwell, W.E.B. Griffin, Nora Roberts, William Gibson, Robin Cook, Brian Jacques, Catherine Coulter, Stephen King, Jacquelyn Mitchard, and many more!

Penguin Putnam Online is located at http://www.penguinputnam.com

PENGUIN PUTNAM NEWS

Every month you'll get an inside look at our upcoming books and new features on our site. This is an ongoing effort to provide you with the most up-to-date information about our books and authors.

Subscribe to Penguin Putnam News at http://www.penguinputnam.com/ClubPPI